The X-Cure

Bruce Forciea

ISBN: 0692536892
ISBN-13: 978-0692536896

To Shan for her love and support.
To my daughter Grace, the most talented writer I know...

.

1

DILEMMA

*"A*lex! Wake up, Alex!"

Alex Winter catapulted out of his sweet somnolent state into a consciousness full of screams, rushed footsteps, and loud crashing sounds. It seemed as if an angry wild boar was rampaging through his apartment. Before he regained his wits, three men wearing ski masks and holding assault rifles bolted into the bedroom shouting in Chinese. In an instant, one man pulled him out of his bed, sprawling him on the floor. A sharp pain shot through his skull from banging his head on the nightstand on the way down, also sending the clock careening into the darkness. Within seconds the men yanked his arms behind him. Any thought of escape became futile with the feeling of cold metal handcuffs snapping around his wrists.

An even deeper darkness fell over Alex as one man yanked a cloth hood over his head. Struggling to breath, and hyperventilating, an electric pain shot through his body, as if the men were ripping his arms from their sockets as they hoisted him from the floor. Feet dragging behind him, and with desperate attempts to regain his balance, the men pulled him along the floor and out of the apartment. His girlfriend's muffled screams faded into the background. He remembered glancing at the bedroom clock on its way to the floor. It read 2:12 am.

As the men forced him down concrete stairs, each step on solid ground lessened the painful pressure on his aching arms. The men seemed powerful, but he sensed fatigue after descending three levels, which made them shove him into a corner while they changed places. He could now bear most of his weight for the final descent of the remaining two levels.

The men shouted at each other as they threw him into the back of a van. More shooting pain, this time from his knees crashing onto the steel floor. The van's squeaky doors slammed shut, enclosing him in a dark hopeless space. In a few seconds it lurched from side to side while speeding off into the damp, black China night. Alex worked to control the panic seeping into the cells and tissues of his body. Thoughts of his execution reeled through his mind. He wondered how much longer he would live.

Confusion and terror poured through his veins as he replayed the events of the past few months in an attempt to make sense of his abduction. China seemed to be a safe haven, but he now realized he should have exercised more caution during these past few weeks. Tando's system of operatives extended their tentacles around the globe, including Beijing.

His body careened from side to side as he struggled to maintain some semblance of balance and to keep from banging his head against the steel walls. His futile attempts at counting the number of right and left turns with the hope that this wasn't a one-way ride ended when the van jerked to an abrupt stop.

The doors again squealed upon rusted hinges as they flung open. Alex felt someone grab his legs, sliding him out and into a standing position. This time he stood under his own accord, disoriented, heart beating as if exploding from his chest, mouth gaping open in desperate attempts to get oxygen, as the leader barked orders to the other men. The unmistakable feeling of a rifle barrel between his shoulder blades knocked him off balance and indicated with certainty that he proceed forward. Indiscernible Chinese voices peppered the air as he entered a building. The floor texture changed from a solid to a hollow sounding substance, like wood. Alex detected no concern in these other voices, as they seemed to perform tasks while ignoring their presence.

Alex turned a corner and entered a room. Something scraped across the floor; it sounded like furniture. His shuffling steps met with a quick push, causing a moment of backward free-fall until his backside met the seat of a metal chair. After another desperate gasp, one of the men jerked the hood from his head, liberating his breathing and allowing the scene to materialize in front of him. He inhaled deeply, taking in a breath of rancid air.

With his hands cuffed behind him, he sat on a metal chair at a metal table in a small, dingy room. The room reeked of a combination of mold and rotting meat. He wondered how many others had met their demise in this putrid concrete room. One of the men talked into a cell phone in broken English, and Alex overheard him say the words 'target acquired'. One of the men set a laptop on the table facing him. He flipped the screen causing it to flicker to life. The small screen displayed a horrific scene. Alex struggled to focus for a moment, identifying the image of a man sitting in a similar room with his arms chained to a similar table. The man appeared terrified and desperate as he tugged at chains holding his arms while his captors screamed at him to stop. Another man stood next to him holding a pistol fitted with a silencer to his head. When Alex recognized the man all the strength in his body drained onto the floor. The man with the pistol turned to the camera, and with a sardonic grin said; "Alex, say hello to your brother."

2
THE 26TH SYMPOSIUM ON INTEGRATIVE
MEDICINE—10 MONTHS EARLIER

*T*he elevator continued to fill with people while making a slow descent to the lobby. The mirrored walls created the illusion of a large crowd, and the effect created an exaggerated sense of claustrophobia in Alex as he awaited the end of the descent. The elevator's inhabitants shifted with every new addition, like members of a marching band performing an intricate formation at halftime. Alex surveyed the choreography of the crowd in the mirrors, his amusement diluted by the fact he'd ended up against the back wall.

For a moment his mind entertained the horrible image of the overburdened elevator stranded between floors. He imagined first responders prying open the doors and hoisting one person at a time through a narrow crack near the roof of the elevator. The ring of the elevator's bell signaled the next floor and snapped him back to reality. The elevator reached the next stop, two floors down, opened and closed its doors with new riders refusing to enter the mashup.

The air, filled with myriad aromas including the usual cheap assortment of colognes and perfumes along with a mixture of mouthwash and coffee breath, choked Alex. Arms pinned at his sides so as not to touch the female standing next to him inappropriately, he turned to display his best forced smile to her. She returned his greeting with her own version of a forced Botox-like smile and added a forced but pleasant "Good Morning" with an upward emphasis on the "Morning" part.

Their exchange added to the collective murmur of casual conversations occurring at a level a few decibels above the hum of the downbeat elevator music. Who knew the Rolling Stones could sound so peaceful? After his impromptu greeting, the awkward silence slowed time even more than the overcrowded elevator. His face tightened into his good morning grin.

"So, here for the conference, Betty?" Alex had read the "Hello My Name is" nametag with the word Betty hand-written in Sharpie across the white space. Betty, like all the others trapped in the small cuboid prison, proudly wore a blue lanyard holding a conference badge.

"Yes, it should be a good one," she said, first glancing at his eyes, then at his blue lanyard and badge. "I see you're a presenter. What are you presenting on?"

"I'm doing a presentation on how radio frequencies kill cancer cells," he said while maintaining his grin.

"Sounds cutting edge; when is it?"

"Tomorrow...in one of the smaller rooms. Stop by, if you can."

She answered but her voice was lost in the final ring of the bell and the opening of the elevator doors. The crowd surged forward toward the lobby while taking in a collective breath of the fresh air that wafted in to replace its stale counterpart. His face relaxed and returned to its usual neutral position, while his body drained the tension from his muscles as he stepped into the hotel lobby.

Doctor Alex Winter had attended countless similar conferences. Many of his professional friends and acquaintances hated these affairs, but he loved them, especially when he attended alone. He loved traveling to new places, networking with other researchers, finding out about some new and promising project, but most of all, he loved hanging out at the hotel. There was something wonderful about not having to make your own bed, cook your own meals, or leaving your room to go for an exploratory walk.

Alex also loved presenting at conferences. Most of the time he worked with a small group of graduate students in isolation, so presenting at a conference made him feel like a star. He welcomed the rush of adrenaline that came with standing in front of a room full of strangers and describing his latest project. His closing words always seemed to result in delightful applause. This contrasted his teaching duties back at the University, where his lectures usually ended with the students rustling books and tapping pencils to get out a few minutes early. He particularly disliked it when students began packing their things right in front of him before his lecture was finished. No applause there.

This year he planned to talk about his work on radio frequencies and cancer cells. His employer, Northern University in Chicago, encouraged him to attend this conference to get some exposure for extending his funding. Money was always an issue with research, with little funding for fringe projects like his. He envied how the government threw money at the large drug companies for their research. He hated the drudgery and constant struggle of locating grants, writing proposals, and being rejected for funding, until one relented and doled out a few dollars his way.

A few years ago Alex had discovered that he could tune certain frequencies to resonate with cancer cells. Cancer cells exposed to these frequencies died. It sounded simple on the surface, but it was anything but simple in getting it to work. Lots of things killed cancer cells in the lab, especially when bombarding them with enough energy. Alex likened it to punching a hole in toilet paper by driving

6

a semi through it. The real trick was getting the precise amount of energy to kill the right cells without harming normal cells.

This particular year had brought more conference attendees than the last three years. London was a cool and sexy city, after all. Previous conferences held at Kansas City, Houston and Pittsburg had provided less inspiring locations. It wasn't that he didn't like U.S. cities; he found them familiar, convenient and comfortable. In contrast, London presented a more exciting location with its mystery and complexity.

He followed the herd of conference-goers past the contemporary sculptures and fountains of the vast hotel lobby. He passed the front desk, busy with late arrivals, and spotted the entrance to the hotel pub in the far corner of the room. For a moment he thought about how different it looked from the previous night. The morning light seemed to drain the magic from the place, like fluorescent lighting does to just about anything. Last night the pub had displayed an atmosphere of warmth, good cheer, loud conversation and lots of English ale; now it took on a corpse-like pallor, as if the life had been sucked out of it with the fluorescent lights beaming, chairs upturned against tables, and the high-pitched, hyper-annoying scream of the cleaning crew's vacuum.

Alex had arrived at the Royal Hotel the previous night at about 9:30 pm. He'd traveled alone, as he liked. Upon arrival he'd kept to his ritual of spending the first evening before a conference in the hotel bar. He enjoyed passing time by striking up conversations with other attendees. Last night, after an eight-hour flight from Chicago, he needed a drink, or two, to take the edge off. The pub, alive and brimming with people from all over the world, provided the ideal place to do so.

Alex had taken one of the few remaining seats at the antique wooden bar and glanced at a plastic-coated menu.

After surveying the dozen or so selections followed by a brief consultation with the bar staff, he decided on Bass Ale, a local favorite, as his drink of choice for the evening.

"Dr. Alex Winter, is that you lurking in the shadows?" A familiar voice broke the white noise. He turned to recognize his old friend Frank McElroy sitting at a table with some coworkers.

"Hi, Frank; when did you get in?" Alex twisted on his bar stool to face his friend.

"A couple of hours ago... How do you like London so far?" The other two gentlemen at Frank's table nodded and continued their discussion.

"This is all I've seen so far, and it looks good to me." Alex held up his drink to salute his friend.

"I'll come over later. I have something to tell you." Alex nodded and twisted back into place. The ale was filling, and he wasn't hungry, so he decided to drink dinner and perhaps snack on some chips or peanuts.

After about an hour, the gentleman sitting next to Alex vacated his seat and Frank moved in. Frank, a project director from a large nutrition company called Biopharmco Incorporated, had known Alex since he'd begun working at the university. Biopharmco manufactured pharmaceutical grade nutrients called nutraceuticals, such as omega three capsules and Coenzyme Q10, as well as a line of potent multivitamins tailored to specific ages. They also dabbled in proprietary supplements for treating chronic diseases. As large as they were, they were no match for the much larger and richer drug companies. Frank kept a close eye on the market, concerned these mammoth companies would take over and squeeze smaller players like Biopharmco out of business. During the past couple of years there had been more scientific research supporting the use of nutraceuticals in treating chronic diseases, and Frank thought it was only a matter of time before the big players tried to squash the competition.

The evening wore on into the early morning hours as

Alex and Frank talked about everything from science fact to science fiction, with a little bit of real life thrown in for good measure. Frank loved to talk about his three children, but the conversation had changed over the years. A couple of years ago it began to morph from happy childhood stories of picnics, playgrounds, and grade school talent shows to what-the-hell-happened. His teenage children, two daughters and one son, tended to shut him out of their lives. He often found it difficult to penetrate the earbuds, cell phones and computers. He witnessed his close child-daddy relationship dissipate into a struggle to maintain any thread of connection amid school activities, friends and social media. This disturbed him as it reminded him of his own advancing age. The loss of his children's childhood provided a slap-in-the-face reality that somewhere between the birth of his youngest child and the present he'd lost a step, grew tired more often, and had begun to wake repeatedly throughout the night to pee. Alex assured him this was typical teen behavior and that they would come around in a few years.

Frank nodded, and after a few moments of staring into space, as if he were visiting some deep memory buried in the gyri of his mind, said, "I almost forgot. I wanted to tell you to make sure to attend Dr. Ling's presentation tomorrow. I think you will find it, and her, interesting. Word on the street is her work on resveratrol is unparalleled."

"Thanks, Frank. I intend to. I think I'm going to call it a night," said Alex while getting up to leave. "See you bright and early."

Alex knew a little about resveratrol, a natural nutritional substance derived from grape seeds. He knew resveratrol was available at any health food or vitamin store and that it had possible anti-aging and anti-cancer benefits. What intrigued him was how a simple nutrient that anyone could buy at a vitamin shop exhibited such a powerful effect on cells? Were there ways to increase the potency, to make it even more effective? What was the optimal delivery system? What was the optimal dose? What was the mechanism for inhibiting cancer? Head spinning with alcohol and ideas, Alex hoped Dr. Ling would have some answers.

With Frank's words echoing in his brain, Alex returned to the present. He passed the pub and continued strolling through the lobby. One particular hallway attracted the blue lanyard minions, and they streamed in from all directions. The space narrowed, instilling a sense of claustrophobia as he made his way down the long corridor to the conference area. The narrow space gave way to a wide open, soaring room with glass walls, escalators and more contemporary sculptures. The morning light beamed through the glass, illuminating one of the fountains and creating a small rainbow in the mist.

Alex scanned the immense space and fixed his eyes on a large blue and white banner that read *Welcome to the 26th Annual Symposium on Integrative Medicine*. Below the banner smaller signs directed attendees to various locations and venues. "Need coffee," Alex muttered under his breath. He waded through the crowd to a table filled with various pastries, toast and the drink of choice. He helped himself to some dark roast and tried not to spill it while getting bumped by other coffee seekers, then navigated to an uncrowded corner and pulled out his conference guide. He surveyed the guide for the programs he'd selected over the past couple of weeks. Today would be all about attending presentations. Tomorrow, he would present his own frequency research.

The first two presentations instilled a modicum of interest in Alex. The first covered antioxidants and cancer prevention. This could have been more exciting if the speaker had presented some of the more controversial research, but he played it safe and stated no opinion one way or another.

The speaker had said, "Some research shows

antioxidants such as Beta Carotene have been shown to inhibit cancer, but there is other research stating that they don't." A cowardly approach.

Alex considered himself a maverick of sorts, at least a geeky introverted researcher sort of maverick. Despite having a doctorate in biomedical engineering from Georgia Tech and a post doc from John Hopkins, with all the major medical equipment manufacturers and research and development firms courting him, he had settled for a position at Northern University in Chicago. Earning half his job-market worth, he considered himself happy since he only taught three courses and directed his own research program. No shirt and tie, no cubicle, no boss hovering over his head, nobody to manage except an eclectic crew of graduate students.

Funds were always an issue, of course, but this year the university had won the grant jackpot and received a large award. They distributed the funds to various projects and had given Alex enough to keep going for at least a few more months. Best of all, his work was his own. Whatever he developed he could patent and reap the benefits. The university had dangled this carrot to encourage startups by professors. It was an effective marketing tool and startup incubator, attracting hordes of young bright-eyed students looking to make their fortunes.

The second presentation, a slight improvement over the first, outlined an integrative approach to back pain by combining traditional medical and alternative approaches such as nutrition and chiropractic care. Previous conferences had featured this topic many times.

Alex found this presentation a little more interesting than the first. At one point, however, his thoughts had wandered from the speaker as his mind traveled back to his university lab surrounded by his graduate students, some playing video games, others troubleshooting circuit boards in an attempt to fix a broken frequency generator. Just as he flipped the switch on his dream state frequency machine, his head jerked forward, catapulting him back into physical reality. He awoke in a slight state of shock and looked around to notice if anyone had witnessed his brief episode of somnolence. Everyone in front of him was still focused on the presenter, his nodding off undetected. His back row seat had afforded sufficient camouflage for dozing, and others near him dove into their cell phones, tablets or laptops. Alex located the clock in the room. He had forgotten to set his watch six hours ahead.

Alex was thankful when the presentation ended a few minutes early and all the participants headed for the lunch buffet in the conference center lobby. After a decent meal consisting of a turkey sandwich, mixed vegetables, fruit and a cookie, he headed for the grand ballroom for the next presentation.

This one featured Dr. Ling and her work on resveratrol, as Frank mentioned. Alex hoped he could find out more about this common but mysterious nutrient. He was interested in how resveratrol affected the DNA of cancer cells. Despite Alex's formidable work on the subject, he still found cellular processes a mystery. Perhaps the Chinese had some new insights.

Dr. Ling and her colleagues had published papers on their work at Peking University. China valued natural healing, as evidenced by an entire school of traditional Chinese medicine complete with full research funding. Alex knew how difficult it was to get funding for his work and envied China's state-of-the-art programs on alternative medicine.

Alex entered the large conference room and took in the rock star feel of it. Six hundred chairs set up in long rows in front of a large stage filled the opulent room. Crystal chandeliers lit with adjustable LEDs cast a warm glow. Ornate gold-framed mirrors hung on each wall flanking the stage and provided the illusion of an immense room. A lectern dwarfed by the vast space occupied the front of the stage. Cinema-sized video screens behind and on either side of the lectern displayed candid images of the conference, beckoning everyone's attention to see if they popped onto the screen. Occasional bursts of laughter erupted from people caught in less than desirable mugs.

Alex found the seats almost full as scientists, doctors, and alternative medicine practitioners flooded in. The noise increased to football stadium levels as the people around him spoke louder and louder as they struggled to be heard.

Alex found a seat about three quarters toward the back of the room on the left side. He could only see part of the lectern but was in a good position to view the large video screen on his side of the stage. Just as a group of people took seats in front of him, further blocking his view, he felt a tap on his shoulder. He swung around to see Frank in the row behind him.

"Hey, Alex, you made it. You okay after last night?" Frank leaned forward, elbows resting on the vacant chair next to Alex.

"Yeah, I'm okay, a bit tired and a little hung over, but I'm looking forward to this one."

"It's always good to check out the competition," said Frank.

"For you maybe, since you're in the same nutrient market. I'm here for any new tidbit on the complex world of the cell," said Alex. "Plus...I think she's hot!" Alex held up a picture of Dr. Ling printed on the program.

"Do I sense a schoolboy crush? I mean, does the esteemed cancer cure researcher and *wunderkind*, and may I also add eternal bachelor, Dr. Alex Winter have a crush on the mysterious Dr. Ling?" Frank chuckled.

"It's starting," said Alex, turning back to face the stage.

The noise diminished as the host began to introduce the speaker.

"We are very excited to introduce this next presenter to you," announced the host in a British accent. "Doctor Xiu

Ling comes to us all the way from Peking University's School of Traditional Chinese Medicine. Dr. Ling holds doctorates in both biochemistry and medicine with an emphasis on nutrition and traditional Chinese Medicine. She has published numerous papers on nutritional substances and their effects on healing. Dr. Ling's presentation is entitled, 'Epigenetic Effects of Resveratrol'. Please give a warm welcome to Dr. Xiu Ling."

The hall erupted in applause as Dr. Ling took the stage and made her way to the lectern. A video camera followed her and produced a shaky image of a young looking, conservatively dressed, and attractive Asian woman heading toward the stage. She was small in stature, about five feet, five inches tall, in her early thirties, about Alex's age, her face brimming with a wide smile and framed by shoulder length hair. A white lab coat cloaked most of her body but revealed a hint of a white blouse and mid-length black skirt. She made her way to the stage and proceeded to shake hands with the host all the while exhibiting a humble and respectful demeanor.

The screen behind her lit up with her first slide and she wasted no time beginning her presentation after thanking and bowing to the host. She spoke with care and deliberation, as if she had practiced the complex scientific terms in English.

She began with an overview of resveratrol. "Resveratrol is a natural substance found in grape seeds, red wine, legumes and the Chinese Knotweed plant. An antioxidant, resveratrol also exhibits properties that can sensitize cells to chemotherapy. In other words, resveratrol made chemotherapy more potent to cancer cells while protecting non-cancerous cells. The key is epigenetics."

She went on to describe a system inside of cells affecting gene expression. Knowledge of this system is what epigenetics was all about. In the past, scientists thought that one was destined to suffer the outcome of the expression of the genes in his DNA. One had zero control over his genes. In other words, if one's DNA contained the gene for a deadly disease, there was nothing in his power to stop it from rearing its ugly head. The new science of epigenetics had changed that thinking. Now, drugs, nutrients and even behaviors were believed to affect gene expression. One was no longer a slave to his DNA. There was hope.

Alex understood a little about epigenetics. He knew if you had, say, the gene for cancer, it didn't mean you would *always* develop cancer. If you chose to live a healthy lifestyle, take the right vitamins and supplements, then there was a chance to keep that cancer gene at bay. The key was in the expression of the gene. Epigenetics was a system influencing DNA to either suppress or express genes. If one somehow manipulated this system to turn off cancer cells, then one would have something groundbreaking. Nothing new here so far, Alex thought. He knew that many substances affected cells by way of epigenetics, and he hoped that she would get into specifics soon.

She went on to explain how resveratrol facilitated DNA error correcting genes like the BRCA1 gene. "BRCA1 helps to repair damage done to DNA by exposure to environmental toxins such as chemicals, food additives and the horrible air pollution in my hometown of Beijing. Damaged DNA produces cancer causing errors. Resveratrol works to correct these errors by turning on BRCA1. In a nutshell, this common health food store nutrient could be the most promising natural epigenetic cancer preventing substance found today."

She continued, "Resveratrol exhibits powerful error correcting effects on DNA. The trick is in the delivery system. We have to get enough of the potent formula to the cell's DNA..."

That's the trick alright, thought Alex. It's great that this stuff corrects DNA errors and inhibits cancer, but getting enough of it past the digestive system and into the bloodstream, then into the cells, that's the real challenge.

Dr. Ling closed her presentation with some information about possible methods for delivering more resveratrol to cancer cells. She bowed her head and thanked the crowed as multiple hands flew up for questions. She answered a few in her calculating and precise way but stopped when the host stepped in to put an end to it. A small crowd followed her out of the room. She made her way off the stage, and Alex felt another tap on his shoulder.

"Interesting stuff, eh?" He turned to face Frank.

"She's got it all; brains, beauty, and fantastic research," said Frank.

"I've got to give it to her," said Alex. "She does know her stuff. Easy on the eyes, too. I'll bet you'd like to find out what kind of delivery system they are working on."

"We haven't cracked that one yet but you can bet we are working on it," said Frank. "I was hoping the Chinese delegation and Dr. Ling were going to share some secrets as to what they thought would work."

"I hear they are pretty isolated...never leave their hotel rooms, especially the females," said Alex with a tone of disappointment.

"Do you want to meet her? We pulled a few strings and arranged a dinner meeting tonight, Biopharmco's treat. Can I count you in?" Frank smiled as he wrote the name of the restaurant and handed it to Alex. "See you at eight!"

A sense of excitement flowed through Alex. Not only would he get firsthand information from the mysterious Chinese delegation, but he would also meet the beautiful, mysterious and elusive Dr. Ling.

Frank broke his pleasant daydream. "Hey, did you check out the Latro Medicor from Tando?" Frank pointed to a row of men clad in dark suits. The men were almost identical. They ranged in age from mid-thirties to about fifty with corporate cropped hair or shaved heads, white shirts and dark blue ties displaying the corporate emblem which consisted of a burnt orange "T" on a dark blue background. They had stayed until the end of Dr. Ling's presentation but were now getting up to leave.

"I know," said Alex. "I have never seen so many at one time. Usually, there are only one or two. They must be concerned about what is going on here."

"These are higher ranking officers, not the usual commando types I've heard about," said Frank.

The Latro Medicor, or Latro for short, was a feared group of mercenaries that worked for the largest and most powerful pharmaceutical companies. The terms Latro Medicor in Latin meant mercenary soldier of medicine. The Latro were guns for hire who worked to protect the interests of their employers. The Latro present at this conference worked for the largest and most powerful pharmaceutical company, Tando Pharmaceuticals.

"Tando must have pulled out all stops and sent the big guns to this one. Have any of them approached you yet, Alex?" Frank was concerned.

"Nope," said Alex. "My stuff must not be much of a threat. No big multinational pharmaceutical corporation like Tando is knocking at my door. But I'm sure they are very interested in Dr. Ling's work."

"I'll bet they are keeping their eye on her alright," said Frank, "I hope she will be okay."

"Come on," said Alex. "I don't think they would bother her."

Frank became more serious. "You remember what happened to poor old Charlie Benson."

"They said Charlie died of natural causes, a heart attack," said Alex. "In all seriousness, do you actually believe Tando knocked him off with their Latro operatives?"

Frank looked around to check if anyone was listening and lowered his voice to a whisper. "Of course I believe they killed him. Charlie was poking his nose a little too far into Tando's business. Rumor says he found some secret documents proving that Tando was sabotaging companies that might be a threat to their business. It's the Tando way, either buy the competition, sabotage it, or destroy it altogether. There have been too many good people silenced or dead at the hands of Tando. I heard Charlie even found a hit list of potential threats."

"I must be spending too much time in my academic bubble," whispered Alex. "Why would Charlie expose this information from the company he worked for?"

"Because Charlie Bensen was one of the good guys. He was fed up with the drug conspiracy and planned to blow the whistle on it once and for all. They found out about it before he could go through with it." Frank worked hard at keeping his voice low.

"Calm down, Frank." said Alex, concerned that Frank might make a scene. He'd heard about large drug companies like Tando, and their questionable methods. They operated much like a drug cartel with various levels of command, and acted as viciously as one as well. The difference was that they operated in secret, and no one knew just how deep, or how extensive their operatives were. Their unscrupulous methods ranged from spying on a target to much worse. They had no problem sabotaging research, threatening scientists with their lives, or making people disappear. They even manipulated the peer review process though bribes and threats to thwart publication of threatening information. They carried out all these terrible things in the name of keeping the flow of billions of dollars into Tando's coffers steady. Why should the public find out about a new cure for a disease if there were billions to be made by selling drugs to treat it? Or worse, why should the public know about how simple nutritional products, available to anyone without a prescription, prevented chronic diseases now treated with Tando drugs? Drug sales provided huge revenues for Tando, and the company spared no expense in protecting its interests.

The   Tando   Pharmaceuticals   Corporation's

headquarters was located in New York but its tentacles extended across the globe including the United Kingdom, Germany and China. Their largest selling products included a line of chemotherapy drugs for a variety of cancers. Billions of dollars flowed into Tando each year from these expensive and proprietary drugs. Tando retained the intellectual power and money to influence the global medical and pharmaceutical industry. Not only could they eliminate the competition but their high priced Washington lobbyists influenced powerful politicians to enact laws to protect their stake in the industry. Their immense power caused heads to turn away when they engaged in questionable activities. The U.S. Headquarters appeared to control the company but everyone knew that the real control originated with wealthy Chinese investors. Their U.S. interests provided the brains of the company through research while the Chinese provided the wealth.

Everyone feared Tando and their Latro goons. Once targeted, people feared for their lives. Their tactics resulted in widespread ramifications causing new scientists to avoid working for competitors or even entering the pharmaceutical field. A few mavericks fought the system with little success but most people avoided them. Charlie Benson was one of those mavericks. Good ole Charlie Benson with a stay at home wife and three kids, two in high school and one in college. Good ole Charlie Benson who always did what he was told, performed the obligatory sucking up to his bosses, and looked the other way when Tando screwed some competitor. Good old Charlie Benson who took shit from his supervisors day after day until he could no longer look the other way, or whitewash incriminating evidence, or cover up the insidious evil doings of his powerful employer. Good ole Charlie Benson, may he rest in peace.

Rumors passed around the conference in the form of whispered conversations and private meetings in the street and local pubs. Secrecy permeated the industry, which resulted in watered down presentations at the conference. The real exchange of ideas happened outside in secret late night meetings in private hotel rooms. The Latro were avoided everywhere, as if each one carried a contagious lethal disease. Heaven help you if you were stuck in an elevator with one of them, or your hotel room was located next to one, or by chance you stood next to one at a urinal in the men's room. Everyone avoided the Latro at all costs.

Alex found them extremely creepy. Last night, when he'd first checked into his room, he had mistakenly exited the elevator on the wrong floor. He turned the corner to witness no less than six Latro operatives walking down the hall, single file, about two thirds of the length of the long hall in front of him. He slowed to a standstill and faked a search through his luggage. The men paired off then entered their rooms. Each toted matching black carry-on luggage and a black briefcase, and each wore the same type of dark gray suit. One would turn with his back against the wall, standing next to the door, as if to guard it while the other slid the key card into the lock. They placed the luggage in the exact same position in front of each of the three rooms. Once each door was open, the man holding the key would enter the room while the other man held the door open and checked the hall in both directions. Then he too entered, pulling the other bag behind him.

Alex wondered if they actually drilled on how to enter a hotel room. He turned and crept back to the elevator as fast as he could, trying to avoid suspicion.

The large hall began to empty, and Alex and Frank were the only ones left in their row. "I'm going back to my room to get some sleep," said Alex. "There is nothing else I'm interested in hearing, and I'm pumped about meeting the Chinese tonight."

"See you then," said Frank. "Hey, one more thing: Do you speak Mandarin?"

"Ha!" said Alex, "The only languages I know are English and computer languages like C, Basic and a little

Java."

"Should make for an interesting evening; maybe we can use sign language. See ya."

Alex made his way out of the now empty row of seats.

3
THE MEETING

*A*fter a refreshing nap and a shower Alex headed out of the hotel and in the direction of the China Imperial restaurant. He exited the large revolving door, turned right, and then began a brisk walk down the crowded sidewalk. The damp cold London air slapped a light mist onto his face. The cars moving toward him rather than away as they would back home created some disorientation. His mild state of confusion magnified every time he crossed the street and looked the wrong way for traffic.

The street took on energy, much like Las Vegas Boulevard, but with narrower streets and much cooler temperatures. Rows of small shops selling a variety of wares, outdoor cafés and traditional pubs lined the streets. All sorts of people in a variety of colors filled the sidewalks. Alex's stereotypes of English people gave way to the diversity displayed before him. Conversations in an assortment of accents peppered the air as the crowd strolled forward, the flow interrupted from time to time by an occasional street performer.

Alex much enjoyed his explorations of new cities. He found this to be one of the most appealing activities when traveling. He loved walking about and observing how people got on with their lives. Sometimes he took off in a random direction to wander the streets of unfamiliar cities in search of unique shops, coffee houses, or in the evening hours, bars. He loved discovering old bookshops containing classic science fiction, or rummaging through second-hand stores for vintage 1980s video games. He remembered his father's old Atari 2600 game system and playing Space Invaders and Pac Man. He rescued the unit from the trash after one of his mother's spring cleaning sessions and maintained it to this day. There was something special about these elemental pixelated games. He appreciated their simplicity and historical value and continued to search for new additions to his collection.

The restaurant, located only a few blocks away, provided a shorter excursion than Alex had hoped, but he'd enjoyed the walk anyway. Exploring the city would have to wait. For now an evening with Frank's Biopharmco crew and the Chinese would more than quench his appetite for adventure. How appropriate that Biopharmco had arranged an intimate dinner at a world class Chinese restaurant for the delegates.

Alex entered the hotel and spotted Frank who waved him over to the group of Americans and Chinese. "I see you found it okay. Any problems along the way?" asked Frank.

"No, I enjoyed getting out in the night air. London is amazing," said Alex as he surveyed the group.

"Excuse me while I tend to our guests; I'll introduce you when we are seated." Frank turned to address the Chinese guests.

Alex felt a little underdressed for this occasion in his opened collar sports shirt, khaki slacks and casual sports jacket. Frank and the Chinese men all wore dark suits and ties. Alex thought the attire was a bit of overkill in formality, but then it *was* a classy restaurant. His discomfort lessened when he spotted one of the other American male guests dressed in casual clothes.

The group moved single file into the restaurant with

Frank and the Americans leading the Chinese. They filed past a series of large round cherry wood tables with accompanying large wooden chairs. Alex reveled at the ornate wall decorations displaying carved dragons and lions painted in traditional Chinese gold and red. The restaurant's clientele included a mixture of ethnic Asians and business types enjoying the quiet ambience of soft ethnic music and polite conversations.

The host led the party through the main dining room to a series of smaller private rooms. Here, a more festive atmosphere permeated the air with laughter, toasting, and celebration. A Chinese family occupied one room celebrating their teenage son's birthday, complete with red envelopes stacked high on a carved wooden corner table.

The host ushered the group into the last room, and Frank began to direct everyone to specific seats around a large round table. Feelings of excitement flowed through Alex as Frank sat Dr. Ling next to him. She wore a conservative looking and feminine high collar white blouse with an open black jacket embroidered with a detailed Asian gold pattern and a mid-length black skirt revealing thin but athletic legs. A small gold pendent displaying a small Chinese symbol hung from her neck. Dark brown shoulder length hair parted to one side framed her round face and almond shaped eyes. Alex marveled at the golden brown tone of her skin which appeared darker than the typical Chinese complexion.

Alex's heart began to beat faster as he extended a sweaty palm to greet her. Her radiant smile acknowledged him as his heart skipped a beat. She spoke in excellent English, careful to pronounce each word distinctly. The introductions to the others occurred so quickly and Alex's focus on Dr. Ling caused him to forget the names of the other two Chinese scientists.

Besides Frank and Alex, the party included two other Biopharmco scientists, Dr.'s Evelyn Waters and Vern Pleshenski, along with two other Chinese scientists, both male, Dr.'s Li Chen and Jianyu Yong. Frank sat on the other side of Dr. Ling. One of the Chinese, Dr. Li Chen, spoke broken English while the other, Dr. Jianyu Yong, only spoke his native Mandarin tongue. This kept Li busy acting as an interpreter for Jianyu.

A few minutes later, food began to flow from the kitchen. The Biopharmco team had done their homework in ordering an impressive array of traditional southern Chinese dishes. A team of waiters descended upon the table, placing dish after dish of delicious looking food at the center of the table that rotated like a Lazy Susan. Frank took charge and rotated each new arrival first to the females, Dr. Ling and Dr. Waters, who rotated the dishes to the remainder of the party.

Alex cared less about the delicious food and worked to keep from dropping it with his clumsy manipulation of chopsticks. He focused his attention on the beautiful Dr. Ling sitting at his right.

Frank began the conversation with the usual polite small talk. "Did you have a nice trip from Beijing?" "How do you like the conference so far?" "What do you think of London?"

She obliged with the usual answers in a polite tone. Alex found her to be calculating and a bit shy. She thought about her answers before phrasing them. Alex recognized this as a quintessential sign of introversion. Introverts tended to analyze what they would say before speaking, a trait he shared with her. She also made eye contact but lowered her eyes at times after speaking in what Alex deemed to be shyness.

After a round of initial pleasantries Frank provided a welcomed segue for Alex to engage Dr. Ling. "Dr. Ling, have you heard of Alex's work on radio frequencies?"

"Yes, I have," Dr. Ling replied turning to face Alex with a demure smile. "And please call me Xiu. We have something in common," she said as she looked into Alex's eyes.

"Oh really?" said Alex acting surprised. "I wouldn't think frequencies would have anything to do with resveratrol."

"But they do," said Xiu. "When you think of it on an epigenetic level, what you and I do to cells and DNA is the same. If you think of your quantum frequencies as packets of information affecting epigenetic information systems, then similarities exist with molecular compounds like resveratrol. Molecules transfer information to epigenetic systems as well. It is all about decreasing entropy in a system. Disease is entropy. Do you agree, Alex?"

"If you think of it that way, you are absolutely right. We are both working to reduce DNA errors, or entropy, by affecting the epigenetic systems that in turn affect DNA. This is a brilliant way to see it."

"I wondered if the quantum information from your frequencies acted as a way to modulate the effects of resveratrol. It would be interesting to discuss this further, Alex?"

"Of course, I would love to." Alex became even more excited.

Xiu turned to face her cohort Jianyu and they spoke in Mandarin. Jianyu smiled and nodded at Alex, and Xiu appeared embarrassed as she turned back toward him and smiled.

"He says she likes you," blurted Li from across the table in a thick Chinese accent. Alex became flush with embarrassment as the entire table stopped to listen.

"I am flattered," said Alex while bowing his head.

"We should have a toast," said Frank as he signaled to the waiter. Within what seemed like seconds the waiters carried in several small white bottles and began pouring drinks into small shot glasses. Alex overheard the Chinese men remark about the drink. "Maotai!" they exclaimed in acknowledgment.

"This is famous drink in China," said Li. "Strong alcohol." Frank raised a glass in a toast and faced the

Chinese.

"To our wonderful guests, Li, Jianyu and Xiu, we wish you much success." Both Chinese men responded with a hardy *Ganbei,* and downed their glasses. Alex and the others followed suit. "It is customary for men to drink bottoms up," said Xiu. "Women only sip."

Alex downed the drink and it made its way down his esophagus, burning all the way to his stomach. "Wow! How strong is this stuff?" said Alex while doing his best to suppress a cough.

"About sixty percent, I think," said Frank.

"Sixty percent alcohol?" Alex thought he'd better pace himself for risk of having to be carried back to the hotel.

"Yup, and it's customary for the men to keep up with the drinking," said Frank with a serious tone. Alex glanced around the table. Evelyn and Vern talked shop about nutraceuticals with Li and Jianyu as Frank split his attention between them and Xiu. But now everything had changed as the toasting war began.

Li proposed a toast next: "We thank our excellent hosts for this fine evening," he said while raising his glass. Everyone followed and shouted *Ganbei* before downing their drinks. Evelyn seemed to be keeping up, but Xiu just sipped a bit more of her original drink.

Alex soon discovered that everyone at the table needed to toast something, so he went next. "To the work of our beautiful guest, Xiu. May it someday help us to cure cancer. *Ganbei!*"

The *Ganbei's* kept coming as tongues became looser and conversations louder. Alex tried to pace himself by excusing himself to visit the bathroom. He also signaled the waiter to continue to bring water, which he drank after each toast. After a while the laughter became so loud that a waiter entered and asked them to be a bit quieter. The noise had pierced the thin walls of the private room and had disturbed some of the more sober guests.

The remainder of the night became a blur. He

remembered Frank calling some taxis to take them back to the hotel, and then walking him to the elevator. What happened between then and the next day was forever lost. But it had been a wonderful evening.

4
ALEX'S PRESENTATION

Alex awoke late the next morning and sprang out of bed when he realized the sun shone through the hotel window. "My presentation! What time is it?" he shouted as he gained full consciousness. The clock next to the bed read 11:00 am. Alex's 11:30 presentation was scheduled in one of the convention center's smaller conference rooms. He bounded out of bed and into the bathroom. His ragged, unshaven, and older than his thirty-one years image stared back at him in the mirror. His angular face had a bloated appearance topped with messy, dark brown, short cropped hair.

He showered and completed an abbreviated version of his morning ritual in record time. A quick glance at the full length mirror reminded him of his rather average physique. He'd never thought of himself as particularly handsome or particularly fit since he spent most of his time in front of computers or working on electronics equipment with little time to exercise.

He arrived with just a few minutes to spare to a filled room. The room held about fifty seats, a big contrast to Xiu's rock star presentation in the grand ballroom. He entered the room and scrambled to get his laptop to work with the projector. The moderator helped him as best he could, but Alex sensed his concern for beginning on time. A wave of performance anxiety washed over him as he surveyed the capacity crowd. He scanned the room and recognized the usual variety of scientists. As his eyes moved over them he discovered what he searched for. Xiu sat in the front row in the last seat on Alex's right. A wave of calmness spread through him as he thought that now everything would be okay.

He began his presentation with a brief history of the origins of his research. A few years ago, he had stumbled upon the work of Royal Raymond Rife, an inventor who lived from the late nineteenth to mid-twentieth century. Rife had produced many inventions, but Alex had taken interest in one in particular, a radio frequency machine that appeared to cure cancer. The machine became a hit in alternative medicine circles but soon fell out of favor when others failed to reproduce Rife's miraculous results. Mystery surrounded the Rife cancer curing machine's demise, while Rife himself blamed it all on a medical conspiracy. Alex conjectured some promise in killing cancer cells based on the original theory of the device and thought that Rife's early work merited a second chance.

He had taken the essential concept of Rife's machine and applied state of the art techniques in frequency modulation and quantum resonance. He'd rebuilt the device from the ground up. The new device bore little resemblance to the faded images of Rife's original device, but Alex hoped that it would kill cancer cells while leaving healthy cells intact by using various combinations of radio wave frequencies. The radio frequencies should not harm healthy cells, unlike traditional therapies such as chemotherapy and radiation.

Alex went on to explain some of the complexities that he needed to address in order to kill cancer cells in humans. One difficult problem involved finding resonant frequencies for each type of cancer cell and creating a quantum pulse to destroy it. The reoccurrence of cancer in the form of lethal metastatic disease after elimination of the initial cancerous cells presented another problem. These metastatic cells contained so many variations that it seemed almost impossible to kill them all.

The solution to the metastatic cell problem would be to kill cancerous cells while disabling cells in the early stages of becoming cancerous cells. Destroying early stage cancer cells proved difficult because of their similarity to normal cells. Using a target frequency on these cells would also destroy too many normal cells. The patient's cells could suffer more damage or die from the treatment.

As Alex neared the conclusion of his presentation, he spied one of the Latro at the back of the room. The tall man, standing over six feet, wore the traditional dark gray suit, white shirt and tie with the orange T. Alex found his demeanor, shaved head and muscular build to be threatening, and he hoped that he hadn't divulged anything that they would be interested in.

He wrapped things up and took questions. Most questions referred to obtaining copies of his research, or what the next phase entailed.

The Latro man in the back stood up. He towered over the group and reminded Alex of an alien since most scientists did not possess such a threatening presence.

"How do you plan to solve the interference problem?" the man asked in an authoritative tone.

"You mean, how do I plan to direct quantum energy without interfering with healthy cells?" said Alex.

"Yes; let's just say we are interested in your approach and would like to learn more," the man said as a hush fell over the small crowd.

"I have some ideas, but they are just theories to be addressed in the next research phase," said Alex.

"We will be in touch." The man turned to leave as a wave of anxiety swept over Alex.

"Thank you all and enjoy the rest of the conference," announced Alex with relief.

As everyone began to file out of the room, Xiu approached Alex. "I enjoyed your presentation, Alex. I am interested in your quantum envelopes. By the way, how are you today?" Alex knew she knew exactly how he felt.

"Not too bad, given that I don't remember how I got back to the hotel last night. I hope I didn't say anything embarrassing."

"No, you were a perfect gentleman. This is how the Chinese male culture is in business, lots of drinking."

"I'll say," said Alex, "Reminded me of my college days. Your companions can certainly put them away."

"They have had a lot of practice," said Xiu. "About your work, you mentioned a new paper discussing quantum envelopes? I would be pleased to read it."

"I will definitely get you a copy." Alex looked into her brown eyes. Xiu turned as Jianyu entered the room and shouted something in Mandarin to her.

"I must go; we will be leaving for China tomorrow," she said as she turned to leave.

"Thanks for coming," Alex called.

He returned to his room and slept the rest of the day. He awoke to darkness in a somewhat confused state. He turned to see 10:00 pm on the clock beside the bed, as well as the blinking red message light on the phone. He picked up the phone, dialed the message retrieval number and recognized Frank's voice. "Hey, buddy, we are going out tonight; if you'd like, join us in the lobby at six. You missed another good meeting with the Chinese earlier today. FYI, they are leaving tomorrow. Thought you might want to say goodbye to Xiu. By the way, she's in room 816. See ya later."

After debating with himself for several minutes and mustering his courage, Alex decided to clean up and pay one last visit to Xiu. He grabbed his notebook and made his way to the eighth floor. He stood outside her door for several minutes while getting up the courage to knock. When he did, her door opened to reveal Xiu dressed in jeans, a plain black T-shirt and sneakers.

She invited Alex into her room. "I wanted to say goodbye and show you more of my work, as you requested," Alex said as his heart rate quickened.

"I'm glad you came. I thought I would not see you again." They sat at the small hotel room table. Xiu scooted the chair next to Alex, her leg touching his. He found this arousing and struggled to focus on his work.

Alex described his project in detail, all the while enthralled with Xiu. She gave her full attention and asked frequent and intelligent questions. After an hour and an half, the conversation changed to more personal topics. "Is your wife missing you?"

"I'm not married," said Alex. "Too much moving around, and school. How about you? I'm sure a beautiful, intelligent and confident woman like you has a husband or a boyfriend." Alex hoped for the right answer.

"I am single. I am what is known in China as a leftover. Leftovers are women in their thirties who have not married because of devoting time to their education or careers. Chinese men are not interested in leftovers."

Hope stirred in Alex.

The night became long and the hours passed as their conversation crossed over from professional to private topics. They discovered many similar interests besides science including video games, science fiction movies and neo-classical music. Alex felt the mutual attraction grow as their conversation continued. He hoped Xiu shared the close bond he felt developing between them. Finally, in the early hours of the morning, Xiu said she needed to get some sleep so she could get ready for her trip in a few hours. She walked Alex to her door and said goodnight.

As she closed the door Alex blurted out, "Wait...I know this is sudden, but, can I kiss you goodnight?"

She smiled and blushed while her eyes first moved to the floor and then met his. She leaned toward him in the doorway. His arms encircled her as he moved in. His heart beat faster. Overwhelming passion spread through him as their lips met, and their powerful attraction made the long and passionate kiss difficult to end. Alex had kissed more than his fair share of women throughout high school and college. He'd even had a couple of steady girlfriends. All of the closeness he felt in these past relationships combined with all of his past sexual encounters did not compare to this one kiss with Xiu. It was as if a powerful inertia had drawn them together, and it stirred him deep inside.

In a few sublime moments the kiss ended. Alex turned and walked down the long narrow hallway, his mind still reeling with Xiu.

5

THE CHICAGO TEAM

*T*he overcast November Chicago sky shone through the third floor block windows of the Northern University lab.

"Good morning, my wonderful team," said Alex with sarcastic enthusiasm. "Ready for another day of science?" Mumbles and groans met his enthusiasm.

Alex's team consisted of a ragtag group of graduate students. Kira Stout, the youngest member, performed the primary computer programming duties. Despite being the youngest, she exhibited by far the most intelligence. After completing high school at sixteen, a bachelor's degree in physics at nineteen and a master's at twenty, she was well on her way to her doctorate in biomedical engineering at the ripe old age of twenty-two. Kira's in-your-face personality complimented her looks, featuring skinny jeans donned over a skinny frame and long dirty-blond hair which was rarely blond and presently a wild mixture of red and orange. When not in pajamas, she wore band merchandise t-shirts and skull jewelry. Her looks contrasted her intellectual abilities and she excelled at programming, solving complex problems regarding spectrum analysis, and quantum resonance.

Alex saw through Kira's counter-culture façade and realized the genius within. He considered her a valued team member despite the difficulties she presented with communication since she always seemed to have earbuds blasting alternative rock. In her spare moments she loved to challenge the guys to video games and held high rankings in all of the popular games.

Kevin Laslo assisted Alex with the frequency machine, and Hans Friedel, a biologist, handled the cells. Like Alex, Kevin followed the traditional path to biomedical engineering. His jet black hair crowned a long narrow face donning wire-framed glasses. Kevin's seriousness and meticulous nature contrasted Kira's carefree and edgy personality. He often remarked at how Kira ran circles around him in math while listening to Linkin Park. Kevin also liked video games and often challenged Kira to Halo, Call of Duty, Destiny and whatever else they got their hands on. They even installed an older X-Box gaming console in the lab. Kira never showed any mercy and Kevin often ended up throwing the controller across the room in a fit of frustration. Kevin referred to Kira as *the kid* since she was four years younger.

Hans carried more than a few extra pounds on his stocky body and looked older than his twenty-six years. His lack of fitness, frequent smoking and receding hairline gave him the appearance of a forty-year-old. Almost finished with his PhD in biology, Hans at times exhibited a negative and dramatic personality causing the others to reel him in when he indulged in a negativity bender. Hans often went missing throughout the day since he took numerous smoking breaks.

Together, the team toiled in a plain, concrete block lab peppered with large wooden tables full of electronic equipment, environmental chambers, computers and an overworked coffee machine that always reeked of burnt coffee. The large garbage cans overflowed with empty coffee cups, soda cans and fast food containers. An old beat-up sofa that Alex and Kevin had found on a curb occupied one wall and faced an old TV, which served a dual role as a break area and gaming station since Kira had connected the X-Box to it.

"He hasn't been the same since the conference," whispered Kira to Kevin. "Must be love," she said in a sing-song tone.

"I know, it's like he's living in some kind of virtual fantasy land, like Second Life meets eHarmony," said Kevin mocking Alex. "I wonder if they have avatars getting it on."

"You wish you could be so fucking lucky," said Kira. "When was the last time you were with a female? And I mean a real human, not some video game amazon sex creature you sit and drool over while manipulating your joystick!"

"Ouch...Kira...brutal...I'm shocked," said Kevin with sarcasm.

"Just sayin'," said Kira.

"Hey, what's going on here?" Alex reached Kira and Kevin's corner of the lab.

"Just a friendly discussion," said a smug Kira. Kevin just shook his head.

"So, is it true that you connect with Xiu like twenty-five hours a day?" teased Kira. Kevin smiled and laughed.

"We do connect every day," said Alex. "Hey, we need her expertise in resveratrol."

"Kevin wants to know if you go on virtual dates with avatars that look like each of you only, you know, enhanced. Like the video game representations of yourselves. Yours would have big bulging muscles and hers would have huge boobs and a tight ass. Unless of course she *has* huge boobs and a tight ass in real life, since we've never even seen a picture of her." Kira displayed a Cheshire smile.

"You are so bad Kira," said Kevin shaking his head.

"Alright, everyone come over here." Alex pulled out his cell phone and began flipping through his gallery. "Here is a pic I took of the Chinese delegation in London when we had dinner together. There, see, she is on the right." The group gathered around and passed Alex's phone so each could get a good look at Xiu.

"Very cute, but no huge boobs though, and I can't see her ass," said Kira.

"Very attractive," said Kevin, and Hans confirmed by nodding.

"Okay, now is everyone satisfied? Can we get some work done?" Alex grabbed his cell phone and took a seat at his work station. The group, satisfied with getting a look at the mysterious Xiu, dispersed and dove into their respective tasks.

Alex's relationship with Xiu indeed blossomed. They Skyped, emailed and chatted daily in an endless exchange of personal information, ideas, and romantic interludes. They seemed inseparable in their own virtual world causing both their romance and professional relationships to develop at a rapid pace. One of the most fruitful developments emerging from their incessant communication involved the discovery that certain combinations of frequencies enhanced the effects of Xiu's resveratrol formula on cancer cells. Both Alex and Xiu were very optimistic about this dual approach.

The frequency generator began to materialize as well with pieces fitting together like a fine stained glass window. Alex spent countless hours hovering over and tending to his baby. The main portion consisted of a hollow tube about three feet long with various coils encircling it. Thick cables attached the coils to racks of electronic equipment which, in turn, streamed more cables to a desktop computer. The tube served as the target site for cell samples. The treatment consisted of bombarding cell samples with various combinations of frequencies.

Alex's team had discovered that each cancerous cell

emitted a distinct electromagnetic frequency spectrum. This quantum resonance signature resulted from cellular processes such as the movement of charged ions inside the cell as well as the vibrations of tiny microtubules. All living cells exhibited a distinct quantum resonance. The team detected this resonance with a special quantum resonance detector built into the frequency machine that sent the information to a computer. Healthy cells exhibited a certain range of resonances while cancerous cells exhibited a different range. Exposing cells to a much higher power signature resonance caused these cells to die.

The team experienced much success with this approach except for one thing. Cells in the process of becoming cancerous resonated close to normal cells. These cells metastasized spreading the cancer around the body. Treating someone with these frequency signatures would also kill their healthy cells. With no way to estimate the damage, the treatment could be lethal. Without solving the problem of eliminating precancerous cells of this kind their cure amounted to nothing more than fancy chemotherapy or radiation therapy.

But this was where Xiu's resveratrol formula came into play. The team found that the addition of resveratrol decreased DNA errors and changed the frequency signature of pre-cancerous cells. The team now identified these cells, obtained the frequency signature and zapped them out of existence. Their tremendous progress since the conference had inspired Alex's team to work around the clock. Alex even supplied cots for the team to crash on as they neared a breakthrough.

"Hey bud, how are things going in the war room?" a voice called out at the door.

"Mark, come on in, we are running a test on breast cancer cells." Alex motioned Mark over to the generator. Dr. Mark Winter, Alex's older brother by two years, displayed a mature, level-headed demeanor lacking in Alex. Alex's happy-go-lucky dreamer personality contrasted

Mark's cool and calculating presence.

Mark and Alex were the offspring of two well-educated parents. Both parents had worked as engineers for the same defense contractor in the Chicago area, where they had met and had fallen in love. They worked hard to provide their two sons with everything needed to stimulate their minds, with no shortage of science and engineering themed activities. The boys attended the best schools and summer programs and entertained themselves with lots of science toys including computers, telescopes, robotics kits and chemistry labs.

Mark and Alex had displayed their science geek personalities throughout elementary and middle school. Mark would pass through a grade with glowing remarks from his teachers, but Alex came along two years later and blew them away. It seemed as though Mark had set the bar high, but Alex had had no problem jumping over it. In high school they both ended up in the engineering club, where Mark held the presidency until Alex took over after Mark graduated. They took on ambitious projects, leaving the other students in the dust while engaging in fierce competitive debates about such topics as how to best simulate Zero-G conditions or which processor to use in a microcontroller board.

The competitive nature of their relationship expanded beyond the school clubs. At home, it emerged in various science projects and video games. The boys spent countless hours playing games as equal opponents, but only for a short time. Mark would take the lead on a new game, but before long Alex caught up and surpassed him. They even engaged in an unsuccessful round of double dating. These dates often ended in cell phone game battles that pissed off their dates with both girls ditching them.

Mark and Alex became roommates at Georgia Tech, where Alex majored in biomedical engineering and Mark in electrical engineering. Both went on to earn PhD's, Alex completing his at John Hopkins and Mark at MIT.

Midwesterners at their core, both brothers returned to Chicago to teach and conduct research programs at Northern University. Alex worked with the school of medicine in the new area of integrative medicine, while Mark worked in the school of engineering on communications research.

Their idealistic lives were not without tragedy. One February morning, when both boys were attending undergraduate school, Mark received a call from their Aunt Joan. She wept as she told Mark of the tragic accident. While Georgia was enjoying sunny warm weather, a severe winter storm battered Chicago. Exhibiting their model employee behavior, the boys' parents had set out to drive to work despite the severe winter weather. The blowing and drifting snow became much worse during their commute, and visibility became dangerously low. Their father had struggled to keep the car on the road and thought that if they made it to work, then the plows would clear the roads for a safe return trip home.

He had continued to decrease his speed while traveling along one desolate stretch of two-lane highway. This portion of the trip included a long steep hill that the SUV climbed with little effort in good weather but struggled to do so in the blizzard. He fought to maintain enough speed to climb the hill without slipping backward. Snow blew across the windshield while the wipers careened back and forth at high speed. As they climbed to about two thirds up the hill, a snowplow coming from the opposite direction began to lose control. The driver apparently hit the brakes while on an icy patch and lost control once the snowplow began sliding down the hill. He did his best to avoid the collision, but his uphill climb along with the SUV's slow speed left little opportunity to maneuver. The SUV, no match for the massive inertia of the snowplow sliding down the hill, slammed into it, and the head on collision had killed both parents.

Both sons grieved the death of their beloved parents, but Mark bore the brunt of the tragedy and fell into a deep depression. Alex tried his best to help his brother, but Mark remained distant. Mark's distance continued throughout undergraduate school. Silence and distance replaced the usual roommate banter and teasing for the remainder of Mark's time at Georgia Tech.

Graduate school afforded some physical distance that seemed to help Mark, and the brothers grew a bit closer during this time. However, the scars of their parents' deaths forever changed the carefree relationship of their youth. Mark found some solace in therapy and antidepressants, and Alex found it in his work.

Now both worked at the same college near their boyhood home, which helped to heal their relationship. Alex still sensed Mark's distance but things had become better since they'd begun spending a lot of free time together. Alex knew that it was wise to be patient and wait for Mark to heal; he trusted that his brother would come around in time.

Hans placed a cell sample on a small petri dish then into the frequency machine's tube. Kira entered commands into the computer. The machine sprang into action emitting a low pitched hum followed by a few loud clicks.

"That should do it," said Kira.

Hans retrieved the cells and carried them to the area of the lab that housed the microscopes. "I'll let you know about this one once my analysis is complete."

"Sure enough, Hans; looking forward to it," said Alex.

"So when are we going to get more funding for the startup?" said Mark.

"Let's talk about it tonight. I have to teach my quantum mechanics course this afternoon but I can meet you after I finish."

"It's a date. See you then. My place or yours?"

"Yours will do. Mine is a mess, as usual," said Alex.

Mark had badgered Alex to form a startup company

over the past year. Alex's initial reluctance subsided when he realized his research funds neared exhaustion. Mark provided a convincing argument, playing to Alex's ego, that his frequency work was an important step toward a potential cancer cure. Mark also hoped the symbiotic relationship with his handling the logical and mundane business duties while Alex handled the creative duties would further help to heal their past.

Mark dove into learning about startups and business by reading books, watching videos and talking to other entrepreneurs in the local startup community. Chicago provided a hotbed of startup activity, so Mark did not need to look far to find as much information as he wished to absorb. He found the world of business quite fascinating and imagined himself a top executive in his and Alex's venture, *if* they could get it off the ground.

Mark wanted to make an equal contribution to Alex's work. The idea of working *with* his brother instead of competing with him kept Mark's hopes alive for healing their relationship. Both brothers wished to recapture some of what was lost with the death of their parents. Until now, neither knew how that could be possible. Their relationship had become superficial during the years following their parents' death. Perhaps working together would deepen it. After all, besides a few aging aunts and uncles, and a handful of distant cousins with whom they had nothing in common, they were the only family that each one had. Mark often thought of how proud his parents would have been if they could just make this work.

6

THE MEETING AT MARK'S APARTMENT

Alex knocked on the old heavy wooden door in the dark corridor of Mark's apartment building. Mark lived in a 1930's apartment complex on Chicago's near north side. His spacious apartment displayed its advanced age with decrepit wooden windows, creaky wood floors and ancient appliances. Alex swore that he'd seen Mark's old gas stove in a museum exhibit about domestic life in the 1950s.

"Door's open," Mark called out from inside. "I'll be right there. Go ahead and introduce yourself."

Alex cracked open the door and noticed two other men standing in Mark's living room. One, a tall preppy looking gentleman with blond hair wearing Dockers and a sweater, stood leaning with his back against the wall near a bookshelf. Alex estimated his height to be at least about six feet and his age to be about forty. The other, a shorter, thirty-something dark complexioned Hispanic man wearing a flannel shirt, jeans and cowboy boots, stood facing the living room window.

"This must be the other infamous Dr. Winter," said the tall man. "I'm Peter North, and this is Xavier Valdez." The men reached out to shake Alex's hand. "Mark told us a lot about you and your work. Fascinating."

"Peter was referred to me by a friend of mine. You

remember Andy and his Internet startup?" said Mark as he entered the room holding a chilled six pack of beer. "Peter knows everyone in the startup community; incubators, investors, you name it, Peter knows about it." Mark pointed to the other man. "You might remember Xavier from my program at the college. Xavier comes to us from Mexico and is a dynamite physicist. He is also an expert on quantum resonance."

"My pleasure," said Alex. "What part of Mexico are you from?"

"I am from Cheran, a small town outside Mexico City. My family still lives there," said Xavier.

"He's been dying to work with you, and I think he will make a fantastic addition." Mark exhibited an air of levity while passing out the beers. "I took the liberty of inviting them because I think it is time to get our little company going."

Alex remembered Xavier from the university but was unfamiliar with his work. He wasn't surprised about his cluelessness about Xavier's interest in quantum resonance because of the university's poor interdepartmental communication system.

"I guess you *do* know me, Mark," Alex grinned. "You know I would keep going on and on with my head stuck in my research and never come up for air. I appreciate the push."

"That's what brothers are for." Mark put his arm around Alex. "Believe it or not, Peter has found an investor who is interested, and Xavier is ready to share his knowledge about quantum resonance. I've already briefed them on the project. Peter thinks we should form a startup as soon as possible. Your funds are running out in a few months, and your project will in essence be dead, so now is the time my genius brother. I propose a toast, to our new venture."

The group raised bottles of beer and took some healthy gulps. "I was thinking of naming our new company

Freetech, Inc. to symbolize our free thinking." Mark looked hopeful that the others would agree.

Alex replied in an announcer's voice, "If there are no objections, I now introduce to you the next ground breaking global innovative company. Gentleman, I give you Freetech, Incorporated!" The others responded by lifting their drinks and swallowing large gulps of beer.

The group discussed the potential cancer cure and how it could revolutionize cancer treatment if they solved a few more problems and were able to get the process to work on humans. They were still a long way from human trials. A much larger problem was the Latro looming in the background. Alex remembered that Tando showed an interest in him at the conference, which had resulted in his development of stringent security measures regarding the flow of information. He even managed to encrypt his emails and discussions with Xiu.

"How are we going to keep this from Tando?" said Alex. "We can't publish any papers, or file a patent because they are always watching. I wouldn't want them to swoop in and destroy us before we even get our feet on the ground." said Alex.

"Don't worry, we even have that covered. We are going to form a sham company that will appear to work on a wellness app for smartphones. This will be our front and will not attract the slightest attention from Tando. They will think that we're a typical band of college startup types developing an app. It's the perfect cover. Meanwhile, we will be working on the real project in secret. This will give us at least a year to prepare before filing corporate financials that might be analyzed and tip off Tando."

"It's brilliant," said Alex. "We can work on both projects at the same time and develop our process in secret."

"I've discussed this with our potential investor and he is good with it," Peter chimed in after gulping another swallow of beer.

"What about Xiu's formulation?" said Alex.

"What about it?" said Mark. "She will continue working in Beijing and sending us updates. Of course she will be a full partner as well."

"I have a lot to talk to her about. I'm sure she will be excited."

"Why doesn't she come to the US?"

"That's a complicated one. It is difficult for the Chinese to get US visas. Plus that may further attract Latro since I'm sure that they are watching her. So we should keep things status quo for now."

"Peter, who is the investor?" asked Alex.

"His name is Sam Foulton. Have you heard of him?"

"Nope," said Alex.

"I wouldn't think you would have," said Peter.

"He is super secretive and would love to stick it to Tando. He has a history with them sabotaging some of his other startups. Good thing he's made most of his money in other ventures. I think he did it with garbage. He owns a huge recycling company and also dabbles in tech and some other areas. They can't mess with his other companies. He is very interested in alternative medicine and health and just about started salivating when I told him about us. He's the one who came up with the sham company idea."

"How much is he willing to give us?" said Alex.

"Somewhere around one million dollars."

"Way more than I thought we'd get," said Alex as he finished off his beer. "

"Hey, we are talking about a revolutionary cancer cure here," said Mark. "You'll be surprised how fast we can burn that amount of cash. Frequency generators, microscopes, lab equipment, computers, environmental chambers and so on...not cheap. Plus there will be enough for each of us to draw a small salary."

The night progressed with detailed discussions about the new company. Mark had found some loft space in the warehouse district north of the city. Peter tipped him off about a recent startup failing to get funding for their second round, which deep sixed them. They signed a three- year lease on the space and were willing to sublet it for half of what they'd paid. Peter pulled out his laptop and showed Mark the detailed financials that he'd produced. Peter and Mark dove into the numbers while Xavier and Alex discussed how to solve the quantum resonance problem.

After two additional six packs, the group decided to call it a night. Alex decided to wait until morning to call Xiu with the good news since it would be nighttime in Beijing. He headed home in the cold November night thinking his ship had finally come in. Life was good. He would be a partner in a million-dollar company that one day might be worth billions, he had a gorgeous Chinese girlfriend, and he loved his work.

7
THE NEXT MONTHS

The cold Chicago winter months passed as the team set up operations in the loft space. They did their best to duplicate the Northern University lab, complete with the beat-up sofa and X-box. Lannon stone brick, wood, assorted pipes and metal ducts replaced the concrete blocks of the University lab. The large second floor windows overlooked a busy industrial street, which resulted in the low sonic rumble from large trucks passing during working hours. The previous startup had left a huge mess to clean up consisting of fast food wrappers, papers, and uneaten pieces of food that had attracted mice during the vacancy. The overflowing garbage bins stood in their original locations, untouched by human hands.

"Hey, Hans," shouted Kira from across the room. Hans turned. "I'll bet you could fill up your rat cages right here. Just set a few traps and get some home grown critters."

"Maybe I'll just come over to your place and get some," said Hans. "I'm sure I would find a few living under your bed."

"At least I don't walk around knee deep in cigarette butts," said Kira.

"Children, children, stop it, or I'll make you hug and

make up!" said Mark.

"I'd pay to see that," chided Alex.

The existing layout consisted of pods of four desks facing each other placed throughout the space, hardly a useful setup for a lab. The team salvaged what they could and divided the space into two sections. The frequency generator team occupied a little more than half the space while the app development team settled in the leftover space. Although no physical structure existed between the two, a kind of invisible dividing line kept each team within their own boundaries. A makeshift break room materialized in one corner, complete with microwave, refrigerator, table and chairs. The sofa and X-Box resided there as well and became the gaming area, which grew with the addition of a couple of old recliners from Goodwill. As much as the team worked in their separate areas, there were no dividing lines in the break room. It was apparent they all enjoyed each other's company.

The frequency generator team led by Alex consisted of Kira, Hans and the new addition, Xavier. The app development team led by Mark included Kevin and newcomer Julie Foley, one of Mark's computer engineering grad students. Like Kira, Julie programmed computers with ease, and working on the app provided little challenge to her. But the similarities between Julie and Kira ended there, as their personalities and styles were opposite. Kira was young, hip and gay with an infectious personality, while Julie displayed introversion and a bit of negativity. Julie wore drab clothes, attempting to hide her overweight body, and it seemed as though she never knew what to do with her long dark hair. She hid her face behind large round glasses and seemed to prefer the company of computers to real people.

Peter played the role of business guru and handled the financial, legal and logistical portions of the business. His involvement in a couple of previous startups, one of them an advertising website, provided him a modicum of success. Peter cobbled together a living by freelancing for various companies. His expertise in social media allowed him to earn money consulting with companies, helping them to begin, maintain, or optimize their social media campaigns. His ability to earn enough for a decent living allowed him to provide child support to his ten-year-old daughter. He adored her and struggled with the guilt of not being with her while she spent time with her mom in his limited placement schedule. He hoped someday to see her more than the every other weekend allowed from his divorce.

Mark studied wellness in preparation for producing the app. The plan for the app included developing software that allowed it to aggregate information from various wellness sites and integrated wearable devices. The team hoped the finished product, a one-stop for all users to access wellness information about diet, exercise, and disease prevention, would fare well in the crowded app marketplace. Another feature allowed users to track their own fitness by logging activities or pairing their wearable devices to the app. The clean, easy-to-use interface automatically updated with all the newest and most relevant articles on health and wellness. The first phase of the project consisted of developing a non-native app connected to a website running on both Apple and Android platforms. The second phase included development of a native app that ran independent of the website. This meant the website development came first, before app development.

Both teams worked at various times throughout the day and night depending on their classes, teaching and university research schedules. Alex's team worked Tuesday and Thursday afternoons while Mark's team worked Monday and Wednesday afternoons. Evenings and weekends brought everyone together. Xavier's interest in 3D online gaming spread to the other team members and work sessions would morph into group gaming sessions.

Sometimes the marathon gaming continued late into the night. This helped the teams to engage in some healthy name calling, dissing and competitive gloating while blowing off steam.

The main game, a first person shooter known as Hadron, took place on the detailed imaginary planet of Hadron. Players created their own characters, male or female, chose exotic weapons and formed teams in different sections of the planet. An interesting feature included the ability of gamers to own properties and build houses. Players did this once they reached a high level. After some intense gaming sessions, Xavier became the first to build his own house, Kira followed by a close second. Everyone played except for Alex, Mark and Peter. Alex tried the game and found it entertaining at first but lost interest when he fell behind the others in skill. He soon tired of becoming phaser fodder after more adept players like Xavier toyed with him like a cat with a mouse before blowing him to bits. Also, his preoccupation with a certain Asian lady didn't help.

Alex continued his daily contact with Xiu. Their relationship grew stronger and stronger as they shared their successes and daily lives. Xiu continued to send samples of her resveratrol formula which Alex's team used in the combined treatment. The project progressed as planned and the team identified the signatures of breast and lung cancer cells. The addition of resveratrol also allowed the team to identify the signatures of precancerous cells. This breakthrough allowed the team to make fast progress. Along with this progress came increased complexity, especially if they wanted to treat several forms of cancer. Alex decided that it would be better to focus on breast and lung cancer rather than to run trials on other cancers. Success in curing these cancers would be a huge step toward developing future cures.

8
THE CALL

Alex sat at his dining room table finishing the last few bites of a bowl of cereal, a morning ritual he'd kept since his childhood. It was 7:00 am and time for his usual morning chat with Xiu. He booted up his laptop and slurped the last bit of milk from the bottom of the bowl. The computer sprang to life and he logged into the chat program he used for communicating with Xiu. After a quick mental calculation he estimated the time to be 8:00 pm in Beijing.

The screen popped on with a disturbing visage of Xiu. The smooth skin of her forehead displayed several furrowed lines and her eyes were half closed in a squint that hid the redness that often comes from weeping. The smile that lit up her face and Alex's heart when they first made contact in their virtual world was gone. Her full lips, pinched together and quivering, were only successful for a moment in holding back an inevitable outpouring of emotion and tears as she began to sob.

"They are stopping my work," said Xiu with a shaky voice. "Today is my last day. They are shutting down my lab," she said as she held back tears.

"I don't understand," said Alex. "Why would they do that when you have such wonderful support from Peking

53

University?"

"I think it might have something to do with Tando." Her trembling voice became more stable. "They think my work is a threat. They probably bribed the University administrators to shut me down. They are reassigning me to teach more courses until I can determine a new research area."

"Do you think Tando is on to us here in Chicago?" asked Alex with a growing concern in his voice.

"No, I don't think so. I just think they were at my presentation in London and decided to shut me down. They do not know about our work together."

"I will be sending the last batch of resveratrol today. I am sorry," said Xiu as the tears began again.

"It is not your fault, we will figure something out. Don't worry. I need to go now and talk to the team. I love you."

"I love you too," said Xiu, and the connection clicked off. Alex pulled out his cell phone and sent a text requesting that everyone on both teams meet later that evening.

The hours crept by, and Alex couldn't stop thinking about Xiu. His schedule included teaching two classes and attending an administrative meeting with his dean. His first class, an undergraduate course in digital electronics, went as usual. He lectured in a medium-size classroom to eager engineering majors. His familiarity with this topic, which included the use of Boolean algebra to reduce redundancy in logic circuits, needed little review. His afternoon course in quantum mechanics did not go as well since he'd begun to feel even more distracted as the day wore on. An inadvertent error on the chalkboard caused the class to spin into a frenzy of confusion. He always hated how undergraduate students spun out of control at the slightest mistake. When he discovered the error a few minutes after writing it, and went to erase it and make the correction, the class responded with multiple sighs and moans. It was as if he'd sprung an unannounced pop quiz on them.

The dean's meeting distracted Alex but he laid low and tried to cruise through it. The meeting interrupted his thoughts of Xiu several times when he needed to report on his participation in various academic committees. Finally it ended, and Alex hurried off campus to get to Freetech as soon as he could. He continued mulling over the problem throughout his journey to the lab.

As he made his way up the warehouse stairs, his sweaty palms slid a bit on the metal railing. He sensed the slight tilt of the steps where they were worn in the center from the multitude of past stair climbers. His awareness of this phenomenon provoked the realization that he had spent most of the day walking with his head down, deep in thought.

The large metal door swung open revealing a serious-looking group. Their anxious demeanor created an even more somber state in Alex as he became evermore aware of his own growing anxiety. Mark and Peter were already there and had arranged the desk chairs into two rows. They sat in the front along with Kevin and Kira. Hans, Julie, and Xavier sat behind them. Alex entered and made his way to the desk facing them. He leaned back against the desk, half-sitting. "Thank you all for coming. I received some bad news today."

"What's wrong, Alex? You look pretty serious." Mark looked concerned.

"I'll just give it to you straight. They are shutting Xiu down. We are getting the last shipment of resveratrol in a few days, and that's it, no more is coming."

"What the fuck?" said Mark. "Is the Latro onto us?"

"Xiu is sure that it's was just about her. She said she thought that the Latro had probably bribed her superiors. She doesn't think they know about us. I believe her, and I'm confident that we're safe...for the time being."

"I'm sorry, Alex," said Mark as he stood and put his

arm around his brother's shoulder and gave him a consolatory pat on the back. "It must be hard for her, and for you."

"So now what?" Peter asked, concerned. "We are dead without Xiu's resveratrol. What about Biopharmco? Can they reproduce Xiu's formula? I mean, I know you and Xiu are an item, but we need that stuff."

"Frank would love to be able to do that, and believe me, he has tried, but Xiu is the only one who can produce it. Plus involving Frank would alert Tando, and then they would be on his tail too," said Mark.

"I've been thinking about this all day, and I think I may have a solution," Alex said as he looked up and saw the concern in the eyes of each of his team members. "I must go to China. I will go to China and work with Xiu to set up her resveratrol lab along with a duplicate frequency lab. This will give us a couple of advantages. For one, we can double our output by having two labs. We already have a secure connection to China, and plenty of money from our first round.

"Why doesn't lover girl come here?" Kira baited.

"It is nearly impossible for Xiu to get a visa to come to the U.S., plus Tando will be watching her closely."

"Actually, that's not a bad idea," Mark added. "It would be great to be involved in producing the resveratrol formula."

"I checked it out; I can leave in about two weeks. There is a Chinese consulate in Chicago, and I can get an accelerated tourist visa. It shouldn't be a problem cloning the lab and setting up Xiu. The real challenge will be in cloning you all. I'm sure we can find some Chinese students or technicians to help, but you will need to continue doing the majority of the work."

Alex continued. "This is where the secure connection comes into play. Kira, I will need you to analyze the data from China. Xavier, you will take my place here and work with Kevin on the frequency generator. Hans will work with his Chinese counterpart on the Bio side. Mark's team will remain the same." Alex's voice gained more confidence. "I need you all to work with me on this."

"I will get going on a list of what you will need," said Xavier."

"I'll work on increasing the bandwidth in our China web connection," added Kira.

"I can encrypt the documents you will need to carry to China," said Kevin while opening his laptop.

"I'll get working on developing biological testing protocols, but now I'm dying for a smoke," said Hans as he headed out the door to light up. They spent the remainder of the evening developing a detailed plan for this new phase of their project.

The team ran few trials on cancer cells during the following two weeks while they prepared for Alex's trip. Xiu worked on finding space and technicians in Beijing. Fortunately, Xiu's uncle, who had some deep connections in local politics, knew people who could find just about anything with the appropriate bribes. Xiu and her contacts had located a space in an industrial area near the sixth ring of Beijing. Beijing, an immense city with a population of eleven and a half million people spanning over six thousand square miles, had eight freeway bypasses or, as the Chinese called them, rings.

9
CHINA

*T*he two weeks flew by and Alex found himself in O'Hare airport waiting for his journey to China to begin. His excitement grew as the time for his flight approached, bringing him ever closer to his beloved Xiu. His direct flight took the northern route over the North Pole and U.S.S.R. which limited his travel time to a little over thirteen hours. The 3:30 pm departure time meant that he would arrive in Beijing at 7:45 pm, two days later.

Alex boarded the plane, dropped into his seat and slid his backpack under the seat in front of him. He tried to calm his nerves over carrying a large amount of cash in his backpack. Peter had decided that paying for everything with cash was the only way to avoid detection by the Latro. This presented a problem with customs, since travelers were limited to ten thousand US dollars or about fifty thousand Yuan. Alex was carrying ten times the allowed amount.

Getting caught at customs and spending time in Chinese detention worried Alex more and more as the flight progressed. At one point he dozed and dreamt about Chinese Customs discovering the cash and detaining him. He did not want to end up in a Chinese work camp in some cold northern province.

After waking from his dream he shifted his attention to reading magazines or watching movies. He decided to try thinking about Xiu and imaged how things would be when they were together again. This helped to take the edge off his growing anxiety.

Throughout the restless night, Alex's head filled with thoughts of Xiu. He found relief from his anxiety by thinking about their time together in London and about the powerful attraction they had experienced. He hoped time and distance had not weakened that mutual attraction. He thought about seeing her for the first time at the conference and how her formality as a presenter contrasted with the genuine sweetness that endeared him to her. He thought about their meeting at the restaurant and how she had smiled every time he'd looked at her and how she moved her long dark hair to one side of her face as if an artist had sculpted the final touches to his masterpiece.

The plane landed on time in Beijing and Alex followed the crowd through the airport to customs to face the impending moment of truth. Alex proceeded past several guards dressed in tan and red uniforms, which made him even more nervous. He began to sweat, and his hand shook when the customs agent handed him the declaration form. He retreated to one of several stands stocked with dull pencils and took a deep breath. "Calm down," he muttered to himself. "Act normal...almost there." He finished filling out the declaration and approached the same agent, a strong looking woman who displayed a serious and methodical demeanor. Alex handed her the form and she snatched it from his hand and glanced over it. The seconds passed like hours. Her eyes passed over him from head to toe several times while maintaining a serious expression.

"Are you in Beijing for business or pleasure?" she asked in a stern tone.

"I'm on vacation," said Alex while working hard to

maintain his composure.

"Where are you staying?" she asked while staring straight into his eyes.

"Um...with my girlfriend, Dr. Xiu Ling," Her demeanor underwent the most dramatic transformation from stern to happy as a huge smile spread across her face.

"Oh, you have Chinese girlfriend; and a doctor too. Have a nice trip." She waved him through. Alex breathed a sigh of relief as he followed the others toward the luggage area, all the while clutching his precious backpack.

A few moments later he found himself ascending a long ramp. Numerous Chinese lined the ramp shouting and waving to relatives and friends who had arrived. Alex scanned the group for Xiu, thinking first that she might be there, standing and waving to him, but then decided that her reserved nature would certainly prohibit such behavior. He surmised that their reunion would surely take place away from the crowd and in the open area ahead. His legs weakened and his stomach tightened again. This time it reminded him of a child's excitement on Christmas morning. His anticipation grew with every step.

The crowd inched its way up the ramp and began to disperse. Alex's eyes searched the crowd but still could not see anyone that resembled Xiu. Doubt began to take root in his mind as he moved with the throng toward the luggage area.

His concern dissipated when he spotted her outline near the large windows facing the street. "Xiu! Xiu!" he called and waved. She spotted him and waved back as she flashed him a wide smile. They made their way through the crowd to each other and were soon face to face. After the thousands of words that they had exchanged in chats and conversations, Alex couldn't believe that she was now standing right in front of him in what seemed like a halcyon reality.

She was as he remembered her. Tight jeans and a button-up blouse caressed her thin but athletically toned body with just the right amount of curves. Her black hair provided a sensuous outline to her umber Asian skin and full lips adorned with a dusty rose pink color. Xiu possessed the perfect balance of strength and sweetness, which Alex found irresistible.

She peered into Alex's eyes and his heart jumped. He had never experienced such strong feelings for any other woman.

He dropped his backpack and took both of her hands into his as he continued to gaze into her eyes. He wanted this moment to linger and hoped she wanted the same. "Xiu, I am so happy to finally be here," he said as he kept his unbroken gaze.

"I am happy you are here too, Alex." He gave her arm a slight pull as if to signal an embrace and she obliged causing them to break the tension of their physical separation. Alex was at peace holding her in his arms. They separated and kissed in the same way they did in London, rekindling the passion of their first. Then they turned and walked toward the luggage area, hand in hand. To Alex, this new and wonderful experience of being a couple felt right. She gave his hand a gentle squeeze as they walked toward the rotating luggage rack.

Alex retrieved his luggage and a Chinese man approached and grabbed his suitcase and motioned for them to follow him to his taxi. Xiu jumped in front of him, wrestled the suitcase from his grasp and motioned him away. Alex, perplexed, said, "What's wrong? Don't we need a taxi?"

"You do not understand China," said Xiu in a gentle manner. "This is a black taxi, government taxis are better." She went on to explain how years ago she had made the mistake of getting into a black or private taxi. These unregulated taxis charged whatever they wished. Government taxis had uniform rates, were cleaner and more trustworthy.

Xiu took charge and directed the taxi to her home off

the third ring in the seemingly endless city of Beijing. Despite the darkness, Alex enjoyed looking at the continuous parade of buildings. The taxi pulled up to a crowed highrise apartment complex. Alex unloaded the taxi, paid the fair and followed Xiu through the door of the large building in front of them. Xiu said, "I am on the fifth floor," and began climbing the darkened stairwell. The unfinished nature of the stairwell surprised Alex as they made their way up the stairs. Plain light bulbs hung from the ceiling, and the concrete walls gapped at the corners.

"Where is the elevator?" said Alex as he sucked in deep breaths.

"There is no elevator."

"You mean you walk up five flights of stairs every day? With groceries and whatever else you bring home?" Alex struggled to catch his breath. "No wonder you are so thin."

After an exhausting climb for Alex, they both reached her apartment. The small apartment included a sleek selection of modern furniture. The door opened to a large rectangular room that served a dual purpose as living and dining rooms. A window overlooked the street on the living room end, and a wall on the dining room end contained a doorway leading to the kitchen. The dining area situated next to the kitchen included a wooden dining table and four chairs. The midway point along the wall across from the door opened into a hallway. From Alex's vantage point he could see a bathroom on one end of the hall and a bedroom on the other. He wondered what the sleeping arrangements would be.

The living room contained a large right-angled sofa on one wall with a TV stand on the other. A variety of plants surrounded a desk located in front of the large living room window. Alex thought the rusted steel bars on the windows detracted from the impressive city view. He had noticed these on many other buildings during their ride.

"Where should I put my stuff?" asked Alex.

"Put it over there, next to the sofa where you will be sleeping." This, of course, answered Alex's question about the sleeping arrangements. "You must be tired and hungry after your long trip. I will cook something for you and you can sleep." Alex sat and leaned back on the sofa and began to relax. He didn't realize how tired he was until this moment and took advantage of the peace and quiet by closing his eyes.

"Alex," Xiu called to him in a sing-song voice. "Wake up; come and eat something." Alex awoke from his brief nap, pulled up a chair to the dining room table and surveyed three plates of steaming food. One contained meat and vegetables, another contained some green vegetables and the third contained something unfamiliar to him. A bowl of rice and hot cups of tea accompanied their meal.

"I cooked three dishes for you. This one is pork and a vegetable; this one is garlic stems; and that one is fungi." Alex recognized the meat, vegetables and garlic stems but he had never seen anything like the fungi before. Xiu explained this popular Chinese dish somewhat resembled mushrooms. Alex ate while they talked and began to feel at home and comfortable with Xiu. After dinner, Xiu suggested that they go to bed. They both completed their bedtime bathroom rituals. Xiu entered the living room with some blankets and pillows. She walked over to him and handed him the bedding. They hugged and kissed goodnight and retired to their respective beds. Alex fell into a deep and relaxing sleep.

Alex awoke the next morning at around 10:00 am to the clicking of Xiu's keyboard. She sat at her desk by the window tapping on her laptop. "Good morning, Alex. How was your sleep?"

"Wonderful, I haven't slept this good in a long time," Alex said as he sat up on the sofa. "This was very comfy; I slept like a baby."

"I thought today we would go to the space for the new

lab," said Xiu as she walked toward the kitchen. "First, we will eat some breakfast. Then my uncle's friend will take us."

"Sounds like a plan. I better get ready," Alex reached for his suitcase. "By the way, do you have a safe spot for this one?" as he held up his backpack to show Xiu. There is about five hundred thousand yuan in it."

"That is a lot of money. I will hide it out of sight. That is all I can do."

"Then I guess that will have to do." Alex handed over the suitcase.

"I will take good care of it," said Xiu. She disappeared into her bedroom.

They enjoyed a hearty breakfast of oatmeal and headed down the stairs to meet Xiu's uncle's contact, Liang. As they waited on the busy street, Alex noticed what he first thought was an overcast day. After a few people wearing masks passed by he realized that the grayness of the atmosphere was the result of smog rather than haze or clouds. The smog, a byproduct of China's recent industrial revolution, made its daily appearance and caused coughing, sneezing, and throat clearing among Beijing's inhabitants.

A black BMW Five series pulled up with two men in the front seat. The man on the passenger side jumped out, greeted them and introduced himself as Liang. Alex was surprised to see such a large Chinese man. His balding head and booming low voice commanded authority when he spoke. His driver remained in place, smiling and nodding his head while speaking in Mandarin. Liang reminded Alex of a kind of drug lord or modern day mafia boss.

Liang opened the door to the back seat and motioned the couple into the car. Alex realized Liang did not speak English, so Xiu took control of the conversation and acted as interpreter.

The car pulled into the busy street. The crowded streets

intrigued Alex with their bicycle lanes filled with three-wheeled bikes, small scooters and bicycle taxis. Cars moving in a disorganized fashion filled the roads. As much as he tried, Alex could not decipher the traffic rules at the intersections. Cars, buses and trucks mixed with pedestrians at the intersections did a complex dance with everyone somehow finding their way through unscathed. "It is not far," Xiu said after conversing with Liang and his driver. "Also near the third ring, in an industrial area. There are many small factories, and it will be an adequate hiding place. It is also reasonable, and we can negotiate. "

The car pulled up to a metal walled building nestled in a group of similar buildings. Liang bolted out of the passenger's seat and opened the backseat door. Alex thought Liang was quite agile for such a large man. The driver stared ahead and said nothing.

Alex got out and surveyed the area. "There are some smaller factories in operation around here but he says this one is vacant," said Xiu. She had been conversing with Liang during their journey. Alex surmised that she discussed the details of the space, especially her specific needs for resveratrol production.

They entered the building. "This is huge," said Alex. "We don't need this much space."

"Yes, it is big but cheap. Liang says they are in negotiations with another factory working for a U.S. company but not for at least eight months. He cannot lease the space to anyone because of this, so he can let us have it for some *guan xi*." Xiu explained to Alex how *guan xi* works in China. The Chinese preferred to use the terms *guan xi* instead of bribe, but it worked about the same. One could get anything in China with enough *guan xi*.

"How much *guan xi* are we talking about here?"

"You will wait while I negotiate." Xiu turned and headed toward Liang.

Xiu and Liang began a wild, emotion filled conversation. Liang would shout something and Xiu would shout something back. Liang would shake his head and turn away, then moments later, turn back and start arguing again. Xiu exhibited a similar behavior and shouted back at Liang. They became quite loud at one point, and Liang appeared to be turning red with anger. Xiu held her own in this negotiation, much to Alex's surprise since she had always displayed her more reserved side to him. Xiu turned her back on Liang and walked to the car, appearing quite angry and shouting at the driver. Just when Alex thought the deal was off, Liang came running after Xiu. She turned, shook his hand and smiled. She turned to Alex and said, "You will need to give him twenty thousand yuan. We can use the building for at least the next eight months for that."

"Gladly," said Alex. "I will as soon as we get back to your place." He shook Liang's hand while Liang smiled and bowed.

Liang turned out to be a huge asset in procuring goods for the operation. He could get anything with his contacts and *guan xi*. Alex also thought him trustworthy, at least as long as he worked for Xiu's powerful uncle. Alex appreciated the loyalty of Chinese families.

Xiu recruited two male and two female graduate students from Peking University to assist in the lab. One of the male engineering students, Duyi, assisted Alex in building the duplicate frequency generator. The other male, Hui, a chemist, assisted Xiu with the resveratrol production. One of the females, Fang, a computer science major, worked with her counterpart Kira on running trials and Lihua, a biologist, worked as Hans's counterpart preparing the cells for the trials.

The lab materialized in record time and they were ready to run their first trials in a few weeks. They ran frequency trials in the morning in synch with the Chicago team since it was the previous night there. Kira developed a secure satellite connection via satellite phones connected to devices similar to old fashioned phone modems. Fang ran the trials and gathered the data. She transmitted the data from each trial to Kira for analysis in Chicago. Hans and Lihua worked together to coordinate trials for active samples and controls. Xiu resumed resveratrol production, which increased efficiency for immediate use in the trials.

Xiu and Alex's relationship continued to develop as well. They spent almost every waking hour together either working, eating dinner out or in Xiu's apartment. For the first few weeks they continued with the sleeping arrangement as well. They agreed that their relationship should proceed at a slow pace. "The best things are built slowly, to last," Xiu would say to Alex.

One night, after running the first successful trials, they decided to celebrate by going out. Not the usual small cafes or noodle shops which they had frequented, but one of the better restaurants in the Wan Fu Jing district. Wan Fu Jing Street was a famous street in Beijing and not far from the Forbidden City and Tiananmen Square. High end department stores lined the street as well as small family owned shops. Narrow side streets containing traditional Chinese markets with vendors selling anything from roasted scorpions to bronze Buddhas intersected with the main avenue. The main street, barricaded to automobile traffic, attracted a large crowd that gathered to enjoy an interesting variety of street performers and vendors.

They arrived at Wan Fu Jing Street by subway. Beijing's amazing subways were famous. They ran non-stop around the clock, moving millions of passengers every day. Xiu did not have a car so they traveled by subway every day. On this cool spring evening the street exhibited an ample crowd of people visiting restaurants and shops. Vendors shouted to streetwalkers as they approached the stands with samples handed to prospective customers. Some vendors recognized Alex as American and called to him in Chinglish:

"Comma comma, looka, looka, gooda food!"

As tempting as this colorful array of street delights was,

they decided to hold out for their destination restaurant and wandered through the open markets. One stall containing a large assortment of jewelry attracted Xiu, and the couple weaved their way through the noisy crowd to take a look. "This one is pretty," said Alex holding up a silver necklace with a Chinese symbol dangling from its chain.

"That is the symbol for love," said Xiu with a look of delight tempered with the slightest bit of shyness.

"Sold," said Alex as he reached around her neck to fasten the clasp. Xiu unbuttoned her shirt a bit to expose her décolletage and the symbol nestled in the upper crest of her cleavage. She gave Alex a light kiss and grasped his hand.

"I will wear it always."

They continued on their way through the cramped market hand in hand with Xiu leading the way. A few blocks later they stood in front of the restaurant. Alex viewed the sign written in Chinese characters.

"This one is famous for Peking Duck," said Xiu.

"I think my stomach will be quite happy here," said Alex.

Gold and red decorations adorned the entrance to the restaurant. Large fish tanks allowed diners to choose the freshest dinner possible. Alex had not only fallen in love with Xiu but also with China's wonderful food. Xiu learned his tastes and ordered several dishes including some vegetables, and the famous Peking Duck which was sliced tableside by a gracious and humble waiter wearing a gold, black and red uniform. They ate as much as they could and finished with a couple of local beers. After dinner they strolled, stomachs satisfied, along Wan Fu Jing Street in the cool evening air.

After taking the subway home and making their way up the steps to Xiu's apartment they entered and sat together on the sofa. Xiu lit a candle and set it on the table in front of Alex. She walked over to the TV stand and put a CD into her player. The room filled with classical music as she took her place next to Alex on the sofa. Alex leaned toward her and their lips met in a passionate kiss. "Do you know how much I love you?" he whispered to her.

"I love you too, Alex." They moved through the darkened room to Xiu's bedroom. Alex had spent his last night on Xiu's sofa.

10
BACK IN CHICAGO

Both Chicago teams made huge progress during Alex's time in China. Mark's team completed the prototype for the website and started work on the app. Peter made biweekly reports to Sam who kept the money flowing and did not ask many questions. Xavier did an outstanding job in taking over for Alex. They made several breakthroughs in determining frequency signatures for pre-cancerous cells and the trials were promising. Now, in early April, they prepared for the next big step. They were ready to move from cell cultures to rats.

Out of everyone on the team, Hans became the most excited to begin this stage of the trials since he handled the lab rats and rats led the way to human trials. Depending on the data, they could begin limited human trials in a few months. Beginning human trials presented problems with secrecy, at least in the U.S., since Tando had access to FDA data. The team decided to get around this by gathering as much supportive data as possible and then beginning secret human trials in China. This would take an additional infusion of cash from Sam, but that would not be a problem if the rat data supported it.

Alex made the decision to begin the rat trials with breast cancer. The Chicago team would conduct the first trial. On the morning of the trial, Xavier carefully loaded the first resveratrol treated rat into the tube of the frequency machine.

"Be extra careful with my baby," said Hans. "I wouldn't want my little darling microwaved like a hot dog!"

"Don't worry, Hans, she won't feel a thing," said Xavier. "These frequencies are nothing like microwaves."

"I think you are getting a little too close to those rats, Hans," said Kira while continuing to stare at her computer screen. "I think we should nickname you 'Willard' from now on." Hans scoffed as he took a seat to watch.

With the rat resting comfortably in its little Plexiglas box, Xavier and Kira obtained the frequency signatures from the rat cancer cells and then applied the appropriate frequencies for both cancerous and precancerous cells. Samples taken from the rats provided data to determine the cancer cell kill rate. So far, all the trials on cells alone resulted in a one hundred percent kill rate.

Xavier removed the rat from the tube and handed it over to Hans.

"Here you go, Hans; one exposed rat," said Xavier.

Hans removed the rat from the box and cradled it like a newborn baby. "Come here, my little girl; let's see what your cells look like," he said as he made a series of kissing sounds while heading to the section of the lab containing the microscopes. Kira rolled her eyes. Everyone became silent as the tension in the room grew.

Hans to crunched the numbers and announced another success. But after a moment, he recanted and exclaimed, "There is something wrong here; we must rerun the trial."

"What do you mean?" said Xavier.

"I don't know. The cancer cells are unaffected. There is something wrong. Xavier, can you recheck the frequencies?" said Hans as his eyes peered up from the microscope, his face wrinkled with distress.

"Okay, but I'm sure that they are correct. They were no

different from the cell samples after we added resveratrol; nothing has changed," said Xavier. He and Kira proceeded to dismantle the frequency machine.

"I need a smoke. I'll be right back." Hans fished for a pack of cigarettes in his lab coat and headed out the door. A few minutes later he reappeared.

"Everything is good on my end," said Kira.

"Me too," said Xavier. "Everything is perfect on my end."

"We need to think," said Hans.

"Okay, what are the possibilities?" said Xavier. "It could be a malfunction of the machine, or more power needed to penetrate the tissue. Or it might be the resveratrol since we are now administering it by feeding it to the rats instead of injecting it into cell clusters. I think what we should do first is check the machine and run another trial." Xavier began taking apart the machine. "Hans, can you get another rat ready in a couple of hours."

"Sure, I'll get started on it right now." Hans headed for the rat cages.

"What about Alex?" said Kira. "He needs to be told what's going on here."

"Well, it's 2:00 pm here in Chicago which means its 3:00 am in Beijing so they will be asleep," said Xavier. "This will give us time to run another trial. Also, Alex will be running his first rat trial in about five to six hours. If we contact him tonight, then we can tell him what happened here and compare notes. Right now, we all need to get to work."

The team sprang into action. Xavier continued taking apart and checking every component of the frequency generator while Kira ran computer software diagnostics. Hans prepared another cancerous rat by taking a biopsy and examining the cells under a microscope to make sure they were cancerous. After two hours, Kira announced that all the software checked out. Xavier said he still needed another hour but so far everything was coming along fine. The wall clock read 4:00 pm, signaling the arrival of the app team. "What's going on here?" Mark entered and detected the frantic mood of the group.

"The first rat trial. Treatment didn't work. Zero cancer cells killed," said Hans.

"Xavier, is this true?" Mark called across to Xavier who was busy assembling the machine.

"I'm afraid so. The machine did not destroy even one cancer cell in our first rat trial. We don't know why yet but we are running another trial in about an hour and hope to find out more. Everything looks good on the frequency machine though," said Xavier in a calm manner.

"Does Alex know?" said Mark as he plopped onto one of the desk chairs.

"We decided to hold off telling him until we run another trial. We'll contact him tonight after we get the results."

"Let me know if we can help in any way. Also, I want to be there when you call Alex and Xiu."

Thirty minutes later, Xavier connected the final piece to the machine and powered it up. A low frequency hum filled the room. Kira ran hardware diagnostics and everything checked out. They were now ready to run another trial. Hans brought in the resveratrol fed rat and gave it to Xavier who placed it into the machine. Kira prepared to enter the frequencies into the machine when Xavier stopped her. "Kira, I think we should take another resonance reading before applying the treatment. Maybe something about the cells changed in-situ." Kira obliged and began the process. A small laser focused on the part of the rat containing the cancerous tumor. The machine made a series of loud clicks as Kira read the data.

"These are different," Kira said with disbelief. "They're not much different, but they *are* different." "They look more like the old trials without Xiu's resveratrol."

"Kira, are you sure?" said Xavier. .

"Yup, they are closer to the resonance of non-resveratrol cells than those with it." Kira stared at the screen.

"Well, that is very interesting," said Xavier. "Go ahead and enter those new frequencies and run the trial." Kira entered the new frequencies and ran the trial. The machine made a few more clicks.

"All done, Hans, you're up." Hans retrieved the rat-container and headed toward his section of the lab.

After a thorough analysis, Hans declared that about ten percent of the cancer cells were dead. Based on this new information the team came up with a new hypothesis. The frequency generator had performed its job, so the problem must have originated in Xiu's resveratrol formula. It appeared that not enough of the formula had made it through the rat's digestive tract, entered the cells and reached the DNA inside the nucleus of the cells. This presented a big problem.

It was now time for the nightly call to Alex and Xiu in Beijing. The team gathered around a video camera attached to the computer connected to the satellite phone hookup. Mark made the call. After a series of scratchy, squeaky sounds and distorted images, a picture of Alex with the China lab in the background came onscreen. "How did the trial go? We are dying to find out over here." Alex seemed pensive, as if he expected bad news.

"Not good," said Mark. "We think something might be wrong with Xiu's resveratrol.

"I was afraid of that," said Alex. "How bad?"

"Zero kills in the first trial. We re-calibrated the resonance and ran a second trial with about a ten percent kill rate and no kills in precancerous cells," said Xavier as he leaned toward the camera.

"Xiu and I talked about this, and I think she is right. It seems like the present formulation does not get enough resveratrol to the DNA to elicit an epigenetic effect. It's a lot different in a living model. She's been working on this and may have a solution," Alex replied with a hopeful tone.

"We're all ears," said Mark. Alex disappeared from the screen as he went to get Xiu. The Chicago team could see them conversing in the background before approaching their video camera. Xiu took over the conversation and explained to the team that she had almost completed development of a new formulation that combined resveratrol with hydrocolloids. The hydrocolloids would act as a transportation system that allowed a high dose of resveratrol to reach the DNA. She had anticipated a problem with the present formulation in living rats and had begun working on the new hydrocolloid formulation.

"So you guys knew?" said Mark, annoyed.

"Not exactly," said Alex. "Xiu had a better idea than I did. I supported the quantum resonance theory and thought that as long as some resveratrol made it to the DNA we could re-calibrate the resonance and it would work. I see I was wrong, though," said Alex.

"When do you think the new formulation will be ready?" asked Mark.

"Xiu figures about two weeks. In the meantime, Hans should prepare more rats. If this works, we will need to run lots of trials on every stage of cancer."

Both teams discussed the plan for the next two weeks and then signed off. Mark said he would report to Peter, who would fill Sam in on the plan. Xavier and Kira said they would work on the larger machine for the next phase of the project, which would include the human trials. Mark and the app team would continue as usual.

11
TROUBLE DOWN SOUTH

The next two weeks provided a refreshing break from the usual action for the Chicago team, while the China team developed the new hydrocolloid resveratrol formula. Peter provided a status report to Sam who seemed to take the news in stride and remained satisfied as long as they planned to move the project forward. He seemed confident that they would overcome their most recent setback and promised another infusion of cash once they did.

Xavier and Kira found it easy to scale the machine and prepare plans for a larger machine for accommodating humans. The new machine would take up an entire room shielded from outside interference. It would resemble an MRI machine, complete with a long tubular structure for holding the patient. One difference included the presence of an additional set of ring-like structures placed over the tube once the patient was inside. The tube, clear plastic instead of white, also included exposed wires and electronics for easy access. The additional rings detected the quantum resonance of each cancerous and precancerous cell. The machine looked like something out of a 1950s science fiction movie.

Instead of building the machine in a separate room, the

team had decided to use a Faraday cage. A Faraday cage contained metal walls for insulating the area inside from interfering waves. The tubular structure would be located inside the cage and the control room consisting of racks of equipment and a desk top computer located outside of the cage. This design allowed for easy access for troubleshooting.

The Chicago team spent their extra time hanging out in the lab playing Hadron. Xavier expanded his virtual land and Kira, Kevin and Julie reached high enough levels to also own land and build houses. Hans played here and there but soon became fed up with playing the role of cannon fodder, plus his frequent smoking breaks became an irritation. Kira created a character much like her own in real life, but also amassed an impressive collection of digital firearms including a laser blaster automatic machine gun with exploding pulses. She enjoyed shooting several pulses into her enemies and then standing by to watch them explode a second later.

Julie's character contrasted her real life persona. She named her character Marata and made her into a muscular female amazon carrying at least five different weapons ranging from ion grenades to heavy grenade launchers. Kevin developed a male version of Julie's character. The prize for the most original character went to Xavier. Xavier constructed a human-size, cigar smoking white rabbit complete with large floppy pink ears. This ominous creature hopped along the virtual landscape wreaking terror and destruction while sucking on a cigar butt. He even programmed it to make a comical bouncing sound every time it hopped, instilling fear in other players whenever they heard the boing, boing, boing signaling the approach of *the rabbit of death*.

On the Tuesday night of the second week Xavier's cell phone interrupted a serious Hadron battle. He excused himself, returned his freaky rabbit avatar to its virtual hole in the ground lair and retreated to a private corner of the lab to take the call. Mark worked nearby on his laptop and overheard Xavier speaking in Spanish. He noticed Xavier's emotion change from surprise to anger to despair as he spoke. This went on for over an hour. Xavier ended the call and began to sob.

"What's the matter, Xavier?" said Mark as he closed his laptop and made his way toward Xavier who sat at his desk with his head in his arms, sobbing. The other team members witnessed his display of emotion and surrounded him.

"What's wrong?" said Kira. "Why are you so upset?"

Xavier attempted to compose himself. "It's my family in Cheran," he said with tearful eyes. "They are in trouble."

"What kind of trouble?" Mark sat across from Xavier.

"It's my brother, Luis." Xavier regained his composure. "He is mixed up in the drug cartel. He betrayed someone important. They are looking for him, but he ran away, so they took my little sister Daniella instead. They will hold her until they find Luis." Xavier's lips began to quiver again. "I want to help but my family says no. They say that if I go, the cartel will kidnap or kill me. My father told me that my place is here, and that I would disappoint them if I came. Family and friends are searching for Luis. When they find him they will tell him about Daniella's kidnapping and how he should make things right with them."

Xavier went on to explain that his family owned a small farm outside of Cheran. The money of the drug trade, especially enticing to the poor, had proved irresistible to Luis. He had worked his way up the ranks which included servicing a sizeable territory. But greed had taken over and he began to skim his boss's cut and to manipulate other cartel members in an attempt to gain more power. He tried to play it both ways but the cartel found out. By then Luis had written and signed his own death warrant. The only hope for Daniella now rested on the family finding Luis and persuading him to face the cartel boss to plead for his life. And there was a good chance both Luis and Daniella would end up dead.

"I will not jeopardize the team," said Xavier with an air of authority. "Especially when I am so close to solving the chaos problem. My place is here. My family has sacrificed so much for me to be here, and to live a better life. I told them that I will not dishonor them by coming to Mexico, but I might not be able to help myself. My family's only hope is to find Luis and convince him to turn himself in. If they find him, I will go."

"We will support whatever you decide to do, Xavier," said Mark. "Just let us know if we can help."

"Thank you all so much. I need to go home now and talk with Becca and my family. I will see you all tomorrow." Xavier shoved his laptop in a backpack and headed for the door.

"Get the satellite connection up stat," Mark shouted to Kira.

"I'm on it," she replied.

"We need to tell Alex about this ASAP. It's 9:30 pm, which translates to 10:30 am in Beijing. Alex and Xiu should be working in the lab."

A few moments later Alex's face appeared on the monitor.

"Hello, hello..."Alex's compressed voice broadcast from the computer speakers.

"Hi, Alex, Mark here." Mark took a seat in front of the computer. "There is a problem with Xavier." Mark told Alex the details about Xavier's brother Luis and about the kidnapping of Xavier's sister Daniella. He also told Alex how Xavier had promised to continue working on the project.

. "I had no idea that his family was connected to drug cartels." said Alex. "In fact, I never even considered that he might still have family connections in Mexico."

"I knew about his family, but not much else," said Mark. "He did mention them to me and said that they were farmers in Cheran. I swear he never said anything about his brother Luis."

"I trust you, Mark. How could you know? Did he say anything else?"

"He said something about a chaos problem he was working on. Do you know anything about that?"

"No, he never mentioned it before. I'm not quite sure what he meant," said Alex. "I wonder if it has something to do with the new resonance settings. I'll look into it. Do you think there is any risk of him selling out to Tando?" The concern on Alex's face transferred to Xiu who stood behind him.

"I'm not sure, but I think we should re-evaluate the security of the lab," said Mark.

"This computer is definitely secure," said Kira as she took a seat next to Mark. "The only way to get data out is through the satellite connection and a secure flash drive. The computer is isolated from the Internet."

"That's all fine, but it also means that anyone could copy files and put them on an encrypted flash drive. I'm sure that there are other leaks as well. Who knows what Xavier's laptop contains?" said Mark. "Any of us could take our information and sell it to Tando."

Alex and Mark decided to continue their conversation in private and asked the other team members to leave. Over the course of an hour they discussed Xavier's situation and potentially leaky security. They agreed to inform Peter and to get his opinion. Then they could decide what to do next. They said goodbye and ended the satellite connection. Mark called Peter.

Mark's call woke Peter from a sound sleep around 11:30 pm. Peter had crashed after a long day of consulting with two of his other clients and taking care of his daughter. Mark told Peter all the details about Xavier and about the perceived holes in their security. He asked what

Peter thought they should do. "I have an idea," said a sheepish Peter. "I think we should take this matter to Sam. He has a lot of connections and runs several companies. He's also managed to avoid Tando for quite some time. I'm sure he will give us some suggestions. Let me set up a meeting with Sam as soon as possible. I'll call you in the morning. Now go home and get some sleep. We have to be sharp tomorrow. Oh, and be sure to tell Alex. We need to keep him in the loop." Peter hung up the phone and went back to bed, but as much as he tried he could not get back to the deep restful sleep from which he had been awakened.

12
MEETING WITH SAM

The next day, a typically overcast, cold and rainy spring day in Chicago, brought the dreaded meeting with Sam. Mark and Peter met in the lobby of Sam's building, a high rise skyscraper in the heart of downtown. Peter arrived first and stood inside the lobby facing the large revolving glass door. Peter checked his watch, and with one minute to spare viewed Mark sprinting through the revolving door. His clothes dripped from the constant soaking rain. "Haven't you heard of an umbrella?" Peter said. Mark was not amused.

"Couldn't find it, and you know about downtown parking."

"Looks like you didn't sleep either." Peter noticed Mark's fatigue. "You look pretty bad."

"Thanks for the vote of confidence," said Mark with sarcasm. "You don't look so great yourself."

The two walked through the wide open space of the immense lobby. Their footsteps echoed off of the marble floor and mixed with others from numerous business people heading in all directions. They headed up a large escalator to the second floor where they caught an elevator to the nineteenth floor. Sam's operation occupied one-third of the nineteenth floor. His Chicago office was the most glamorous of his three. The others were located in New York and Los Angeles but he considered Chicago his home. Born and bred in the windy city, Sam took pride in his Midwestern roots but fantasized about being a cowboy or an oil tycoon. He donned a cowboy hat and on occasion his Midwestern accent took on a bit of a drawl.

Sam dabbled in many businesses with the majority of his interests centered on a company much less glamorous than the surroundings in which Peter and Mark found themselves. His largest company encompassed waste removal and recycling. He made billions on this company alone causing people in business circles to dub him the 'Trash Czar'.

Sam stood only five feet, six inches tall with long flowing gray hair and a matching trimmed gray moustache and beard. No one knew his exact age, but his wrinkled face indicated a man in his early to mid-sixties. His round body was the result of his love for food and his disdain for exercise. He always wore the traditional CEO uniform; a dark suit and white shirt and a tie that strained the buttons when he sat due to his substantial belly. Sam exhibited a jovial personality; nothing seemed to bother him. However, his demeanor could change in an instant, from an easy going pal to a serious courtroom judge. One experienced his serious mood when he tilted his head downward and stared with eyes that pierced the soul.

Peter and Mark opened the large gold-lined glass doors to Sam's office and walked into a reception area containing the finest in waiting room furniture. The décor included a mixture of hardwoods and marble with dark floor tiles also trimmed in gold. A large mahogany wood desk staffed by a gorgeous blond receptionist occupied the middle of the room in front of a large matching hardwood wall containing a modern wavy gold sculpture and the words "Foulton Enterprises" in a bas relief modern gold font.

As Peter approached the receptionist's desk, his eyes focused on the receptionist's nametag displaying one word,

Sheri, in a prominent location on her chest. Even though they had met on a few other occasions, Peter fought to control his gaze. After a brief hesitation, he lifted his head to focus on her eyes for fear of getting caught admiring her large breasts. On the one hand he wanted to act like a gentleman, but on the other he suspected she liked this kind of attention.

Sheri wore a bright blue business suit with a crisp white blouse and gold pendant around her neck. Peter pegged her to be in her mid-forties and admired her exceptional shape. Her makeup, applied with a sense of artistry, revealed only a hint of a few wrinkles. Short blond hair framed a thin headset and microphone and her delicate hand displayed a huge diamond ring on her right third finger. Her level of casualness around Sam indicated their history together spanned more than a few years.

"We are here to see Mr. Foulton, Sheri," Peter said as he placed his elbow on the desk.

"Go right on in gentlemen, he's expecting you," she said in a perky but professional voice.

During previous visits to report on Freetech's progress Peter wondered about the relationship between Sam and Sheri. It seemed that no matter what kind of news Sam had to deal with, he always displayed a big smile whenever she entered the room. On a few occasions Peter witnessed Sam exiting his office, approaching Sheri and placing his arm around her shoulder while giving her instructions. Peter thought this behavior from a bygone era in the business world would in many cases lead to a lawsuit these days. Sam and Sheri kept it alive though. He concluded they were merely two divorcees having a bit of playful office fun. The thought did however cross Peter's mind wondering if Sam would ever have a chance with a lady like Sheri if he were just a middle class slug.

They passed through another glass door that led to a short hallway. The hallway divided into right and left sections with Sam's office on the left. The other section opened onto a cubicle farm on the right. They turned left and spied Sam's door cracked open. They walked inside to see Sam sitting behind his large desk. He wasted no time getting up to greet them. Sam gave his full attention to every person he met.

Mark always found the spectacular downtown Chicago view from Sam's office inspiring. It even impressed him on a rainy day like today. Both shook Sam's hand as he said, "So, I hear there's trouble brewing with one of your partners? Mr. Valdez, I presume?" Peter had briefed Sam before the visit.

"Yes, as I said on the phone, there is no trouble yet, but there is potential for problems," said Peter.

Another man occupied a chair in the corner of Sam's immense office. The man ignored Peter and Mark and kept his head buried in a laptop while clicking on the keyboard. "Oh, let me introduce you to Simon." Sam turned to face the man, who responded by closing the laptop and standing up to greet them. "Mark Winter, Peter North, meet Simon Black." Simon shook both of their hands and muttered a nondescript greeting. About the same size and shape as Sam but much younger, Mark estimated Simon's age to be late twenties. His mid-length hipster dark hair cast a frame around his pudgy face, complete with a goatee. He appeared comfortable in his black jeans, black polo shirt and sneakers. Mark thought he might be Sam's son.

"Simon is one crackerjack security expert." Sam walked over and patted Simon on the back. "I know he doesn't look like much. No offense Simon. But he is one hell of a cyber-security guru. Simon heads up my cyber-security division. I want Simon here to analyze your lab to find any leaks that might need to be plugged." Sam morphed into one of his personality changes, a more serious tone. "We don't want any leaks of our precious data, especially with Tando sniffing around as they always do. Men in desperate situations are capable of doing desperate things, and

Xavier strikes me as a desperate man." Sam reached for a drink from his office bar. "Care to join me, anyone? Nothing good here since I quit drinking, well...at least cut down on drinking, but there's a nice selection of mineral waters and diet soft drinks."

"No thanks," said the others.

"I hope you understand about my desire to protect my investment this way."

"No problem," said Mark in a convincing tone. "We welcome any help we can get, right Peter?"

"That's right. When can Simon start?"

Simon smiled at Mark and Peter and said, "No time like the present. Lead the way, gentlemen."

Simon rode to the lab with Mark. It struck Mark as odd that someone with such intelligence and acumen as Simon hadn't learned to drive. As Mark drove, Simon peppered him with questions about the project, focusing on Kira's satellite link. He seemed particularly impressed with that piece of engineering and wanted to meet her. Mark chuckled to himself when Simon asked if Kira had a boyfriend since she wasn't the least bit interested in men. It wasn't long before they reached the lab.

"Here it is, our humble little quantum resonance lab," chided Mark. Kira clicked away on her laptop playing games, and Hans tended to his precious rats. The app team would arrive in a few more hours. "This must be the lovely and intelligent Kira," Simon said as he walked over to her and extended his hand.

"This is Simon, our new security expert," said Mark as he attempted to keep from laughing out loud. "He wants to go over your satellite link and how we store our data." Kira remained sitting but peered up from her laptop.

"Where's Xavier?" said Mark.

"Not here today. Don't know when he is coming in. Didn't he call you?" said Hans while looking into a microscope.

"I guess he needs a couple of days off to deal with his

family issue," said Mark in defense of Xavier.

"This should take me a couple of hours at most. First off, I will need to know the chain of custody of all data from the time it originates to where it is stored," said Simon. "You and I will need to work closely." Kira rolled her eyes and said "whatever" and proceeded to the main computer that held the data.

"Don't get any ideas," chided Mark. Kira smiled at him and extended her middle finger.

Kira explained to Simon about how the satellite system worked. She hacked a traditional satellite phone to act as a modem for the computer. They could then use it for VoIP communications for both audio and video conferencing. A geosynchronous satellite transmitted data to China. "Nice hack," Simon said. "What kind of encryption do you use?"

"GMR-2" replied Kira.

"Well, that's a problem," said Simon. "Everyone knows satellite phones are insecure."

"But our data is also encrypted *before* it hits the phone," said Kira in a defensive tone. "Our audio and video data may not be secure, but our frequency data should be. Our main computer here contains a TPM (Transfer Process Module) processor and we use BitLocker for encrypting our hard drive and flash drives."

Kira continued, "As you know, BitLocker has no backdoor, which prevents anyone from hacking into our signal while we are transmitting. The satellite connection provides the only means of transmission since this computer is isolated from the Internet. It would be difficult for someone to hack into our satellite signal during the limited time we are transmitting, then hack into our hard drive and somehow steal our data."

Simon became enthralled with Kira as she spoke. He replied, "Not probable, but not impossible for someone to hack in. It would need to be someone as good as me, and that's not too likely. Do you want to go out for a drink after this?"

"Why would I want to do that?"

Simon leaned in closer to Kira. "Because all this tech talk is making me so hot."

"In your dreams..." She struggled to contain her laughter. "You're not my type anyway, even if you are some tech guru."

"So what is your type?" Simon leaned back in his chair. "All I'm going to say is not you. Now let's get back to work."

Kira showed Simon the data on the encrypted hard drive. "So who can access this?" said Simon.

"Everyone on the team has access, but there are only three encrypted flash drives that can also copy data."

"So who, my dear, has them?" said Simon in a flirtatious tone.

"Well, let's see...that would be Mark, Alex and Xavier." Concern washed over Kira's face. "You don't think one of them would defect to Tando, do you?"

"I hope not," said Simon. "Especially since my boss invested a mil and is ready to write a check for another. So much for the computer, now how about cameras, hidden microphones, other spy stuff. Are there any other security devices around?"

"No cameras or anything else. It's just us here, and we all trust each other. I don't think anyone would betray the team."

"Your naivety and innocence are as captivating as your beauty." Simon sat back and stretched his arms over his head. "Everyone's got a price; what would you do if someone offered you a million dollars or ten million for what you have here?"

"I wouldn't betray my friends for a billion dollars." Kira became agitated.

"I've seen enough." Simon stood up. "Where's Mark and Peter? I'm ready to make my report."

Peter had joined Mark on the app team's side of the lab. They sat at a table drinking sodas when Simon made his way over to them. "So, what do you think?" said Peter as Simon pulled up a chair to join them.

"I think there are some not so shitty and some very shitty things about your security."

"Okay, so tell us." Mark reached back for a soda. "What's your pleasure, Coke, Mountain Dew, or water?"

"Mountain Dew." Simon sat down and laid his backpack on the table then proceeded to report that he thought the satellite connection was weak and could be beefed up with some better encryption. He also recommended installing software he had developed for monitoring the main computer. This consisted of what was in essence a secret key logger program that recorded every keystroke on the computer as well as all read-writes. He recommended that only Mark, Peter, and Alex know of its existence. During the next satellite call he would remotely install the same software on the sister computer in China. Alex and Xiu were the only ones with access to the China computer. Simon also suggested that they install video cameras.

"No cameras," said Mark. "I don't want to go that far, plus it would raise suspicion. We have a fun team here, and I don't want people to feel inhibited."

"It's your show; I'm just the lowly consultant." Simon took a healthy swig of his Mountain Dew.

Peter stood up. "I've got to pick up my daughter from school. Mark, can you take Simon to wherever he needs to go?"

13
THE SPY

Xavier returned to the lab the next evening looking like he hadn't slept or bathed. Mark greeted him. "Good to see you, Xavier. Heard anything from your family? Good news, I hope."

"It is the same; Daniella is still missing. My family assembled a group of neighbors to search for Luis. They think he might be somewhere in Mexico City. They are going there to try to find him. I came to work to try to get my mind off the problem. I can't sleep, I can't eat. All I can think of is Daniella, and what they might do to her."

"We are all here for you, Xavier; whatever you need, just say the word," said Mark as the others gathered around him.

"I am so lucky to have you all," Xavier said. "How is the new resveratrol coming?"

"Good news on that front," said Mark in an upbeat tone. Alex said it's on its way and should be here in a couple of days. I think we should all take a deserved day off tomorrow and have some fun. Maybe meet for lunch and drink until we can't see anymore." Everyone agreed. Xavier said he would rather stay home to deal with his family situation.

"I do want to get some work done tonight though. I

am close to solving the resonance problem."

"You do whatever you need to do. Take a couple of days; we will see you on Monday. Hopefully, there will be good news from your family by then," said Mark.

Xavier and Kira analyzed the data from the last few runs and Xavier alternated between a stack of papers dense with mathematical equations and his laptop. He was so deep in thought that Kira figured he would not flinch even if the fire alarm sounded. It was getting late and both teams decided to call it a day.

"We are starting the party Clancy's bar down the street if you want to join us," Kira said as she put on her coat.

"That sounds good, maybe when I finish; we'll see," said Xavier.

"Well, you know where we'll be." Kira and the others made their way out of the lab. Xavier could hear their voices diminish as the inverse square law predicted. He turned back to the world of quantum resonance, a timeless place where hours passed like minutes.

He surfaced at 2:00 am. I think I figured it out. Imparting a resonant frequency without modulating the pulse in a specific sequence will produce a chaotic effect within the cell's DNA. This inherent chaos will build over time creating more errors, which could manifest as more disease. The last step I will need to complete is to determine the correct sequence of modulation. This will eliminate the chaotic effect. No sense in telling Mark; he would not understand. Alex would, but it would be better to finish the calculations to complete the solution than to bring up another problem. I will tell Alex when I have the solution Xavier closed up shop and left for home, thinking about his precious Daniella all the way.

"Let's do a shot of Fireball; it's on me." Kira said well on her way to feeling no pain. "Bartender, shots of Fireball for the geek team here!" The young man behind the bar responded and soon a tray of shot glasses appeared.

Everyone grabbed one and Kira announced, "To Xavier, we wish his family the best!" The group raised their glasses and downed the shots. "Poor Xavier," she continued as her words took on a slight slur, "I feel for him. He is such a good person. I hope they find that bastard brother of his."

"They will." Mark put his arm around Kira. "I'm sure they have some good leads and will find him soon. Hey, what did you think of Simon?"

"Ha, for being such a genius he sure lacks gay-dar. The guy hit on me the whole time."

"Yup, he couldn't stop talking about you the entire trip back to Sam's. He asked me if I thought you would go out with him." This made Kira laugh.

"Yeah, maybe to a geek fest like Comic Con as a brother-sister combo, but that would be about all I would consider."

Light conversation and laughter filled the tavern. Kevin and Hans got into an Angry Birds battle on their cells phones while Julie and Kira kept company with Mark. The group continued to party until beyond last call, beyond the flashing lights and until the bouncers came to usher them out. Mark kept a reasonable composure and ordered two cabs. He occupied one with Julie and Kira and Hans and Kevin took the other.

14

THE NEW FORMULA

*E*veryone anticipated the arrival of the new resveratrol hydrocolloid formula from China. It was Monday, after a long weekend off, and the team dove into the work. Xavier reported no new information about his sister and he appeared better than the previous Friday. The sample arrived on schedule at 10:00 am, and Hans took charge of it as he prepared a new sample of rats by feeding them each a measured dose. Alex discovered a damaged component while checking the Chinese machine for problems, and Liang had not been able to come through with a replacement yet so all eyes were on the Chicago team to run the first trial. Alex and Xiu were on the computer screen via the satellite link. You could see their empty lab given the late hour in China. After about thirty minutes Hans said that they were ready. Xavier had the frequency machine ready to go.

Hans placed a rat into the small Plexiglas container and handed it to Xavier who placed it into the machine. Kira entered the start code and the machine clicked as it first calibrated the resonance and then clicked again as it administered the frequencies. "All done," said Kira. Hans removed the rat for biopsy. The lab became quiet as everyone waited for Hans as he rushed to prepare some slides. Seconds passed like hours until Hans announced, "All good! They are all dead! I think it worked! The new resveratrol reached the DNA of the cancer cells and we are back in business." Cheers erupted from the team. The small computer monitor displayed an image of Alex and Xiu hugging and kissing.

"Looks like we have a cure for cancer!" said Alex, still holding onto Xiu.

"We did it, brother," added an ecstatic Mark. More cheering, hugging and congratulating followed. Xavier, however, exhibited a less enthusiastic response as he sat in front of the machine shaking his head and saying over and over again, "I can't believe it, I can't believe it."

The team ran a number of trials and each one resulted in killing breast cancer cells at various stages of development. Xavier took the liberty of dismissing everyone at about 10:00 pm. "I think we've accomplished a lot today," he said with pride and exhaustion. "Please, go and get some much needed rest. We can continue tomorrow."

"I agree with Xavier, let's get some rest. Tomorrow is another day," said Mark from across the room. "Let's shut her down." Both teams shut down their machines except for Kira since she needed to transfer the day's data to Alex in China via the satellite connection.

Everyone made their way out until only Kira and Xavier remained. "Go home and get some rest," Kira said to Xavier as she tapped on the central computer's keyboard.

"I have some more work to do," said Xavier."

"Don't you think we've accomplished enough ground-breaking science for one day?" Kira continued to keyboard.

"I am not convinced the results are real." Xavier sifted through papers riddled with mathematical equations as if he were searching for one in particular.

"What do you mean? Dead cells are dead cells. Do you

think they will rise from the dead and become some kind of zombie cells eating the nuclei of all the healthy cells?" Kira's sarcasm was lost on Xavier.

"It's complicated," said an aloof Xavier. "It involves chaos... Where is that sheet of equations? Here it is. Yes, one of the models predicts chaos. I've been working on a solution."

"You mean that butterfly stuff?" said Kira as she finished the transfer.

"If you are referring to the butterfly effect, where the flapping of a butterfly's wings in one area of the world can cause a hurricane in another part of the world, you are correct." Xavier peered up from his papers. "The epigenetic system we are influencing is a non-linear deterministic system and is prone to the effects of chaos. In other words, there is a probability that small changes in the information of the system can perturb it enough to cause chaos."

"Oh, this is weird quantum stuff, isn't it?" Kira sat back in her chair having completed the transfer.

Xavier continued, "Actually it is chaos theory, which is different. It is difficult to explain, but trust me, I need to make sure we are not imparting chaos into our system."

"Well, my work is done here, and I am leaving." Kira reached for her coat. "Don't work too hard," she said as she headed for the door.

"It helps me to keep my mind off of Daniella. Good night, and see you tomorrow."

The door closed behind Kira and Xavier sat down at the central computer to access his mathematical modeling program. He had written this program to help him to model chaos in the rat DNA. He tinkered with the input data in order to run several scenarios then sat back and admired the numbers flowing by on the screen, too fast to read. After four runs he had his answer. It was midnight and he decided to head home.

The next week flew by as the team ran trial after trial with the new resveratrol. The new treatment killed breast cancer cells in all stages of development as well as precancerous cells. Tumors seemed to melt away in the rats treated at the beginning of the week. Enthusiastic optimism permeated the atmosphere with talk about what it would be like to be millionaires. Kira said she would buy a Lamborghini. Hans wanted a big house in the northern suburbs. Kevin wanted to sail around the world despite never having been in a sailboat, and Julie wanted a mansion out west somewhere like California, Washington State or Colorado. Mark and Xavier, remaining practical, abstained from the dreaming session. Deep down everyone knew all Xavier wanted was his sister back home.

Mark and Peter also met with Sam and presented their results. Sam, ecstatic, pledged an additional two million dollars for development of the machine for human trials. He told them to give everyone a well-deserved raise. They asked when they would be meeting again with Simon, and Sam informed them that Simon had been sent to Europe to deal with another security issue and was to return in two weeks. They reported that Xavier appeared stable and focused on his work and was keeping his negative feelings about Daniella to himself. They also mentioned their concern over Xavier's late night activities and were anxious to see what Simon's security software revealed.

Mark reported that the app team had made good progress and the wellness website had received some traffic as people signed up for free memberships. The mobile app was just about ready but still required some testing. The camouflage that the app team provided worked well at keeping Tando off their backs.

They discussed the next phase of the project in detail, which included human trials once the rat trials were finished. This phase could not be completed in secret, at least not in the U.S. Sam informed them of a secret way to perform human trials in China. He said that he had been working with one of his powerful Chinese contacts to arrange this. This meant that China would host the next phase. Their plan included building both U.S. and Chinese machines, with the Chinese machine conducting the trials. Once completed, the human trials would establish that they indeed had a cancer cure. They could then bring their creation out in the open and launch into the largest phase of the project, which would include full scale development of a series of treatment centers. They would build at least twenty machines for use in private clinics placed throughout the U.S. This phase also entailed the filing of patents. Sam said that launching everything simultaneously would make it nearly impossible for Tando to do anything to stop them.

Mark and Peter left with a visible skip in their steps, and feeling like millionaires. "We have to keep this real," said Peter. "But the best thing about this for me is that I can give my daughter a good life."

"I'm looking forward to finding that special lady, settling down and starting a family of my own," said Mark.

"I never pegged you as a family man," said Peter as he climbed into his car.

"Well, you know, I'm getting older, and I'm tired of the single life," Mark entered the passenger side. "Although, I haven't had time to date with all of this work."

"Just wait until you are driving your Maserati and living the millionaire lifestyle. The ladies will be lining up for you." They both laughed and headed back to the lab.

15
BACK IN CHINA

Alex and Xiu, ecstatic about the news and new infusion of cash, thought things were going extremely well. They grew closer as a couple, and Xiu produced the new hydrocolloid formula and they successfully duplicated the Chicago team's trials. Alex enjoyed his life in China and had become used to the idiosyncrasies, food and the fascinating culture, but the crowds and choking pollution still annoyed him. He found their lives to be simple and pleasant. After work they rode the subway home with millions of people doing the same. Often they stopped for a simple dinner of spicy noodles with some vegetables and meat in a small noodle shop near Xiu's apartment. Afterward they would walk hand in hand for the rest of their journey home. Relaxing at home included reading, talking or making love.

Alex's feelings for Xiu continued to grow, as did his seriousness about the nature of their relationship. So much so that he had begun to take secret excursions to shop for an engagement ring. He loved her and felt the same from her. He learned about the cultural differences regarding courting as well. Courting was a bit more old fashioned and conservative in China. There was less dating around or playing the field than in America. Women chose men based on how the man made them feel, as well as how well they could provide for them. Men took charge of the situation, even organizing the wedding. It was important for a man to achieve some success in life before taking a bride. A woman having sex with a man was a sure sign she wanted to be with him forever. Despite Xiu's success and experience in the West, she still carried some of these traditional values. Alex respected her culture.

Alex wanted nothing more than to marry Xiu, but he wanted to wait until the project was a complete and undeniable success. Weddings were a big event in China and required time and planning. Plus her Chinese citizenship complicated things. Would they live in China, in the US, or both? Would she even consider living in the US? Should their wedding be Chinese or American, or both? The overwhelming nature of their work afforded little time to discuss such issues. Xiu deserved the best, and Alex wanted to give her the best life possible. If they had to wait a few more months, then so be it.

Mark communicated all the details regarding Xavier, Sam and Simon to Alex, who gave them his blessing. Mark also informed Alex he must meet Sam's contact in China who would deliver some much needed cash and discuss the next phase of the project. Alex was uncomfortable with such meetings because their mystery contrasted with his straightforward nature. The meeting's unknown location further added to Alex's apprehension. The plan was for a black car similar to Liang's to pick him up and take him to a private meeting in an undisclosed location.

Alex's apprehension grew as the meeting hour approached. He stood on the street in front of Xiu's building watching for Li Quang's car. Alex removed his pollution mask despite the smoggy day so that whoever picked him up could get a good look at him. He waited for a black Mercedes Benz which was to arrive at noon for the 1:00 pm meeting. Alex surveyed the endless traffic stream in front of him. The bicycle lane between the sidewalk and traffic was busy with bicycles, scooters and peddlers pulling carts on bicycles loaded with all sorts of wares. Many of these peddlers spent their entire day chanting to potential customers to buy their goods. The sounds of these chants added to the white noise of the street.

Alex thought it unusual that no one approached him as he stood alone on the sidewalk. Perhaps the mask had made him appear less Western. Since his arrival he had been a walking target for every kind of trinket, map or scam. One time while visiting Wan Fu Jing Street he decided to get a Coke while Xiu shopped. The street was alive with all sorts of Friday night activity. The street, cordoned off to automobile traffic, allowed for flocks of streetwalkers who wandered about exploring its delights. After parting with Xiu at a large department store, Alex headed up the street to his favorite Coke vendor about four blocks away. He liked this particular vendor because it had outdoor street-level seating, and he loved watching the people stroll by.

About twenty yards into his journey he felt a tap on his right arm. "Hello, hello, are you American?" Alex turned to face an attractive young Chinese woman walking by his side. She appeared to be in her early to mid-twenties, well dressed in a nice blouse and jeans.

"Yes, I am an American." He continued his pace.

"Do you mind if I walk with you to practice my English?" she said as she kept pace with him. "Where are you from?" she asked before he could answer her first question.

"Chicago," he said, not exactly sure what she was up to.

"Do you want to get some tea and talk so I can practice my English?" She grabbed Alex's right arm.

"No, my girlfriend would not be happy about that." He moved his arm away causing her to let go.

"It's just tea."

"No, I can't, and please leave me alone," said Alex in a strong tone. She understood and backed off.

It wasn't long before an attractive young lady again approached him. "Hello, are you American? I am student studying English. Do you want to get some tea so I can practice my English?" She smiled and walked next to him. What is going on, he thought? This must be some kind of scam.

"No, I have a girlfriend and she would not be happy."

"Is your girlfriend Chinese?" she asked.

"Yes," he said, agitated. As soon as he said this the girl backed off and disappeared into the crowd.

By the time he reached the Coke stand young women had approached him no less than four times. He purchased his drink and took a seat facing the street so that he could keep an eye on the crowd. After a few moments he spotted one of the girls who had approached him a few moments earlier. He watched her walk up to another Western looking man much older than Alex with a big gray beard. The man dismissed the young girl and she again disappeared into the crowd.

Later Alex told Xiu about the incident. "Were these girls prostitutes?" he asked.

"No, this must be the famous Beijing tea scam. Good thing you didn't go with one of them."

"Why, what would happen?" Alex was curious.

"They would have taken you to a restaurant in some private room with a door and closed it behind you. You would order tea from the menu, and they would sit and drink tea and talk to you."

"That's it? Doesn't seem too bad to me. No sex or robbery or anything of that nature. What's the scam then?" Alex was curious now.

"After the tea you would get the bill and it would be for lots of money. They know that foreigners don't know prices, so they will charge a high price for the tea. They would not let you go until you pay, or until they get your credit card number so they can charge lots of money to it. I have heard that they charge as much as one thousand yuan for a cup of tea, which is about two hundred U.S. dollars for one cup."

"Wow, I'm glad I didn't give in to the young street beauties then," said Alex.

"You are a good man. That's why I am with you."

Alex became aware of some commotion on the street and swung to his left. A black Mercedes sped toward him. He panicked and jumped out of way, but the car stopped just before hitting him. A short Chinese man dressed in a white dress shirt with no tie and black dress slacks exited the driver's side and motioned for Alex to get into the car. "Alex? Comma..Comma," he said while waving. "We go to Li." The man ushered Alex into the back seat. Alex obliged and the car took off into the busy Beijing traffic.

Alex had no clue as to their destination, but it seemed as though they were heading deeper into the heart of the city.

This seemed odd. He had imagined meeting Li Quang in some private rural area away from crowds. "Where are we going?" he asked the driver.

"We go see Li." Alex deduced the driver's limited knowledge of English so he gave up asking questions. He felt safe, so he decided to sit back and enjoy the ride.

After about an hour in the impossible Beijing traffic, the car pulled up in front of a property resembling a park and located in the heart of the city. The driver once again pulled onto the sidewalk and parked. He then opened the car door for Alex and motioned to him to follow him into the park. The attendant recognized the driver and let them through without hesitation. Alex followed the driver through the turnstile and into a beautiful park.

They walked down a tree lined path as the sun shone through the trees creating dappled patterns of light on the stone walk. "Temple of Heaven" explained the driver. "Comma Comma. Ming and Qing emperors pray for good harvest here."

Alex remembered Xiu explaining about how good luck was an important part of Chinese culture. The Chinese practiced countless rituals in the hopes of increasing good luck. He realized that Li probably had chosen this location because of its history as well as its seclusion. Li must be at least a little superstitious, thought Alex, since he apparently thought that meeting in this place of good luck would bring him some as well.

The path led to a series of long wooden buildings. The buildings were open shelters with wood floors, red wooden railings and ceilings, and filled with carved decorations. The ceiling's support beams displayed painted repeating patterns in blue and green. Older men playing games sat on the flat red railing at intervals surrounded by onlookers. "Chinese chess," the driver said as they walked past. One battle in particular drew a large crowd. One of the players made his move and slapped his piece on the board as the crowd gasped. The other player sat motionless as onlookers attempted to coach his next move.

Another wooded path extended beyond the buildings. This path featured a series of metal lamps to light the way in the dark. They passed a lady singing a Mongolian folk song with a few bystanders looking on. Families with children sat on benches enjoying an afternoon picnic. What a strange place for a meeting, thought Alex.

Alex could see the hint of a large temple through the trees further down the path as they continued their brisk walk. Finally, the trees parted and they came to a courtyard containing three temples. The largest was a magnificent structure with a three-gabled conical roof. The temple rested on a base constructed of three circular marble platforms. "Temple of Heaven," the driver said while pointing to it. Two rectangular temples stood on either side of the large structure with tiled roofs. "Comma Comma," the driver said as he directed Alex through the courtyard and onto another path. "We go this way."

Disappointed for not stopping to examine such wonderful historical architecture, Alex understood that sightseeing was not on today's agenda. They continued their fast walk down the path and came to a large rectangular temple with a blue tiled roof. "East Annex Hall," the driver said while pointing straight ahead. Alex spied several ropes and signs placed across the pathway leading to the temple blocking it off to visitor traffic.

The driver led Alex to a small doorway which opened after an exchange in Chinese. Alex entered the dark space. It took a few moments for his eyes to adapt to the low light. His first few breaths revealed a musty smell, and he began to make out the ornate interior full of glass displays containing models of temples and paintings of emperors. Two Chinese men faced him. One gentleman, quite short and dressed much like the driver with a white dress shirt and dark dress pants, appeared to be the boss. The other, tall and muscular, wore a jacket with a curious bulge that Alex assumed concealed a firearm. The taller man held a briefcase.

"*Ni hao*! Welcome, Alex. I am Li Quang, and this is my assistant, Liu Jie. You have already met my other assistant who drove you here, Zhang Jun. We are pleased to meet such an esteemed scientist. Sam has told me a lot about you."

"*Ni hao*, and pleased to meet you, too" said Alex. "I was surprised by the location of the meeting."

"Tando is everywhere, even in China. It is better to hide in plain sight. What better place than one where the emperors prayed for good harvest? This place will bring our venture much good luck. Also, I can never be completely certain of the loyalty of any of my employees. It only takes one betrayal to ruin all I have worked for. Now for business...come and sit." Li Quang took a seat at a carved wooden table that appeared to be hundreds of years old. Alex pulled up a chair and sat across from him. The other two men remained standing and avoided eye contact. "I hope Liu Jie does not scare you with his ominous presence. I assure you, he is here to protect us both."

Alex and Li Quang discussed the materials needed for the next phase of the operation. Alex opened his briefcase, which prompted Liu Jie to reach into his jacket. Li Quang held up his hand, and Liu Jie relaxed. Alex pulled out some papers and slid them across the table to Li Quang. "This is a list of what is needed to assemble the machine for human trials. I hope you can get everything." Alex's words fell off at the end of his statement.

Li Quang surveyed the papers and responded, "This should not be a problem. It will take some *guan xi*, but it is possible to obtain these items."

Relieved, Alex said, "I understand that you can help us to run secret human trials as well."

Li Quang stared at Alex and appeared to be calculating his response. "I can arrange that as well. One can make just about anything happen with *guan xi*, and our friend Sam is providing plenty."

Li Quang motioned to Liu Jie to hand him his briefcase. Liu Jie placed it on the table next to Li Quang's and opened it. Alex saw that it contained stacks of Chinese yuan.

"This is five hundred thousand yuan," said Li Quang. "A fortune for a Chinese man, and a magnet for thievery and danger. This is for your expenses for the next phase." Li Quang closed the briefcase and slid it across the table toward Alex. "Liu Jie will drive you home. I want you to understand that once you take the money, it is out of my hands and my responsibility to Sam is finished." Alex nodded and slid the briefcase off the table.

This would buy a pretty nice wedding, he thought as he went out the door.

16
SUSPICIONS

The next morning the satellite call from the Chicago team came as expected. Alex still had trouble accepting that it was the previous night in Chicago. These calls always made him feel like he could look into some kind of alternate universe. He held an intense fascination with the Schrödinger's cat experiment, whereby a cat is locked inside a box, isolated from the rest of the universe. Inside the box is a vial containing poison. The vial represents a quantum event. This puts the cat in an indeterminate state. Either the cat is alive or the vial has broken, causing the cat's death. The only way to know for sure is to open the box and observe the cat. The problem is that the act of observing the cat collapses the indeterminate state into either a cat alive or cat dead state. One solution to the problem is whichever state the system collapses into, the other state exists in an alternate universe. The universe splits into two separate universes, one containing the living cat and one containing the dead cat. Alex felt as though his life had split into two distinct universes, one the somewhat odd Beijing universe and the other the alternate Chicago universe. To him the fuzzy video calls were like looking into the other universe.

The team discussed the day's trials along with the data

transferred for Alex's analysis. They also compared Alex's data with their own. "The trials are going along nicely," said Mark. "But there is something else I want to talk about. Will you be around in about an hour? I want to speak to you in private."

"I'm not going anywhere," said Alex, concerned. "I will wait for your call."

The satellite phone began to buzz about an hour and a half later and Alex rushed to answer it. "Yup, I'm here Mark. What's up?" Alex saw the concern on Mark's face. "Seems important..."

"It's Xavier," said Mark in an ominous tone. "I think he might be a spy." A wave of anxiety shot through Alex like an electric shock draining the strength from his body. For a brief moment he imagined everything they had worked for destroyed.

"Are you sure?"

"No, not yet, and we haven't talked to Simon either, but Xavier's been working late every night, and the situation with Daniella is not any better."

"But you don't have any proof, just suspicion at this point," said Alex.

"Yes, but the conditions are right for him to sell out."

"I suppose so, but he is such a key player. What do think we should do?"

"I'm not proposing anything yet. Let's just keep an eye on him and see what Simon comes up with." Mark grabbed his chin with his thumb and forefinger. "I just want you to be aware."

"Thanks, Mark. I'm glad you are there keeping an eye on things." The satellite phone clicked off and Alex returned to his Chinese universe.

17
THE GURU

Sam's office was barren and foreboding at night. The steady hum of the air conditioner replaced the usual office noises. The reception area appeared vacuous, as Sheri had left for the day. Peter peered down the hall to Sam's office; the other passageway led to a dark and vacant cubicle farm, the blue glow of computer terminals mocking the city lights reflected in the surrounding windows. It seemed as though the only other people on the entire floor were Sam and Simon. Peter and Mark entered Sam's office through the open door. Sam sat at his desk lost in his computer with Simon at his side.

"Come in, gentlemen," Sam said with the slightest hint of a Texas accent. "You remember Simon." Sam continued staring at his computer. "Can I get you something? Soda? Water?" Both Mark and Peter greeted Sam and Simon and declined refreshment. They each picked up on the serious mood in the room as Sam had not displayed his usual jovial demeanor but had switched into his eye-piercing serious expression. Both took seats in front of Sam's desk and attempted to contain their anxiety.

"Simon thinks that we might have a problem with your partner Xavier," said Sam.

"I analyzed the key logger data and it appears that

Xavier has been accessing a lot of data very late at night."
Simon poked at the keyboard of Sam's computer and said,
"Here it is. Virtually every night during the past week
someone accessed the main computer's data after
midnight, which I think would be after everyone has gone
home. I think we can assume that this someone is Xavier.
It appears that he leaves when you all close up shop and
returns late at night. The logs show that he not only
accesses data, but there is also a good deal of data transfer
to an outside source."

"I knew it!" Mark said as his anger grew. "I thought
something might be up with him. You know, they haven't
found his sister or his brother yet, and he is becoming
more and more desperate as the days pass."

"Wait a minute, Mark," said Peter. "Xavier is a loyal
guy. He even put us before his family by staying and
continuing his work."

"True," said Mark. "But think what you might do if this
happened to you. Your brother gone, your little sister
kidnapped with a ransom on her head, and you have access
to data worth millions." Sam got up from his chair and
turned to face the Chicago night scene outside the window
behind his desk.

"The man's got a point," said Sam.

"Hold on" Peter said. "Simon, did you say something
about a data transfer?"

"That's right," said Simon. "My records show a
complete data dump at 1:00 am last night to an unknown
location."

"But why would he use a flash drive since we can easily
track any read writes? Wouldn't that just implicate him?
Peter appeared very confused.

"That is correct," said Simon.

"The only way one could actually get away with this
would be to use the satellite hookup." Peter became more
confused.

"Exactly," said Simon. "That is exactly what happened.

There was a satellite transfer to an unknown location lasting exactly seventeen minutes and thirty-two seconds. This transfer occurred at exactly 1:13 am this morning, more than enough time to transfer every secret file, every plan, every last detail of your project to some unknown location."

Simon's last words hung in the room like the odor of a dead animal. Mark took in a deep breath and said, "Please, excuse me. Sam, where is the men's room?"

"Right around the corner." Mark disappeared down the hall. Peter's face had turned pale and he muttered to himself underneath his breath. "When Mark gets back we will need to talk about our options," declared Sam as his eyes pierced Peter's. "I've got close to two and a half million riding on this deal, and so far we've been avoiding any attention from the Tando fuck crew, but now I'm really concerned."

Mark rejoined the meeting. His shirt was drenched, as if he had wet his face.

"Pull yourself together." said Sam.

"I'm okay." Mark was still shaken.

"Well, it is obvious what the first order of business is with regard to this issue," Sam said as his intensity grew.

"We must find Xavier! Any ideas where he might be?" said Mark. "He didn't show tonight. At least he wasn't there when I left."

"Well you'd better find him," Sam said as he balled both hands into fists.

"We are on it," said Mark as he and Peter rushed out of the room. The elevator ride to the lobby seemed endless, as both men were deep in thought. Mark finally broke the silence: "I will contact Alex if you will track down Xavier."

18
THE PREVIOUS NIGHT

*T*he team decided to close shop at around 11:00 pm and began to pack up. Hans had already left, as had Mark and the app team. Kira and Xavier were the only ones left, and Kira was shutting down and gathering her things. "Another long night, Xavier?" she said while stuffing her laptop into her backpack. "Doesn't Becca feel like you are ignoring her?"

"Yes, she is a good woman, and I am grateful for her," said Xavier sitting at his desk. "She is under much stress with me right now."

"Well, you might want to take a night off and take her out or something. I'm sure she would appreciate it," Kira said as she put on her jacket.

"I will do that soon," said an aloof Xavier.

Kira left and Xavier continued to work until about 12:45 am. He then packed up and headed out, locking the lab as he left. The stillness and quiet in the building bled into the street below. He made his way along the dark sidewalk to the lot where he'd parked his car. But realizing that he'd forgotten his jump drive, he turned around and headed back to the lab.

Xavier climbed the steps to the lab. As he turned the corner in the hallway leading to the lab, he discovered that the door to the lab cracked open. A wave of confusion passed through him.

The sound of a man's voice broke the stillness. The voice carried into the hallway and Xavier crept toward the door to listen. He recognized the voice. It was Mark's.

"Everything is a go on this end. Time is 1:13 am. Initiating transfer. Yes, I have the encryption key and will deliver it after my meeting with Sam tomorrow. Nobody has a clue here. They will think Xavier did it. You said you would take care of him? Okay, I don't want to be involved—that was the deal. I provide the data and you take care of Xavier. You must get his laptop and flash drive."

Xavier's initial caution and curiosity grew into panic as he rushed down the hallway and down the stairs taking three at a time.

A loud crash awakened Becca as Xavier bolted through the door and ran across the room to their bedroom. "Becca, get up, get up! he shouted. "We must leave. We must leave right now! Get up and pack some things."

"Xavier, what's wrong? You look terrible." Becca sat up in bed.

"They will come for us...Tando's Latro. Mark has betrayed us and he is trying to frame me!" The tears began to well in Xavier's eyes. "Becca, you must leave right now, my love. I don't want anything to happen to you. I love you so much." After pleading with Becca for over thirty minutes, Becca finally accepted the gravity of the situation. She knew Xavier well and was certain this was real.

"Where can you go, Becca? I can't think straight right now."

"The only place I can think of would be my parents' place in Florida, but that's a long way." Becca sprang into action and began throwing things into a suitcase.

"That is far enough away; they will not find you." Xavier began to calm down a bit.

"What about you?" Becca began to cry. "Are you coming with me to Florida?"

"No, I cannot involve you. You don't know what they are capable of. I will hide close by and tell the other team members." Xavier was now able to think more clearly.

"There is one thing I must do to help Alex. I hope he can figure it out," said Xavier as he opened his laptop. Becca continued to throw whatever she grabbed from drawers and closets into her suitcase and finished in about twenty minutes.

Xavier handed her a package addressed to Mexico and said, "Becca, make sure this gets to my family in Mexico. Promise me you will do that, my love."

"Okay, I will. But what about you? I can't leave you here." Becca sobbed. Xavier grabbed her suitcase, put his arm around her and ushered her to her car.

"This has to be. I will contact you. Do not call me. Do you hear me? Go to Florida, mail the package and wait for me. I love you, my dear Becca."

"I love you too, Xavier," she replied as he pushed her into her car and watched her drive away.

Xavier returned to his apartment and finished packing his things. He shut the door, took one last look at their humble home, then left.

He needed to get away, to find a motel somewhere far away and hide out until he could contact the others. He decided to take the interstate to Indiana, and a weird sense of safety spread through him as his car sped through the darkness. Was there really safety in another state?

Somewhere near Gary, Indiana, he exited the interstate and began to search the deserted industrial streets for a motel—any motel. Suddenly, he became aware of something peculiar: someone seemed to be following him. He made a right turn to confirm his suspicion and the other car obliged. He made another turn and so did his follower. Xavier stepped on the gas, and the other car accelerated too. They both raced down the dark street until

Xavier spotted a red traffic light in front of him. He pushed his foot hard onto the gas pedal and the car lurched forward as he tried to run the red light. The last thing he saw was a glaring pair of headlights coming at him from his left.

19
PETER. 11:35 PM

*U*nable to connect with Xavier after calling his cell phone numerous times, Peter decided to go to Xavier's apartment. Xavier and Becca lived on the first story of a two story duplex in an old working class neighborhood not far from the lab. The late hour made navigating the vacant and narrow streets easy as Peter pushed the speed limit. He arrived and pulled up to the curb and spotted a darkened living room window.

He walked to the front door and rang the doorbell several times before realizing it was not functional. He began knocking and calling out to Xavier. No response. He listened for any sound indicating that someone was inside. He pounded on the door a few more times while calling louder: again, no response. He stood in silence for a few moments thinking about what to do next and then pulled out his cell phone to call Xavier one more time. Perhaps he would hear the cell phone ring inside the flat, an indication that Xavier was just avoiding him. More silence.

In a last ditch effort he once again pounded on the door. It rattled back and forth in its frame. This time his efforts did receive a response. The lights went on in the upstairs apartment and a window opened. He stepped back off the porch and looked up to see an angry man. "Can you please stop the banging? My kid's asleep up here," the man yelled to Peter.

"I'm looking for Xavier. Have you seen him?" Peter retreated farther from the porch to get a better view of the man. The man stood at the window with a woman looking on. Both wore robes.

"Is he in some kind of trouble?" the man in the window asked, his anger subsiding.

"It's extremely important; I must see him," said Peter.

"Well, I think you're out of luck, pal. He and the missus took off in the middle of the night." Peter's heart sank. Mark was right. Xavier was a traitor. He and Becca were probably sleeping in some luxury hotel in downtown Chicago, compliments of Tando Pharmaceuticals. "Thanks, I'm sorry I bothered you." Peter turned and walked to his car to the sound of the upstairs window slapping shut as if a judge were banging his gavel for the final time in pronouncing the guilty verdict in the treason case of Xavier Valdez.

On the way to the lab, Peter decided to call Mark. Perhaps Mark might be able to make a satellite call to China to brief Alex on the new information about Xavier. He became annoyed when his repeated attempts to connect with Mark failed. Mark's cell phone seemed to be off. Peter continued to try during the entire drive to the lab with no avail.

Peter rounded the corner to enter the street where the lab was located but what he found shocked him to the core of his being: a police barricade was blocking the street. Fire engines and police cars were everywhere, red and blue lights danced off the nearby buildings and water drenched the streets. Police worked to keep a gathering crowd contained. Small groups of firefighters ran into and out of the lab building in organized chaos. Two fire trucks with ladders extended to the second floor directed their hoses at the lab, dousing it with a continuous flow of water.

Smoke stung Peter's nostrils before he noticed it billowing from the second floor lab. He pulled his car over and rushed to get closer to the police tape. A small crowd of onlookers permeated the air with comments and conjecture about the fire. Peter pushed his way through the crowd to the tape and shouted to a nearby police officer. "That's my building! What the hell is going on?" The police officer came over to him.

"Explosion on the second floor. Bomb squad is up there now."

"Who is in charge?" Peter shouted above the crowd noise. "Can I talk to the person in charge? That's my lab in there."

The officer shouted, "Wait here...I'll see what I can do." A few moments later a man appeared wearing a worn suit and a police badge on his left lapel. "This is detective Vince Marini. He will fill you in." The officer then disappeared into the maze of firefighters, police and flashing lights.

"I'm Peter North. That's my lab up there. What the hell is going on here?"

"There was an explosion about an hour ago. Took out a good portion of the second floor. No one was hurt."

"Thank God!" said a shocked but somewhat relieved Peter. "Was it a bomb?" The detective turned back toward the building where a group of men wearing heavy protective suits walked out and waved to him.

"Wait, here comes the bomb squad now...all clear. I guess it's all over." Detective Marini continued. "The preliminary report from the bomb squad said it had all the hallmarks of a precision explosive device. They think it was a professional job."

Kira had just arrived home from a late night at the clubs when she got the call from Peter. "Christ, Peter, it's like 3:00 am! What's up?"

"The lab's been bombed," said the excited voice on the other end. "We've lost everything. Plus there is more bad news." Kira's jaw dropped and she collapsed onto her sofa.

"What the fuck could be worse than that?" Kira snapped into sobriety.

"I'm pretty sure Xavier is a traitor and has sold out to Tando."

"I don't believe that," said Kira. "Xavier is a good man. He would never do something as evil as that."

"I know it's unbelievable, but Xavier's brother is in trouble, his sister was kidnapped, he has access to our data, then he disappears and here I am standing in front of a bombed out lab."

Peter instructed Kira to meet him at his place as soon as she could get there. He said he would contact the others as well and that she should continue to try to contact Mark.

Hans was the last of the group to arrive at Peter's apartment. Fortunately, Peter's daughter was with her mom. It was now 4:00 am. The stunned group sat in Peter's living room.

"As you all know," began Peter, "earlier tonight a bomb went off in our lab. I was not able to go into the lab because the police were not letting anyone in, but the detective I talked with said it looked like a professional hit, and I think you all know what that means.

"You mean Tando found out about us?" said Julie.

"How the hell would something like that happen?" said Hans reaching for a cigarette. Kevin shook his head in disbelief.

Everyone sat in silence as Peter continued: "Also, just before this happened, Mark and I met with our financier Sam and his security liaison Simon, who you probably remember did an assessment of our security system. We had evidence that Xavier had betrayed us. I went to Xavier's apartment right after our meeting and discovered that Xavier and Becca had left in a hurry earlier last night.

Lastly, I've tried reaching Mark with no luck. Kira, did you hear anything from Mark?"

"No. And you know what's weird? For the first dozen times or so there was no answer, but then the message switched to something about the phone not being in service." Kira dialed Mark's number again and held up her phone to broadcast the 'out of service' message.

Peter continued, "The last strange thing is that I also tried to place an international call to Alex's cell phone with no answer. There are a lot of very bizarre things going on, and I'm confused." Peter sat down on a recliner chair next to his sofa.

"So we are dead in the water?" said Kevin.

"All that work for a cure for cancer and Tando comes in and steals everything and bombs our lab?" Kira chimed in. "We should bomb the Tando building. That would show those fuckers!"

"How can they get away with this?" said Hans, an unlit cigarette dangling from his lips.

"You know how everyone looks the other way with Tando and the Latro," said Peter. "They can get away with just about anything. Xavier is probably with them right now planning the first set of cancer cure clinics."

Kira interrupted Peter. "Has anyone tried calling the police to see if they can find Mark or Xavier? Maybe they were taken to an emergency room or found dead in some alley somewhere."

"Good idea," said Peter.

"I'll try calling Becca," said Julie. "Maybe she will answer and actually knows something."

The group made many attempts to contact Mark and Alex to no avail. Julie, however, successfully contacted Becca. "Becca? This is Julie from the lab." Peter signaled for Julie to hand over her phone.

"Hi, Becca. Peter here. We are trying to locate Xavier." The group overheard Becca sobbing on the other end of the line. "What's wrong, Becca?" Peter tried to calm her but she continued to sob. "Tell me what's wrong," Peter insisted.

After a few gulps of air Becca sobbed, "Xavier is dead!"

"What!" Peter was shocked.

"He is dead. My poor husband is dead!"

Becca went on to explain that she had received a call from the police about an hour ago saying an ambulance had taken Xavier to an emergency room in Gary, Indiana after an automobile accident. The police said that a semi had crashed into Xavier after he had run a red light. They said that he had died instantly. Becca said that she was heading there now. Peter had put her on speaker phone and the last thing she said sent chills down everyone's spines: "Xavier said that Mark had sold your secrets to Tando, and that we had to leave town. He thought Mark was trying to frame him, but Mark was the real traitor!" The news stunned the group even more. After a few more words Peter said goodbye to Becca. Becca said she would not go home but stay at a friend's house until after the funeral. She would then go to her parents' home in Florida.

The group decided it would be best to all go home and wait until they could get into the lab or hear from Alex. They were to stay on alert keeping their cell phones on and within reach at all times. Peter said that anyone who wanted to was welcome to stay at his place. He planned to drive to Indiana to meet Becca at the hospital and offered to take anyone who wanted to go with him. Kira obliged. Julie and Kevin decided to stay at Peter's, and Hans went home.

Peter and Kira spent the day with Becca at the emergency room and the police station. They participated in the gruesome task of identifying Xavier's mangled body and obtained as much information from the police as possible. The police report contained little information other than the semi driver who had struck Xavier's car saw Xavier running a red light. The police officers who were first on the scene also stated that the driver remarked about another car stopping right behind Xavier. He said that the car had stopped and two men approached Xavier's car. The driver thought they were coming to help, but once they discovered Xavier's dead body, they had driven off. The driver did not remember any other details about the men since he had rushed to try to help Xavier.

This horrible day concluded with a visit to a funeral home. Peter and Kira helped Becca with the arrangements as best they could. They planned to cremate Xavier's body, and there would be a service later that week. Peter and Kira returned to Peter's apartment to find Julie, Kevin and Hans, who had just returned from Xavier's home. "I drove past the lab on the way here," said Hans. "The police were still there and not letting anyone inside. It's pretty bad; the entire floor was blown out."

Peter gave an update regarding Xavier's funeral.

"We examined Xavier's body. It was very disturbing. Part of his skull was smashed." Peter filled in the group on the details of Xavier's account of Mark's betrayal. He had just about finished when his phone rang. It was Alex.

20
EARLIER THAT SAME DAY IN CHINA

Alex sat at his desk while the China team worked hard performing another successful series of rat trials. Xiu was working in her section of the lab preparing a batch of resveratrol when all hell broke loose. A loud crisp bang shattered the quiet as the kicked-in door flung open and several men wearing ski masks and carrying automatic assault rifles rushed inside. The men entered with the efficiency of a well-rehearsed precision strike force. Four men rushed in single file and spread out with weapons drawn and shouting at each other in Chinese. The fifth man entered holding his assault weapon in a neutral position with the barrel facing upward. He wore a red ski mask and spoke into a walkie-talkie. Before Alex could decide what to do the men had surrounded them, weapons pointing at them.

Duyi had been in the process of shutting down the frequency machine when one of the armed men ran toward him yelling. Duyi dropped to his knees as well as did Hui, Fang and Lihua. The men motioned to them to hold their hands behind their heads, move to the center of the room and lie on their stomachs.

Alex, in a state of confusion, stood up from his chair and witnessed the horror enfold. He thought the men were going to execute everyone right before his eyes. Some of the men leveled their weapons against the heads of the Chinese lab assistants as if they were going to shoot. The leader spotted Alex and walked over to him while pointing his weapon at his head. He shouted in English. "Get on the ground...NOW!" He raised his weapon, aiming slightly above Alex's head, and emptied a few rounds into the ceiling.

Alex checked to make sure that Xiu was okay as he joined the others on the floor. Lihua and Fang cried and pleaded in Chinese for their lives. The armed men shouted back at them to be quiet. Alex took a place next to Xiu and assumed a prone position. Before he could say a word he found his arms forced behind him and bound with some sort of plastic device. A soldier ordered him to get up and stand along a wall with the others. The leader barked commands to his soldiers who bound everyone and herded them to the door. They lined everyone up against the wall near the door. Alex thought he would at least die next to his beloved Xiu.

The leader shouted another order and the men drew their weapons and pointed them at their prisoners in firing squad fashion. Alex turned to Xiu, who appeared to be in a state of shock and horror, and told her that he loved her. She turned toward him and said she loved him too. Lihua and Fang continued to sob with their heads down, while Duyi and Hui struggled to show brave faces to their captors.

The leader drew his weapon and pointed it at the group. Alex braced himself for the fatal barrage of bullets. He detected a sick and twisted smirk through the mouth hole in the leader's mask and thought about how cruel it was for them to taunt their prisoners. He took in a deep breath and held it all the while clenching his muscles as if to magically shield his body from the bullets. Just as he thought he saw the leader's finger twitch to pull the trigger, the man pivoted and began shooting into the lab.

Alex and the others witnessed the men fire with abandon into the lab, shattering equipment, destroying computers and killing all the rats. The men seemed to relish in the destruction. After wreaking destruction by spraying the area with bullets, they took aim at specific targets. Alex stood by as bullets ripped apart the frequency machine. They hit Xiu's resveratrol production area next, and glassware shattered into tiny pieces and crashed to the floor. Xiu turned away as the men took aim at the rats. They exploded into blood and body parts with the heavy caliber bullets. Some of the rats escaped their cages, and automatic weapon fire followed them as they scurried away.

After the mass destruction the men shouted more commands in Chinese and walked Alex, Xiu and their team outside and loaded them into two black windowless vans. "What's going on? Where are you taking us?" Alex screamed at the leader.

"No questions. Cooperate and you will live," the leader yelled while standing a few inches in front of Alex.

Alex panicked when he saw Xiu forced into the other van. "Xiu...No! Don't separate us!" Alex jumped out of the van and one of the soldiers took aim at him.

"No!" the leader said holding up his hand to the soldier. He caught up with Alex and wrestled him to the ground. Alex turned on his back and began kicking the man while yelling, "You can't do this...You can't do this!" The leader smiled and raised the butt of his rifle. Alex felt a sharp pain on the side of his head and descended into unconsciousness.

Alex awoke with searing pain in his head. He sat on a chair with his head resting upon a metal table. He lifted his head. His hands were chained in front of him. "Hello? Hello? Is anyone here?" he cried out. His words echoed in the empty room. A full glass of water stood on the table in front of him. He scanned the room and discovered one wall contained an embedded mirror. This is an interrogation room, he thought.

The door squeaked as it opened and a Chinese police officer entered. "How are you feeling?" the officer asked in English.

"I am okay, except for my head," said Alex as he tried to touch his head against the restraints. The officer unshackled him.

"This is just a precaution for your own safety," said the officer in a friendly tone.

"Where am I?" Alex put both hands on his head.

"You are in a police station."

"Where is the lady I was with? Is she okay?"

"She is here along with the others who were with you. She is okay."

"How did I get here? I don't remember anything."

"You were found on the side of the road in an industrial park about two kilometers from the terrorist bombing."

"That was no terrorist attack. It was the Latro from Tando Pharmaceuticals. It was a coordinated hit on our lab. Wait a minute; I don't remember a bomb..."

"An entire building was destroyed by a bomb. We are investigating."

"They bombed everything? I must see Xiu."

"You are free to go. I will take you to the others."

"Aren't you going to question me?"

"There is no need to ask questions. We are investigating," the police officer repeated.

At that moment Alex realized that the police also must be cooperating with Tando, and there was no use pursuing the matter. He only wanted to know that Xiu was unharmed. The officer escorted him out of the small room and down the hall to a waiting area. He spotted Xiu and the others sitting on a row of wooden chairs. "Xiu, are you okay?"

"Alex, you are okay! I thought they killed you!" Xiu

began to sob. "Everything we worked for is lost."

"I know, I know." Alex attempted to console her. "I'm just glad you are okay. Do you remember getting here?" Xiu sobbed into her hands.

"No. All I remember is getting into the van and the doors closing. Then the doors opened again and someone threw a canister into the van. Then there was gas. I choked and thought I was dying, and the next thing I knew I was here. I thought I had died."

Alex put his arm around her. "I'm so happy that you are alive. I don't know what I'd do without you."

"Me too," said Xiu.

Alex and Xiu naturally concluded that the attack was a systematic extermination of their project by Tando. A random act of terror, as the police were calling this incident, made no sense whatsoever. They would not be alive if this were truly an act of terror. Evidently, the attackers wanted to keep Alex, Xiu and the China team alive. A Latro attack made perfect sense. The Latro, known for their efficiency, only killed when necessary. This raid constituted more than just destroying a competitor. They wanted to either send a message to others not to compete with Tando, or to keep Alex and company alive in case they wanted more information from them.

Equally perplexing to Alex and Xiu was the destruction of the lab. At no time whatsoever did anyone from the China team see any of the attackers take anything from the lab. If they were smart, then they would have known that we had valuable information and data supporting a bona fide cure for cancer. Something Tando would give just about anything to possess. Alex took some comfort in this and thought that at least they could begin the project again. Alex wondered how Tando had discovered their covert operation. He thought they had gone to great lengths to keep it secret. Perhaps Liang or one of the Chinese lab assistants had tipped them off.

"I have to get to call Chicago. The satellite link is gone. What time is it?" Alex surveyed the room and noticed a clock on the wall that read 10:33. The darkness displayed in the windows further indicated it was 10:33 pm.

Alex and Xiu first made sure that the others from the China team were okay and then rushed out of the police station. They had no problem hailing a taxi on the crowded street in front of the station. Xiu directed the driver to her apartment where she had a backup cell phone that they hoped would make an international connection. For the next forty minutes they sat in silence, still in shock from what had happened. Finally, Xiu broke the silence.

"What will this mean for us?"

After what seemed like a long time Alex spoke. "I need to take this all in."

The taxi pulled up to Xiu's apartment and they bolted up the stairs to the fifth floor. Xiu's apartment door hung open, revealing a ransacked mess within. "Apparently, they've been here too," remarked Alex. Xiu sat on the sofa and began to cry. Alex sat next to her and put his arm around her.

"We will get through this," he said while holding back his own tears to appear strong. After a few minutes, Xiu calmed down and they both surveyed the mess. "It doesn't look like they took anything," said Alex while searching through the items strewn about the floor. "I suppose if all they wanted was information, there would be nothing here of value to them. They even left the money." Alex referred to the remainder of the last cash infusion from Sam. They had not spent it all and the remaining sum was quite substantial.

"My laptop!" Xiu pointed to a shattered mess of plastic pieces on the floor.

"They destroyed mine as well," said Alex holding a twisted piece containing a few keys. "I guess this is what they were after."

"I found it!" Xiu held up the cell phone. She rushed it

over to Alex.

Alex dialed Mark's number, making sure to include the additional digits for international calls. He looked puzzled.

"What's wrong? Can't you make the connection?"

"That's odd," said Alex. "It says Mark's number is disconnected. I've tried several times and I get the same recording. I'll try Peter."

21
ALEX AND PETER CONNECT

Peter picked up his phone and shouted, "Quiet everyone, quiet! It's Alex!" He raised the phone to his ear. His hand was shaking.

"Alex, are you okay? What's going on over there?"

"We are okay but the lab...it's been destroyed. It was bombed. They came in broad daylight. I thought they were going to kill us, Peter."

"I'm glad you are okay, but we have similar bad news here. First of all, and thank God that no one was hurt, but our lab was also bombed. We lost everything...and worse. We think Mark betrayed us and sold out to Tando."

"What? Mark?" Alex was stunned. "Why do you think Mark would have done this?"

"Well, there is something else you need to know. Xavier is dead. He was killed early this morning in a car crash."

"Xavier is dead? What happened?" Alex was shocked and confused.

"Well, Xavier was running from something, or someone. I talked to Becca and she said Xavier saw Mark making an unauthorized data transfer using the satellite connection. She also said Xavier overheard a conversation between Mark and someone else claiming they were trying to frame Xavier as a traitor. Kira and I talked about it and we think Xavier suspected Mark. If Mark discovered this, then he needed to get Xavier out of the way."

"I can't believe it! Mark is my own flesh and blood. I've known him my entire life. There must be another explanation for all this."

Julie blurted out, "Hey, turn on the six o'clock news! I just got a text about something happening with Tando."

"Hang on, Alex; I'm putting you on speaker." Kevin rushed to the TV and tuned in to the national news.

"Good evening. Today, breaking news from Tando Pharmaceuticals, who just announced that they have discovered a revolutionary, ground-breaking treatment for cancer. We take you now to Chuck Brimsley standing by in Chicago."

The scene switched to a live news conference held at a downtown Chicago hotel. A man stood at a podium displaying the Tando emblem. Reporters from all the major media outlets filled the room and the clicks of multiple cameras and flash pops reinforced the importance of the event. The reporter began:

"We are here at the Wexley Hotel in downtown Chicago where a news conference is about to begin. Jim Barnes, CEO of Tando Pharmaceuticals will be announcing what is purportedly a new cure for cancer. They are just about to begin."

The scene cut to the conference room.

A man dressed in an impeccable suit and red tie stood at the podium smiling and nodding to the crowd of reporters. Someone signaled him from the side and he began speaking into the microphone. "Today is a day that will change the course of history in science and medicine. Today is a day we can look back on and say we began to win the war against one of our most deadly diseases. Today, Tando Pharmaceuticals will announce a ground-breaking treatment for cancer. To explain more I will introduce the lead researcher and new vice president in charge of cancer treatment for Tando Pharmaceuticals. Please welcome Dr. Mark Winter."

Mark stood at the podium, almost unrecognizable in a suit and tie. A flurry of photographs and flashes caused him to squint and blink as he was about to begin. He took a moment to compose himself then began:

"We at Tando Pharmaceuticals are excited to announce a new cure for cancer. Our work combines a state of the art approach that uses radio waves at various frequencies along with a proprietary nutraceutical substance that when used together eradicates all cancerous and precancerous cells. We plan to test the new treatment in a series of human trials in the coming months and make it available as soon as we open cancer cure clinics in major cities throughout the U.S. We are confident that the human trials will be successful and we are on a fast track with the Food and Drug Administration to provide this cure to anyone who needs it. Our plan is to make the cancer cure available to breast cancer patients first and then expand to other cancers such as lung, pancreatic, liver and prostate. That's all I have for now, and I will take just a few questions."

The group sat in stunned silence as the news unfolded. Here stood Mark, their teammate, cofounder and Alex's brother selling out to Tando and betraying them right before their eyes on national television. Peter continued to repeat, "I can't believe it, I can't believe it." His cell phone was silent with Alex on the other end, listening. Kira said, "Shhhhhh!" to Peter as the program continued.

A reporter from a major national news outlet asked the first question: "You say you have only tested this new treatment on rats, so how are you sure it will work on humans?"

Mark replied, "Good question. It involves a revolutionary new mechanism which is proprietary, but this new procedure will eradicate all cancer in a living system. We are confident that our treatment will scale to humans." Mark pointed to another reporter.

"When do you think this will be available to the general public?"

"We think we can open the first cancer cure clinic in about six months. We have time for one more question, over there."

The reporter asked, "Is it true that Tando uses questionable tactics to obtain information including hiring mercenaries?"

Jim Barnes jumped in front of Mark and said, "I don't know what you are talking about. I've never heard anything about this. No more questions. Thank you all for coming." Mark exited the stage in a further flurry of photographs, and the program cut to a commercial.

"I can't believe what I just heard," said Alex on Peter's phone. "Was that really Mark up there? For Christ sake, he's my brother. What is wrong with him?"

"I don't get it," said Peter. "I just don't get it. It explains a lot, though. Mark had access to everything and was able to run the app team and collect information. He probably made several data transfers to Tando using our satellite link while we were all working together. It wasn't until Simon put the heat on us with his monitoring program that Mark could do as he pleased. He needed someone to blame to keep us off his back after Simon installed his surveillance software. The problem was that it backfired, and Xavier is now dead."

"Yes, once he had all our information for the cure, he called in a hit on both labs to erase any evidence connecting us to it," said Alex.

Kevin added, "He may be a bastard son of a bitch asshole traitor but you've got to give it to him for planning this whole thing and carrying it out with such precision."

"I think we should go down there and confront the fucker." Kira, like the others, was full of anger.

"That wouldn't do any good," said Peter. "Mark is

probably on a plane to California or New York or some far away secret location surrounded by Latro bodyguards. We can't even accuse him of anything since we have nothing but two burned out labs. Anything we say is just hearsay." Peter's phone lit up with another call. A look of dread washed over his face when he recognized the number. "Alex, I have to put you on hold; it's Sam."

"What the hell is going on over there?" Peter had never heard Sam so angry. "Why did I just watch Dr. Mark Winter announce *our* project to the world on behalf of Tando? I thought Xavier was the traitor. Hell, you and Mark were just in my office last night."

"I know Sam. We are all as confused as you are. Xavier is dead."

"What? How the hell did that happen?" Peter went on to explain Xavier's death and his and Alex's take on what Mark had done. Sam said he would need some time to process this and talk with his attorneys but he didn't think there was much recourse at this point. He left the conversation saying that he would soon be in touch.

"Alex, are you still there?"

"Yes, I'm here. What did Sam say?"

"No surprises," said Peter. "I filled him in on what happened to Xavier and our theory and he said he would meet with his legal team and get back to us. He wasn't very hopeful though."

After a long silence Alex said, "I don't see any other option than for me to come back and help get things straightened out. I'll get on the next plane to Chicago. See you in a couple of days, Peter."

Alex hung up.

22
ALEX RETURNS TO CHICAGO...

Alex was unable to procure a flight to Chicago until four days later. The call finally came for a standby seat on a United Airlines flight. He and Xiu arrived at Beijing International Airport and remained together as long as they could before boarding time. Alex thought about his arrival and how far he had come with the project, and in his relationship with Xiu. He'd spent the past four days rehashing what had happened and deciding what to do next. Alex was adamant about Xiu returning her work at the university, as if nothing had happened, and to lay low for a while and fly under Tando's radar. Xiu requested that Liang investigate what had happened as well. Liang had done so and told them not to pursue the subject. Tando was powerful and dangerous and any attempt to fight back could provoke a lethal retaliation. He assured them that the police were in on it too.

Alex took the entire incident as if he were responsible. How could he not know that Mark, his own flesh and blood, was capable of such a thing? He searched his thoughts for possible signs that he might have missed. He thought about how he and Mark had grown up together and how hard Mark had taken their parents' death. With the exception of Xiu, Alex had never been closer to anyone else in his entire life. Mark knew more about him than anyone. Now, everything had changed. Mark's betrayal and Xavier's death had annihilated their relationship forever.

Alex's tremendous guilt and obsession with the tragedy tortured him. Xiu and the others tried to console him but their efforts did little to stop him from feeling that this entire mess was his fault. Depression and anger replaced Alex's usual optimism. He remained locked inside his head and allowed no one to enter. After all, Mark was family, and he had betrayed not only the team, but the love of Alex's life. To Alex, Mark's betrayal was his betrayal.

As the departure time drew near, Alex and Xiu realized that time was running out and that they needed to say goodbye. They stood facing each other holding hands. "You must go now, but I will be with you in spirit," said Xiu while holding back tears.

"I will be with you, too." Alex struggled to look into her eyes. "I love you, Xiu."

"And I love you, Alex." They kissed, and Alex turned and walked to the security area. He soon became lost in the crowd. He turned back to see Xiu waving at him and wondered if he would ever see her again.

After a couple of days the police allowed the Chicago team to visit the burned-out lab. They assembled in front of the building and made their way inside. Alex was the first to smell the strong odor of burnt wood and plastic as he and the others entered the main hall. Fortunately, the fire department had declared the building's structure was still intact. The first floor appeared unaffected with only the pungent odor to indicate damage. The stairs appeared off limits, the entrance blocked with yellow police tape. The elevator stood with its doors open and beckoned them inside. The team entered and pressed the button for the second floor causing the doors to close. "Must not be too bad if the elevator still works," commented Peter.

The elevator came to a halt and its doors squeaked open to reveal the first signs of the explosion. The heavy metal door to the lab hung open on one hinge and the hallway was half-filled with rubble that had blasted through the door.

Alex led the team into the charred lab. The blown-out windows and twisted metal, glass, and plaster from the walls strewn on the floor created an eerie post-apocalyptic scene. It was as if he entered an alternate reality, a movie set from a battle scene. This was real however, and the reality crept in after a few moments.

"It's like being in a video game, except it stinks," said Kira as she followed Alex through the blown-out door.

Alex noticed that the soot from the post explosion fire was more concentrated near the frequency machine and resveratrol production areas. He surmised that there had been two precision explosions, one each targeting these areas.

They continued their survey of the wreckage. Rubble stood in place of most of the equipment. A twisted metal frame with burnt goo hanging from it stood in place of the sofa where the team had once engaged in vicious video game battles. Hans made his way over to what was left of the rat cages. He shook his head and mumbled something about his poor rats. Various shades of black, brown and dried red rat blood covered the walls. Mangled and twisted desks, chairs and other furniture created a maze through which the group navigated. Kira found an intact video game controller but that was about the only thing salvageable.

"I guess this is a total loss," Peter said as he stood in the center of the rubble.

"No way could anything survive this," said Kira as she and Julie sorted through the rubble looking for the main computer.

"Maybe we can get something off the hard drive," said Julie in an attempt to convey some hope. Her hopes were soon dashed after she found only a few charred pieces.

Alex broke down and began to cry. "I am so sorry..." The others tried to console him.

"It's not your fault, Alex." Kira held back her own tears. "How could you possibly have known?"

"I should've seen something. There must have been some clue, something I missed that would have tipped me off," said Alex.

"You cannot take responsibility for this, Alex. I knew Mark too, and I didn't have a clue. Don't beat yourself up. We need to figure out a way to move forward."

The team met at Peter's home later that evening to discuss their next steps. They concluded that the dramatic use of bombs by the Latro had served two purposes: they had destroyed any evidence that another project existed; and it served as a formidable scare tactic for anyone in Freetech to stay away and leave this issue alone. Plus, it served as a warning sign to any others who might try to compete with Tando. Peter also contacted Sam, who had now met with his legal team. The news was bad here as well. Sam reported that his lawyers thought that they had a very weak case against Tando. No evidence existed except for Alex and Xiu's early work on frequencies and resveratrol that they had each presented at the London conference. Since this information was not proprietary, Tando could use it to their liking. Also, because of Freetech's secrecy, the bombing appeared to affect only the app startup. A case against Tando could only be based on hearsay.

Peter offered to revive the app team since they had had a modicum of success with their wellness app and asked who would be interested in joining him. He said that they still had some money from Sam, and he preferred that they try to recoup at least some of the loss. Fortunately, they all retained copies of the software, so it would be an easy project. Julie and Kevin said that they would join Peter, but Kira and Hans declined. Kira said that she was finished and fed up and would now focus on her doctorate. Hans made a similar decision; he wanted to lay low and get lost in his graduate studies.

"How about you, Alex?" Peter said with hope.

"No thanks, Peter. I appreciate the offer but I need a break to process what has happened. In fact, I'm handing in my resignation to the university tomorrow."

"What? You can't!" said Peter and Kira simultaneously. "Let's face it, I've lost everything: my work, my hope to be with Xiu—everything!" Alex was serious. "I can't work. I can barely function."

"Why don't you take some time?" Peter tried to be rational.

"I don't know if I could ever do this again," said Alex.

That night Alex returned home and spoke with Xiu. She had resumed her previous life at Peking University. He told her about Peter and the app team. She told him that her uncle had advised her again to leave the issue alone, and that she would be safe at the university. Alex said nothing about his resignation, or about his plans. At the end of their conversation they affirmed their love for each other. Alex said one more thing: "Xiu , I want you to know that I will come back for you someday." Xiu, perplexed by his statement, figured Alex was not rational and that he would come around in a couple of days. They said goodbye and Alex reached behind him to grab his backpack. He tossed his phone onto the sofa. He walked through the door of his apartment, turned back to look at it one more time, and then said "goodbye."

He closed the door leaving his old life behind.

23
THE FUNERAL

Peter opened the large wooden doors of The Schultz Funeral Home and walked up the concrete steps to the foyer. He surmised the numerous cars filling the parking lot were for the other of the two funerals held that day. Besides his students, one could count Xavier's friends on one hand. It was 6:00 pm and Peter knew the service would begin in an hour. He followed the sign in the foyer directing him to the room on the left.

There were ten rows of chairs in two sections, which seemed like too many for the handful of mourners that were expected. The chairs faced a display consisting of two easels holding poster boards full of pictures of Xavier at various stages of his life. The center, bisected by a single marble column about four feet high, contained an urn holding Xavier's ashes. About fifteen people milled about forming small groups and conversing in hushed voices about Xavier. New age ambient music helped to set the somber tone of the affair.

Becca, stationed at the front of room along with two older Mexicans, greeted the mourners. The mourners formed three distinct groups. One group consisted of the Chicago team, another of Xavier's students and a third included Becca's parents. Peter migrated over to the first group. "Are those Xavier's parents?" he asked in a hushed tone.

"They flew in today from Mexico," said Kira.

"Where's Alex? Didn't he come with any of you?" Peter's question met with head shakes and shrugged shoulders.

"We thought he was coming with you." Julie took the lead for the group. "None of us has been able to contact him. It's really strange."

"He might still show up," said Peter. "He's in a bad place right now, you know, taking responsibility for everything."

Peter broke away from the group to give his condolences to Becca and to Xavier's parents. Becca stood next to Xavier's mother, comforting her as she broke into tears at regular intervals. Both parents stood not much taller than five feet and spoke little English. Becca assisted as translator. Xavier's mother wore a black dress with a black scarf covering her hair. His father wore a piecemeal outfit consisting of a dark gray blazer, white shirt and black slacks. Peter noticed their poverty and figured that they had had to spend a good portion of their savings to come here. "I'm so sorry, Becca." Peter choked up when he saw the grief in her eyes.

"Thank you for coming." Becca appeared to have been crying so much that there were no tears left. She introduced him to Xavier's parents, Alma and Carlos. Peter gave his condolences to them as well and they responded with sincerity.

Becca said, "Have you heard the news about Xavier's sister Daniella?" With all of the commotion of the last few days Peter had almost forgotten about Daniella's kidnapping by the drug cartel. "Daniella was found and is home safe. The people in Cheran rose up against the cartel. Evidently, they have had a lot of problems with the drug lords, and Daniella's kidnapping was the last straw. Xavier's family and some strong local women led the uprising. A local farm boy who told them Daniella's location tipped off the vigilantes. The group of armed farmers stormed the place and rescued her." The good news made Peter happy.

"What about Luis? What happened to him?" said Peter.

Becca continued: "Not so good news about Luis. The cartel got to Luis before the farmers and murdered him in a Mexico City hotel room. It was a professional hit. Luis had a long history of getting into trouble. Xavier used to admire his big brother, but after he came to the States they grew apart. Luis took a dangerous path in his life."

A priest entered the room and made his way to the immediate family. "I will talk to you later Becca." Peter turned and rejoined his team. Peter remembered that Xavier's family practiced Catholicism and that a priest would conduct a prayer service. As the time for the service grew near, the mourners took their seats. Peter sat next to Kira.

"Where's Alex?" Peter whispered to Kira who shook her head and shrugged her shoulders.

The priest conducted a brief and solemn service consisting of an overview of Xavier's life along with some prayers and a blessing of the ashes. Xavier's parents folded their hands with fingers pointing skyward and bowed their heads in prayer as if they had experienced this sort of thing many times before. Peter understood that the purpose of funerals was to impart a sense of closure for friends and family. Unfortunately, the events surrounding Xavier's death gave him no such solace. He wondered if they would ever discover the true details about what had happened during Xavier's final night.

24
PETER'S LETTER

Peter and the others repeatedly tried to contact Alex over the next two days. Peter visited Alex's apartment a few times and tried knocking on the door, just in case Alex returned. At first he assumed that Alex had dodged Xavier's funeral because of his guilt. But he became much more concerned when Alex didn't answer his texts or calls. Xiu even contacted Peter as her concern grew into a near panic. Peter did his best to calm and reassured her and told her that Alex would contact her soon.

After several attempts, Peter convinced Alex's landlord to let him inside the apartment. Suicide not completely ruled out, he expected the worst and braced himself for the potential horrifying sight of Alex's dead and decaying body. The landlord unlocked the door and Peter swung it open. He scanned the living room and picked up Alex's discarded cell phone.

At least we know why he hasn't been answering his calls, he thought. Proceding with caution through each room, he saved the bathroom for last. An image of a dead Alex lying in the bathtub came into his mind causing him to hesitate as he nudged the door open. A wave of relief washed over him when, after getting up enough nerve, he drew the shower curtain back to reveal an empty bathtub.

Upon returning home, Peter recruited the other team members to organize and contact the local police and hospital emergency rooms. After a full day of talking with police and hospital staff, Peter, starving, decided to pick up a pizza on the way home. When he arrived home he stopped at his mailbox to collect the day's mail, and then carried it up to his apartment. After plopping the pizza onto the dining table, he retrieved a beer from the refrigerator, pulled up a chair and sat down to enjoy his bachelor's dinner. With a piece of pizza in one hand, he leafed through the mail with the other. After sorting through the usual coupons, ads and the latest issue of *Wired* magazine, he spotted a hand-addressed envelope with no return address. Peter ripped open the envelope and unfolded the single page. The letter read:

Dear Peter, Kira, Kevin, Julie and Hans:

I am so grateful to you all. The time we spent together will always be precious to me. I have never had such friendship as you all have given me. I would have loved to continue to work with you but I must decline. I can't bring myself to even face you all again. I take full responsibility for what happened with Mark. He was my brother and I should have seen some indication of his betrayal stopped it. I was blinded by my own selfish needs and now all is lost and Xavier is dead.

I am going away. Please do not try to find me or contact me. For how long I do not know. I will be okay.

Forever grateful,
Alex

Shocked, Peter fumbled for his phone to call Kira, who was working at the Northern University lab. Kira answered on the first ring.

"Peter, I'm glad you called. I was going to call you. I just found out that Alex resigned his position with the university."

"I know," said Peter. "I just got a letter from him. It says he's gone away. Doesn't say where or when he's coming back. I'm not one hundred percent sure this is not a suicide letter."

"Oh, my God!" Kira was very upset. "I guess that explains why he didn't show up at Xavier's funeral. I hope he didn't do anything stupid. He knows none of us blames him, doesn't he?" Kira's voice cracked.

"I think he's okay," said Peter. "There's no way to be sure, but maybe he just needs to get away for a while and will come back in a few days, or a couple of weeks."

"But he resigned, which means he may not be back."

Peter and Kira decided to contact the others to fill them in on the news. Peter said he would contact Xiu, and Kira would call Hans, Julie and Kevin. Peter's call to Xiu was difficult, as Xiu became hysterical at one point despite his attempts to calm her. He could think of nothing else to say except that they would work their hardest to find him, and that the letter had said that he was okay. She listened, regained her composure and thanked Peter. He ended by saying that he would contact her the moment they heard anything.

25
XIU'S LETTER

A week passed with no word from Alex. Peter and the others continued to work on the wellness app project and tried to forget the awful chain of events. The constant reminders in the form of non-stop media coverage didn't help. Unless one lived in a media vacuum, there was no avoiding the incessant stories about Mark, Tando and the new cancer cure. As over the top as the coverage was, it became worse with the news that the human trials were to begin soon.

Xiu received Alex's letter the week following Peter's call. She recognized his handwriting on the envelope and tore it open. It read:

My loving Xiu Ling:

I am so sorry for all that I have put you through. The time we spent together I will forever hold dear. My hopes and dreams for us have been replaced by guilt and despair. How could I ask you to be with me when I have nothing? In Chinese culture a man must be successful in the eyes of a woman, and I hoped I would be worthy of you. But now, with everything lost, I cannot even face you. I take full responsibility for this dismal state of affairs. Mark is my brother and I should have paid closer attention to him.

Please go on with your life and try to forget about me. I am going away for a while and do not know when or if I will return. I only know I cannot endure such pain.

All of my love,
Alex

Xiu stood by the mailbox and began to weep. She was trapped in China and powerless to do anything to find the only true love she'd ever known. At that moment she wanted nothing more than to tell him how important he was to her. She longed for their lives together in China when everything was good. And she now feared that she had lost him forever.

26
THREE MONTHS LATER

*T*he months flew by and Alex passed the time by
drowning his feelings in a world of drugs and booze. It
wasn't long after he'd arrived at Manitou Springs, Colorado
that he found a job as a bartender. His new life consisted
of working late into the night, partying with the other
service people, and sleeping most of the following day.
Alex had fallen in love with the Rockies years ago when
presenting at a conference in nearby Colorado Springs and
had wanted to return. Now, in his devastated state, he
found it to be the perfect hiding place.

After staying at the Golden Saddle motel for a couple
of weeks, he rented a room in an old house occupied by an
eclectic group of people. Angie, who worked as a fortune
teller/psychic in a small closet size space between a
souvenir shop and an art gallery, made Alex uneasy at
times with her supernatural chatter. Adam and Bill, a gay
couple in their mid-forties who owned their own
struggling art gallery, seemed nice enough, and Alex found
them to be good roommates. Alex's most interesting
roommate, however, was Tommy. Tommy, a dwarf,
performed standup comedy at the local clubs in town and
surrounding areas. Tommy's shtick centered on self-
deprecating humor with a lot of sex thrown in. He knew

he could get away with telling dwarf jokes since he was one, and it worked. Tommy's audiences loved him, and he enjoyed a loyal following of adoring fans.

Alex loved it when Tommy sat at his bar and made loud comments for everyone to hear. A common one was, "Hey, Alex, ask that girl over there if she wants a little." Another was, "Hey, my girlfriend asked me to go up on her last night." Tommy became the life of the party, especially after a few drinks. And Alex often bought Tommy drinks just to get him going. Once he did, customers bought him drinks all night long. Customers dubbed the experience the 'Alex and Tommy Show'. The owners of the bar loved the free entertainment. Alex formed a special bond with Tommy, since they both seemed to be on the same path to destruction. While Alex attempted to bury his terrible feelings of guilt with his new reckless and alcoholic lifestyle, Tommy did the same for his lifelong feelings of rejection, shame and low self-esteem stemming from his dwarfism.

This misfit group of roommates provided a never-a-dull-moment atmosphere. Adam and Bill argued about their business with a fair amount of drama. Their different tastes in art fueled many a battle. Most of the time, it began with one of them selecting an artist that the other deplored. In one instance, Adam allowed a young male artist to display some of his work in the gallery without Bill knowing. Bill discovered the pieces and became livid. He even accused Adam of accepting the artist's work because he was young and cute.

"I'm just trying to help a young, starving artist," said Adam.

"I'm sure you are," said Bill. "You're trying to help the poor young thing into your pants!"

Angie exhibited a quiet and somewhat strange personality. As a child, her strange nature had provoked a fair amount of bullying throughout her childhood. In an attempt to draw her out of her introverted shell, her parents had done their best to give her all the accouterments of a middle class lifestyle. She'd attended good schools in suburban neighborhoods, completed high school and some college, majoring in fine arts before dropping out. Her eccentric behavior stemmed from her alleged psychic abilities. She would stare into space for brief periods and then elicit oddly profound statements. Alex thought she was harmless but creepy, especially when he first met her and she blurted out, "Family trouble with this one...big family trouble." He avoided any circumstance in which he would be alone with her. Angie was in her late thirties and never had held a regular job. Her parents helped her start her small fortune teller business and she made enough to get by.

The group performed a kind of rite of passage where Angie would read a new person in their lives. Alex avoided this as long as possible but one night, after relentless chiding, he gave in. They all sat around the dining room table after a makeshift dinner that Adam and Bill had put together when Tommy said, "I think it's time for Angie to read Alex." Alex did his best to decline, but Tommy persisted. "Come on, you've dodged this long enough. Hey, we've all been through it. I'll even buy you a drink afterward."

Alex relented. "Okay. Okay. I'll do it for you, Tommy." Tommy stood up on his chair and gave Alex a big kiss on the head while the others laughed, except Angie who wasted no time staring into space.

Angie continued her trance-like state for a few moments then blurted out a few statements: "Big...big. Things with this one...much despair...I get betrayal...I get lost love."

"Hey, join the crowd," Tommy butted in. "I think all of us were in a romance that ended up turning to stone."

Angie continued: "No, not the usual kind...this is big...big...like changing the course of history big." She looked at Alex, her eyes looking into his mind and causing a shudder to trickle down his spine. "Not to despair; after the fire comes rebirth," she said.

A strange feeling came over Alex. Shivers ran up and down his spine, and he fought the powerful emotions bubbling up from deep inside. It was as if Angie had connected with his soul and ripped it out for everyone to see. He hated his vulnerability and wanted to bolt out of the room and run as fast and as far away as possible. He had worked hard at burying his despair, and now Angie apparently had no problem dredging it up and plunking it on the table like a Thanksgiving Day turkey. Angie dropped her head and began to sob.

"Angie, are you okay?" Bill said as he and Adam moved to console her.

"I've seen her do a lot of these readings, but I've never seen her look like that," exclaimed Tommy. The carefree tone of the room turned dead serious.

"I'm okay." Angie pulled herself together. "Strong karma with this one..."

Alex, shaking and dripping with sweat, broke the tension by turning to Tommy, who was now displaying a serious and pale face, and saying, "Did you say something about buying me a drink?" In a few moments they were out the door.

27
TANDO PHARMACEUTICALS PROJECT MEETING, LOS ANGELES

*T*hirteen men and women filed into the large glass-walled conference room taking seats around a large oval glass table. The extraordinary panoramic view of the city displayed through floor to ceiling glass windows from the thirty-fifth floor of the Tando building in downtown Los Angeles added to the classy corporate atmosphere of the affair. Attendees included a mix of project leaders, vice presidents and CEO Jim Barnes. The Beijing team patiently waited in an identical conference room linked by Telepresence monitors along one wall. Their virtual presence emphasized the gravity of the event.

Jim Barnes sat in the center facing the monitors flanked by his vice president of operations on one side and Mark on the other. Jim greeted the Chinese delegation and began the meeting.

"We are here to discuss the latest developments in the Cancer Cure project and future projections. We should begin with a report from our new vice president, Dr. Winter."

Mark, a bit uneasy, took a deep breath and began his presentation. A multicolored graph popped up on one of the monitors capturing the group's attention.

"Here we see the data from the first set of human breast cancer trials. As you can see, the treatment eliminated the cancer in all of the subjects. This occurred without side effects and without recurrence of the disease, although it may be too early to make any formal determinations. We also received word from the FDA stating the treatment will be cleared for breast cancer in the next month or so. This means we can complete phase two in short order."

A spattering of applause, accompanied by smiles and head nods, spread through the room. Mark could almost feel the atmosphere grow heavy with greed as he moved on to his profit projection slide. The cure would bring in additional billions to Tando's revenues making everyone in the room including Mark millionaires many times over.

Tando had been building the Cancer Cure Clinics during the past couple of months in anticipation of the successful trials. The clinics were ready to open at a moment's notice once given the green light by the FDA. Tando had poured over a billion dollars into the project but they stood to make billions more on their investment. Mark had done quite well too; he was paid a million dollar bonus and a three million-dollar-a-year salary. After the breast cancer phase, new phases were in the works targeting prostate, lung and colon cancers. Tando stood to dominate all cancer treatments worldwide. Its stock had already soared, making billions for the shareholders.

Everyone exited the conference room at the conclusion of the meeting except for one gentleman. "I thought you would be interested in what your brother is up to," the man said as he closed the conference room door. Mark packed up his papers and shut down his laptop.

"Did you find Alex?" asked Mark. The man opened his briefcase, picked up a set of photos and dropped them onto the table.

"Your brother has been located. He is living in Manitou Springs, Colorado. He tends bar at the Mountain View Brewhouse and lives close by. We have him under close surveillance. As far as we know he has not contacted any of the Chicago team or Dr. Ling." Mark scanned through the pictures which showed Alex in various surroundings.

"Nice job," said Mark as he handed back the pictures. "Remember, you are not to intervene or harm him in any way. That was the deal. He is not to be harmed."

"I understand, sir," the man said while closing his briefcase. "I have specific orders. The target is not to be confronted." The man turned and left the room. Mark sat down and took a deep breath. He hated these meetings with Latro operatives.

Mark's rigorous schedule of television, radio and web interviews left him exhausted. He made appearances on all the national shows and conducted interviews for all of the newspapers. His life became a whirlwind of activity in dealing with the media in addition to keeping tabs on the project. Along with the non-stop media blitz, he ran the entire cancer cure program, also a formidable task, even with an elite team of scientists and engineers at his disposal.

Occasionally, feelings of guilt seeped in to Mark's consciousness. He appreciated his demanding schedule because it helped to bury the unpleasant feelings about his betrayal. This worked, but only to a point. Nights were the most difficult. Most nights he would wake from a sound sleep in his high-rise luxury L.A. condo. Heart pounding and dripping from sweat and unable to return to sleep, he would lie awake in a futile attempt to get some rest so he could face another grueling day. The next morning brought the kind of fatigue reminiscent of his all-night study sessions for the college final exams. Mark had slept little during final exam weeks and ran on adrenaline and caffeine. Once exam week was over he would crash and sometimes sleep for up to three days straight. Now, his adrenaline originated from work and fear. The excitement of having so many brilliant people working for him and building the high tech cancer cure clinics combined with the fear of the ever-present Latro operatives provided sufficient stimulus to keep him going. As much as Alex drowned his feelings in alcohol and drugs, Mark did the same with work.

Mark's face began to show the effects of his new lifestyle. His usual glow degenerated into an ashen color, and wrinkles emerged on his forehead. Most of his shirts gapped at the collar, and his clothes began to hang from weight loss. Mark had begun to feel as though he'd made a deal with the devil. He'd spent his life in the shadow of his brother, until now. Now it was time for his star to shine, but at what cost? Most of the time he enjoyed the recognition, attention, and of course the money, but there were times, usually late at night or when he lay in bed in the early hours of the morning, when doubt began to creep into his mind. During those times of despair he found comfort in revisiting his logic behind his decision. He thought about the events that led him to this place. At the core of these events was his life with Alex.

Alex, the real star in the family, constantly reminded Mark of the painful fact that he was smarter and more competent. Alex had chipped away at Mark's self-esteem each time that he'd bettered Mark's grade point average, scored higher on some exam, won first place to Mark's second, or defeated him at video games. Alex received praise from his parents while they told Mark, "You'd better watch out, your brother is going to pass you right up," or, "Alex beat another one of your records; isn't that great?"

Now it was Mark's turn to be on top. He'd finally prevailed with this one victory that no one could take from him, especially Alex. He alone would bring the cancer cure to humanity. He alone would command a billion-dollar project. His efforts would be rewarded by saving the lives of thousands of people, and he would re-write history.

28
BACK IN CHICAGO

Three months after Alex's disappearance, Peter and the team still continued their search for him, but at this point their efforts consisted only of asking anyone they knew if they had seen him. Alex's landlord had cleaned out his apartment for lack of rent payment and placed Alex's furniture, clothes and other items in a temporary storage unit.

The app team succeeded in producing a native wellness app and sold it to a large insurance company for inclusion in their wellness program. Universal Health Insurance purchased Freetech for 1.2 million dollars. Sam took half and divided the remainder among the Chicago team. Sam also offered positions to each of the Chicago team members. Peter accepted but Julie and Kevin had declined to focus on their graduate studies.

Peter continued to contact Xiu as she continued to work at Peking University teaching classes in traditional Chinese medicine. She missed Alex and waited with steadfast loyalty for him to return. She even continued working to obtain a U.S. visa without success. She felt the Chinese government and Tando kept close watch on her and monitored her Internet activity as well. She did a good job laying low and did not engage in any suspicious activity.

The Cancer Cure Clinic story still dominated the news with each event broadcast on every media format. Mark's picture still occupied the front page of every newspaper as well as many magazine covers. At one point, Julie taped a picture of Mark to one of the walls of the new Freetech space, which acted as a target for darts. They devised a point system as well. Ten points for each eye, five for the forehead, and two for the mouth. Once they destroyed the picture, they had no problem finding another.

Tando was on the verge of completing the first round of human trials for breast cancer. The results were stellar. They built a series of futuristic Cancer Cure Clinics in all major U.S. cities, as well as several Chinese cities including Beijing, Shanghai, and Hong Kong. Their plans included building more clinics worldwide during the next year while running human trials for lung, prostate, and colon cancers. The initial projections for each clinic featured two machines scheduled to run sixteen hours per day with each treatment lasting thirty minutes. Tando could charge somewhere around $50,000 for each treatment, which came out to around $3.2 million for each day for each clinic, or $96 million per month. The first group of thirty clinics would gross somewhere around $2.8 billion per month, or $34 billion per year.

People clamored to get on the waiting list for treatment. Tando took referrals from oncologists, and the clinics were booked almost six months in advance. Peter often drove by the Chicago clinic to check on its progress. He watched as the futuristic modular clinic took shape over the period of a few weeks. They spared no expense in these high tech buildings. The Chicago site featured a free standing circular white building resembling a space ship. A series of small oval glass windows wrapped around the building's walls giving it sleek lines. A white granite tile walkway led to the glass door entrance.

Peter managed to pull a few strings and slip into the

clinic during one of the physician tours. The main doors opened into a waiting room area with curved white walls and white marble floors. A receptionist sitting behind what appeared to be a glass and stainless steel desk greeted patients. The waiting area contained curved rows of overstuffed cream-colored, soft leather chairs along with a series of strategically placed plants. A large aquarium stocked with exotic tropical fish dominated one wall.

"Doctors, please follow me," announced an attractive female tour guide dressed in a white lab coat displaying the Tando logo. She led the group through one of two doors on opposite sides of the waiting room leading to identical treatment areas. The doors opened into a hallway with two small but comfortable treatment rooms on each side. The tour guide said that these were for the first part of the treatment, which consisted of an intravenous injection of the resveratrol formula. She said this portion of the treatment lasted about thirty minutes. The frequency treatment, lasting about the same amount of time, followed. The hall led to another door that opened into a larger room containing the frequency machine.

The frequency machine resembled an MRI scanner but a bit smaller in size and standing upright. The patient walked into the machine and turned around in a standing position with her back against the table. The table reclined and two large half-cylindrical devices closed around her. Finally, another set of circular coils surrounded the cylinders. This portion of the treatment also took about thirty minutes to complete.

The tour guide offered to let anyone get into the machine; a few doctors obliged but Peter declined. The control room occupied one side of the room. The technicians viewed the patient through a large window. Inside, a large table with a glass top acted like a huge touch screen. The technicians had full control over the frequency machine. The wires and exposed hardware that Peter was accustomed to seeing were gone, hidden either in the floor or walls.

The tour concluded with refreshments in the waiting area. The doctors enjoyed champagne, smoked salmon, a variety of small sandwiches and other delights. Each doctor was given a tote bag containing a white Cancer Cure Clinic coffee mug along with assorted promotional materials including a pack of finely embossed prescription pads.

"We have our first patients scheduled for November first," the tour guide announced. She introduced the gentleman standing next to her. "Doctors, I would like to introduce Doctor William Baker, Chicago Cancer Care Clinic Director. He will be happy to answer any of your questions."

Dr. Baker fielded a barrage of questions, most having to do with insurance issues, from the visiting doctors. Peter's anger made him want to blurt something out about stolen technology, but he managed to hold his tongue.

29
THE BOTTOM

*T*he nonstop party lifestyle had begun to wear on Alex. His drinking now extended into most days resulting in ending his shift in a drunken state. After work, he and Tommy would disappear to the after party scene and continue throughout the night. Tommy was a lot more experienced at this kind of lifestyle than Alex and often encouraged him to keep going despite Alex's desire to go home. Tommy's addictions did not stop at alcohol; he never turned down a line of cocaine or a snort of crystal meth when one came his way. He always offered whatever came his way to Alex as well, but Alex remained steadfast about not doing hard drugs. Tommy often said things like, "You are the better man, my friend," or, "Sometimes I wish I hadn't done the hard stuff."

Alex's life took a serious turn one Friday night in September when Alex and Tommy ended up at a house party after hours. Tommy made his usual celebrity entrance to shouts of "Hey, Tommy's here, let's get the party started. Hey, Tommy, tell us a joke." They began chanting, "Tommy....Tommy...Tommy" until he had a drink in his hand, then raised it and drank it all in one gulp with everyone erupting in cheers.

Tara, a waitress from Alex's bar, approached Alex. "I

was hoping you'd come, Alex...I'm so glad you did. You wanna get high?" Alex smiled and put his arm around Tara. "Lead the way, my dear." Tara ushered him into a bedroom and closed the door. She opened a box on the bedside table and took out a joint and a lighter. She handed the lighter to Alex who lit the joint in Tara's mouth. "Allow me," Alex said while flicking the lighter. Tara sucked in a deep hit and passed the joint to Alex, who did the same.

"I've been watching you, Alex," Tara said after she exhaled her first hit. "There is something special about you; I can feel it." Shyness came over Alex. Tara was a young attractive brunette about twenty-five years old, and Alex had admired her fit body at work. He knew she worked the weekday shifts at the bar, and word was she also worked as a stripper on weekends. Despite her questionable profession, her personality was not what one would expect, as she possessed a kind of sweetness about her which Alex found very attractive. Now, sitting alone with her intensified his feelings, he desired her.

"I'm glad you think I'm special. I think you are special too." Alex sat close to her on the bed, their thighs touching. Tara reached over and rested her hand on his thigh.

"You can correct me if I'm wrong, but I think you are a lonely person, Alex." The combination of alcohol, marijuana and the beautiful Tara turned Alex on.

"I think we are all lonely at some point in our lives." Alex continued to take hits on the joint.

"This is true, but I think you are especially lonely," Tara said while leaning in closer. Her breast touched his arm. "I'll bet you could use some female company."

Alex turned to face Tara, and before he could reply they began kissing. Tara leaned back on the bed and Alex found himself on top of her. He savored the comfort Tara's charms provided and yielded to his nature. It had been a very long time since he'd succumbed to pure lust, and it felt good. He knew the transient pleasure of this encounter would pass and dissolve into feelings of guilt, but he didn't care. For that moment, he and Tara were one. Tara gave him a special gift that night, a moment's reprise from his misery, and for that he was grateful.

Afterwards she got out of bed and walked into the adjoining bathroom. Alex admired her naked body illuminated only by a small candle on the nightstand. A few minutes later she returned with a mirrored glass tray containing several small lines of cocaine. "Please, do a line with me, Alex," she said while rolling up a twenty dollar bill.

"I've never done this before," he said.

"I'm honored to be with you for your first time," Tara said, and inhaled the line. "Let me give you some tips. First of all, be sure to take it easy when you inhale so it doesn't go down your throat. You have to get used to the taste. Second, do one nostril first, then the other. Go into the bathroom afterwards and rinse out your nose, because it can burn the membranes."

Alex followed her instructions and inhaled his first line, and then his second. In a few moments his heart began to pound and dizziness overcame him as he headed for the bathroom.

He rinsed his nose as some of the substance ran down his throat, causing him to gag and cough. "You were right about the burning," he shouted to her.

"You'll get used to that...eventually," Tara said while doing two more lines. "The high only lasts for about thirty minutes to an hour."

"Wow, this is pretty good!" Alex walked toward Tara while looking around the room as if he were surveying new surroundings. "If I were to describe this, it would be that I feel like I could do about anything right now, like I have so much energy." Alex realized that the drug gave him the illusion of some higher gear. He talked faster and wanted to rejoin the party in the living room. He did, and found himself talking nonstop to anyone who would listen, and dancing to whatever music played. His newfound high was matched only by the newfound low he experienced when the drug wore off about an hour later.

The new low he experienced sent him looking for more of the magical cocaine. He soon found some in the kitchen, where Tommy hung out doing lines with some other partiers. Tommy and Alex now had something new to share. Not only were they both seeking to keep the horrible feelings deep within them at bay, but now Alex took one more step closer to catching up with Tommy on his path to total self-destruction. A path all too familiar to Tommy, it was a new experience for Alex. He found it terrifying and yet strangely attractive.

Alex and Tommy grew closer as they shared their brotherhood of seeking new highs and surviving new lows. They both fed each other's vices by encouraging and justifying their behaviors with their party-like-there's-no-tomorrow philosophy. The substance abuse lifestyle seemed to suit Tommy's career, and he used his dysfunction to his advantage in his comedy routine. "Everyone likes to hear about what a fuck-up I am, because it makes them feel better about their own miserable lives," he would say to Alex.

Alex's life took a different turn than Tommy's. Over the next month he almost lost his job over his drunken behavior. His boss sent a warning by rescheduling his hours to the weekday shifts instead of the more lucrative weekends. The subsequent loss of money made it more difficult to get drugs. Alex could only rely on Tommy's popularity and goodwill to a point. His happy-go-lucky attitude gave way to mood swings in which he broke into fits of rage followed by fits of crying. Alex's life was falling apart before his eyes. His face bore witness to his unsuccessful attempts to drown his sorrows in booze. He could not even bear to see the ashen gaunt face sporting a feeble attempt at growing a beard staring back every morning in the bathroom mirror. He seldom showered, and even Tommy told him to clean up his act.

Alex came to the conclusion that it was time for him to end this charade. He figured the best way to go would be to overdose on heroin; at least he would be able to experience a profound euphoria before he fell into a deep and lethal sleep. He was relieved when he made his decision and seemed a bit happier. The plan was to take some of the little money he had left and visit a drug house he knew of in town where he would buy a lethal dose of heroin.

The final night arrived and Alex sat on his bed fiddling with his phone. He wanted to make one last call to Xiu but couldn't get up the nerve. Plus, he thought she might try to talk him out of it. He thought about how at one point he had had it all, and how it had fallen apart. He thought about what a fool he had been not to know about Mark, and he thought about how his plan to numb the horrible guilt inside had backfired. He surmised that the only way to stop feeling this way was to stop feeling on a permanent basis. He threw the phone against the wall and began to cry. After a few minutes, he pulled himself together and went to the bathroom to rinse his face with water. He looked in the mirror and said, "We have to do this...it's the only way." He headed out the door and into the night.

He reached the drug house at around 12:30 am. It was a clear September night and he made his way along the beat-up concrete path littered with broken glass and empty beer cans to the front door. The old house appeared somewhat inviting, like a house from his youth but more rundown and decrepit.

He knocked on the front door. A large man answered. Alex could see some people behind him sitting on a sofa in the living room watching television.

"Yeah?" the man said.

"Tommy sent me," Alex replied.

"Then c'mon in..." The man opened the door and Alex

walked into the living room. "Don't mind them," the man said. "They're coming down."

"What do you need?" the man asked.

"I need a gram of H," Alex replied.

"Two hundred," the man said while holding out his large hand. Alex reached into his pocket and handed over the money. "You a first-timer?" the man asked.

"Yeah, how did you know?" replied Alex.

"Don't see no tracks, and you don't have the look," the man said. "Need help? Cindy will show you."

A woman of about fifty took Alex's hand and led him to a dark room. There were old chairs and mattresses scattered about on the filthy beige carpet speckled with cigarette burns.

There were several addicts either sitting in chairs or lying on the mattresses. One was moaning, but the others sat either staring into space or with their eyes closed. The room, lit with a small child's night light, flickered with a dim yellow glow. A small wooden table laden with various drug paraphernalia stood at the center of the room. Cindy led Alex to a chair and put a tourniquet around his left arm. She took the powder and placed it on the table next to a spoon.

"How much do you want to do?" she asked.

"I can take it from here," Alex said.

"Okay, but if you need help, just holler." She left the room. Alex was sure he could prepare the heroin, as he had seen it done at least a hundred times at parties. Alex took all the powder and placed it in the spoon, careful not to drop any. He took some water from a bottle on the table and poured some over the powder. He picked up a lighter lying on the table, flicked it and heated the mixture until just a few bubbles surfaced. A few moments later he placed a cotton ball into the spoon. The lethal liquid disappeared into the cotton ball. He reached into his pocket for a syringe that he had stolen from a box of syringes at the last party that he and Tommy had attended.

He drew all the liquid into it.

Alex looked around the room at the other addicts and wondered how he had ended up there. There had been so much hope for him. He'd grown up with a loving family who had given him every advantage that they could. He had fallen in love with a wonderful woman who he knew loved him, and he had enjoyed success at everything he'd ever attempted. He even loved his brother Mark despite Mark's betrayal. How could it come to this? How could he now be sitting in a drug house with a lethal dose of heroin in his hand?

He placed the needle next to a bulging vein in his left arm and put the thumb of his right hand on the syringe. He looked around the room one more time. The needle touched his skin on the surface of the vein, and his right hand began to shake.

Come on... Come on... Do it... Do it!

Just as he found the strength in his right hand to push the syringe something deep within him began to stir. It began as the most infinitesimal feeling, almost imperceptible but enough to take hold like the smallest seed beginning to germinate in fertile soil. As fleeting as it seemed, it did not dissipate but began to grow. Alex had no perception of its origin, which must have been somewhere deep within his subconscious, or even deeper still. Perhaps it emerged from a universal force, a product of the events and the people of his life making some sort of ethereal, nonlocal connection with him. Whatever it was, Alex felt its strength.

The feeling continued to grow and materialize as if his neurons where responding to some quantum information from the universe and forming a connection with the macro world manifesting as a communication. One word of potential salvation took shape and emerged from his subconscious to enter the conscious world in which he presently existed. That one word was *Fight!*

Alex's mind split into two minds. One was working

hard to force his thumb to complete the lethal task, while the other fought hard to stop it. He began to sweat as his right arm began to shake. His face constricted from the torment of the moment, and his shaking became worse, spreading throughout his entire body.

The battle raged on for what seemed like hours but what in reality was only seconds. The word 'fight' continued to repeat in his mind. Finally, he lifted his head and saw a most peculiar image on the wall. The visage pulsed into and out of existence, as if escaping to another dimension after revealing itself.

Alex studied the shape as his mind struggled to make sense of it. It had a definite structure consisting of an oval central section with two large extensions on each side. The lower portion seemed to dissolve into the wall, as if the shape had emerged from some dark otherworldly place. It emitted no light, causing Alex to ponder whether it had come from his imagination, from the shadows, or from some odd combination of both.

The shape gained definition as it rose along the wall. The oval section and extensions rendered into what Alex recognized as a bird with mouth open and wings spread. The bottom portion of the bird lacked definition, as if it had coalesced from another object or place, never fully coming into focus as it made its upward journey along the wall.

An overwhelming barrage of feelings rushed through Alex the moment he defined the image. The part of his mind wanting to end his life gave way to feelings of hope. He imagined Xiu, and again felt the love that they shared. He imagined Peter and the others and felt his love for them, and he felt a hope they he would somehow be able to right this wrong. He even thought of Mark, and how he loved his brother.

Alex dropped the needle and pulled off the tourniquet as he left the room and made his way out of the house. He had a newfound energy. Everything around him was crisp and beautiful. The night sky shimmered with stars, the cool air and the outline of the nearby mountains had never appeared so pristine. He carried the image of Xiu with every step he took. He knew that he must see her. And he knew that he must fight to make things right.

30
CHICAGO...A FEW DAYS LATER

Peter had returned from dropping off his daughter at her mom's place and was settling down to a quiet night of TV when he heard a knock at his door. "Just a minute," he shouted across the room as he flicked off the TV. His jaw dropped when he opened the door to find a thin but smiling Alex.

"Alex? Where have you been? Come in, come in!" Alex walked inside and set his backpack on the floor.

"I'm so sorry, Peter. I just couldn't...I felt so bad," Alex struggled to explain his disappearance in a few words.

"That's okay, sit down and relax. Tell me where you've been. I almost didn't recognize you. Sit down while I get you something to eat."

Alex sat while Peter made him a ham sandwich. "I went on a journey, Peter. I felt so guilty about everything. I couldn't face Xiu, or you, or the others. How is Xiu? I'm sure she is angry at me for what I have put her through." Peter put the sandwich in front of Alex.

"Xiu is fine; but she is more worried than pissed, as we all were."

"I'm so sorry," Alex said as he chewed the sandwich. What did Xiu say about me?"

"She was heartbroken, but after the first few weeks she

pretty much went back to her old life at the university. She was told to lay low." Peter sat on his sofa and faced Alex.

"Mark is another story. He has turned into something I don't even recognize. He is heading up the Tando Cancer Cure Clinic project. I'm sure he is enjoying his fortune, and they are ready to begin using our treatment to start curing breast cancer. From what they say, they will be ready to open around the first of November." Alex finished his sandwich while Peter talked.

"Now it's your turn, Alex. What happened to you?"

Alex sat back in the chair and took a deep breath. "Well, I couldn't deal with my horrible feelings of guilt, so I left not knowing where I would go or what I would do. I ended up in Colorado, where things got worse until I just about killed myself a couple of days ago. Then I had a vision that stopped me millimeters short of suicide. You are the only person I could come to who would understand this, Peter, so that's why I'm here."

"My God, Alex! None of this is worth killing yourself over. There is always a way. Have you spoken to Xiu yet?"

"Not yet. I am still getting up the courage to call her." Alex sighed.

"You should call her right now," exclaimed Peter and handed Alex his phone. "Let's see, it should be about noon in Beijing." Alex dialed Xiu's number. The phone rang several times before her sweet familiar voice answered.

"*Ni hao...* Peter, is that you?" Alex took a moment to compose himself.

"Xiu, it's me, Alex." Silence followed then he heard the sounds of sobbing.

"Alex, we thought you were dead. My dear Alex, what has happened to you?" Alex spent the next hour explaining himself to Xiu and asking her forgiveness. He told her he could not face her after their loss. He told her all about his journey, and he told her about his vision of hope.

"I hope you can find it within your heart to forgive me, Xiu," he said while holding back tears.

"Of course I forgive you. I want to see you again. When can you come to China?" she said.

"I will come as soon as I can," replied Alex. "There is one more thing I have to do first." They talked for another hour before saying goodbye.

Alex and Peter spent the evening catching up on all the details of the past few months. Alex found out that his share of the Freetech sale was almost $50,000, and Peter had kept it for him in a savings account. Peter described the Cancer Care Clinic in as much detail as he could remember. "Looks like they thought of everything," said Alex.

"It's quite impressive," replied Peter. "You should see the human version of the machine. It was spectacular. They talked until the early hours of the morning, and when Alex could no longer talk, he fell asleep on Peter's sofa. He dreamed of Xiu, and China, and their precious time together. He knew someday he would again be with her.

Alex awoke the next morning to the pleasant odor of frying bacon. Peter's breakfast amplified the emptiness in Alex's stomach. "Have some bacon and eggs, Alex. Hope you slept well on that old sofa."

"Slept like a baby," Alex said while heading to the bathroom. You wouldn't believe some of the places I've slept lately."

"I can imagine," replied Peter as he served breakfast.

Alex pulled up a chair and tore into the bacon and eggs. Food hadn't tasted this good in a long time. Alex had been sober for a few days now, and his senses began to return. "What's the plan now, Alex?" Peter said while pouring a second cup of coffee.

"Well, there is one thing I have to do before anything else. I have to go to Mexico to give my condolences to Xavier's family. I felt terrible about missing his funeral."

Peter told Alex all about the funeral, about Xavier's grieving parents and about how devastated Becca had been. He also told Becca's story about Xavier catching

Mark in the act of betrayal and how she thought that she and Xavier were under threat.

"They were right to get out of town," Alex said.

The sun reflected off the small dining room table and lit up the room on one wall. Since Alex's close brush with death, everything had taken on a new vibrancy and sharpness.

"I want to go with you to Mexico," Peter said while picking up the dishes. "We can't lose you again, Alex."

"No, definitely not; I must do this alone." Alex was adamant about his plan. He wanted to pay tribute to his fallen partner. "After all," he said to Peter, "if it weren't for my brother's deception, Xavier would probably be alive."

31
MEXICO

The five-hour flight from Chicago to Mexico City gave Alex time to contemplate the events of the past few months. Mark's betrayal had been long in coming. During his entire life Mark had lived in Alex's shadow. Alex remembered how he used to gloat and taunt his older brother with his superior accomplishments. Any retaliation on Mark's part met with punishment by their parents. Alex remembered one time in which he had competed with Mark in an engineering fair.

Mark's project had had to do with capturing energy from the Earth's rotation and using it to charge a low powered battery. He'd developed a series of Foucault pendulums. A set of electromagnets captured the energy. He'd attempted to prove that under low friction conditions in a super-cooled environment he could demonstrate a way to capture the energy from the angular movement of the pendulums due to the Earth's rotation. His device captured a minute amount of energy, and he fiddled with it to decrease the amount of energy loss, but his results were not as good as he predicted.

Alex had competed in the same science and engineering fair, but his project was very different than Mark's. Alex had produced a working exoskeleton using electroactive polymers. Electroactive polymers were materials that contracted and expanded in response to electrical currents. Alex saw the opportunity to produce an exoskeleton sleeve fitted over a human arm. The sleeve mimicked a few basic arm movements that allowed paralyzed patients to trigger a computerized controller to produce a series of standard movements. The program included a mimic feature that allowed a user to perform a movement either by himself or with assistance, and was able to reproduce the movement.

Needless to say, Mark's project, as brilliant as it was, won a first place award. However, Alex's project won the grand prize. Their parents tried hard to rein equal amounts of praise on each of their gifted and talented sons, but Alex received far more attention from the media for his accomplishment. This was the norm for Mark throughout his life. As much as Mark tried, he could never win against his brother, at least not until now.

Alex contemplated what he had learned over the past few months as well. Despite his destructive lifestyle and suicide attempt, he was still alive. Despite his atheist beliefs, he now sensed that something protected him—if not a spiritual force, then perhaps sheer intention. He thought it possible that his life played a part in a bigger plan. Instead of dying in a drug house, he had decided to continue moving in a positive direction. Before his ordeal, he could not have faced Becca or Xavier's parents; now he found the strength to do so.

His decision to live had set in motion a higher ordered plan of sorts. He believed that all human interactions comprised a complex system consisting of an astronomical number of choices or decisions. There were certain probabilities governing these systems, but in essence all states of existence before making a decision were indeterminate states. From quantum physics he knew that information (in the form of decisions made by observers) influenced indeterminate states by solidifying them into reality. In other words, we determine unknown states by our decisions.

One example was his possible death. If he had made the decision to die, then the result of that decision would include a greater probability of Mark and Tando getting away with stealing the cancer cure. However, if he were alive, then there was a presumably smaller probability of that circumstance playing itself out, The end of the whole mess was still not determined, and if information in the form of decisions influenced indeterminate states, then his decision to stay alive would move the system, albeit a minute amount, toward a more favorable outcome. It was as if there was one future, in a set of all possible futures, where things could work out.

Alex found comfort in thinking this way, even though his friends and family did not understand his reasoning. To Alex, science, math and spirituality created a fabric in which the universe existed. To him, intention had the same effect as prayer. Intention encompassed decisions, and decisions were real things. Decisions exhibited powerful effects not only on physical events but also on people's lives. Decisions brought the universe into existence.

Xavier's parents lived in the city of Cheran which was about a five and a half hour trip by car from Mexico City. Alex planned to spend the first night at the Grand Hotel de Mexico and leave first thing the next morning in a rental car. He would spend a couple of days in Cheran.

The tune "Morning Flower" burst from Alex's phone at 7:00 am, and he awoke to the sun shimmering through the window. A sense of calmness and purpose flowed through him, as if he were on a mission to make right a very serious wrong. Today he would face Xavier's family in Cheran and express his deepest sympathy over their loss. His trip would entail a drive on several highways through the Mexican countryside, and through several small cities. He looked forward to the adventure.

After a light breakfast, Alex headed out of Mexico City toward Toluca. This part of the drive passed through mountains and a national park. The last portion of the drive zig-zagged west and south, taking him though Panindicuaro, Cantabria, Zacapu, and finally to Cheran.

Cheran, a city of about 16,000, was located in the western part of the State of Michoacan. Alex arrived in the early afternoon. A small sign marked the city limits, and a large school painted a dull pink color emerged on his right. More buildings appeared as Alex proceeded into the city. Many of these buildings had large metal garage doors displaying graffiti pointing to the streets with cars and trucks parked in front. Alex passed by more shabby buildings with glassless windows and tarps for walls and doors. As he approached the heart of the city, he witnessed open markets and street vendors selling all sorts of colorful products to customers. Many of the shops displayed their goods outside on the sidewalk. Buildings constructed of red bricks dominated the streets.

A large church with a red tiled roof loomed over the downtown area. The streets became very narrow in the center of the city, and one street led to a plaza. Alex struggled to understand the Mexican rules of the road. Cars converged from side streets and seemed to merge at random, and he finally surmised that whoever was in the lead, no matter how small, had the right of way.

Xavier's family lived on a small ranch outside of town. Their ranch consisted of a modest stucco farm house and a small barn. A few cattle roamed a large grassy area bordered by barbed wire.

Alex parked his car on the side of the dirt road and made his way to the wooden porch of the small house. The floor creaked as loose floorboards buckled with every step. He wondered if they would recognize him from the pictures Xavier had sent home. He also hoped that they would accept him as a friend, despite Mark's actions.

32
TANDO HEADQUARTERS, L.A...ONE WEEK BEFORE

Mark returned from the L.A. Cancer Cure Clinic site and headed toward his office on the twenty-sixth floor of the Tando building in downtown L.A. when his assistant, Maggie, rushed to his side with an urgent message. "Dr. Jeff Bradley is on the line. He says this is of the utmost urgency. Something about the human trials we ran back in June." Mark, puzzled, did not break stride.

"I'll take it in my office. No interruptions!" Mark increased his pace to his office and closed the large hardwood and glass door behind him. The door shut with a suction sound indicating a soundproof seal. Mark made his way around his metal and glass desk and plopped down on his leather chair while wondering what the urgency was all about. Dr. Bradley was in charge of the human trials project that they had run back in June. Why would he be upset? Mark took a moment to catch his breath and then picked up the phone.

"Dr. Mark Winter here."

"Hi, Mark; it's Jeff Bradley. I have some bad news."

"Let's hear it, Jeff." Mark's heart began to beat faster.

"I'll give it to you straight, Mark. It looks like we've had our first casualty. Yesterday one of the breast cancer patients we treated back in June was taken to Tampa General Hospital where she passed away today." At first Mark thought that this was bad, but not too terrible given that people die from various causes every day. Since the first group of patients totaled one hundred, it was reasonable to assume one casualty from some cause other than the treatment.

"Okay, Jeff, but what did she die of?" There was a moment of silence before Jeff replied.

"That's the real mystery, Mark. The docs here in Tampa are saying that they have never seen anything like this before. They said she had multisystem organ failure. All her organs failed at the same time." The color drained out of Mark's face.

"Did they come up with any reason as to what would cause this?"

"I've had pathologists examine her cells and they say she suffered from a kind of spontaneous cell death. It was as if her cells just exploded." Mark paused and thought for a minute.

"Was there any infection, sepsis, parasites, or anything else that might have caused this?"

"Nope, she was clean. Her husband said she was fine. She even ran a triathlon last week. He said she collapsed last night. He called 911 and the paramedics took her to Tampa General. The ER docs said she was in a coma and put her on life support until all her organs failed this morning. But that's not the worst of it, Mark."

Mark leaned forward at his desk; he began to sweat under his shirt and tie. "What else, Jeff?" he said in a weak voice. Jeff paused as if he were getting up the courage to speak.

"Well, you know how the first trial consisted of one hundred female breast cancer patients treated at the Tampa location...and they were given the treatment in five groups of twenty over a five week period with twenty receiving the treatment every week along with control groups?" Jeff gained his nerve as he spoke. "Well, it seems all twenty are now hospitalized with the same thing...multisystem organ failure, and they are all critical!" Mark's jaw dropped and he struggled to maintain his composure.

A barrage of thoughts raced through Mark's mind as he sat at his desk attempting to process this devastating news. They could attribute one case to a heart attack, stroke or allergic reaction, but twenty cases could only have been caused by one thing: the treatment. "This sucks!" said Mark.

"I know," Jeff said. "I have a team working on isolating the cause. They are working on samples right now. I also have eyes and ears on all the patients, and I'll keep you posted. The media is another issue. We can explain away one death, but twenty is another story. I would get ready if I were you. Also, if the treatment did cause the deaths, then we could see another twenty next week and so on." A sick sensation began to percolate in Mark's stomach and spread through his body.

"Thanks, Jeff. Thank you for everything. Please keep me posted on any new developments."

"Will do," said Jeff before hanging up.

Mark sat looking out of the floor to ceiling windows at the L.A. skyline. The sun began to set casting a pink glow against the steel and glass buildings. As he pondered what had happened, the intercom interrupted his thoughts. "Dr. Winter?" It was Maggie. "Mr. David Brysen is here to see you."

Mark did not want to see anyone at this moment, especially Brysen. David Brysen, the commander of his Latro operation, always invoked fear in Mark. He thought for a moment and decided he needed to cooperate with Brysen in any way he could. Mark hated the cloak and dagger special ops part of his work and never trusted any of these guys. He figured he would try the honest approach to show his loyalty to the company. At least that way they might stay off his back.

"Let him in," Mark said after pulling himself together. A trim but athletic black gentleman with a shaved head standing about six feet tall entered the room. He wore the standard issue black suit, white shirt and blue tie displaying the Tando logo. Mark could tell by the way Brysen moved that he was ex-military, probably special ops or similar. Brysen displayed a confidence that on some occasions made Mark feel safe. This was not one of those occasions and Mark dreaded seeing him, especially after the bottom had dropped out of everything. He wondered if Brysen was aware of what was happening in Tampa.

After greeting each other Mark directed Brysen to a small conference area in one corner of his office consisting of a sofa and two overstuffed chairs. Mark offered mineral water but Brysen refused before taking a seat on one of the chairs. Mark sat on the sofa facing him.

"I will get right to the point, Dr. Winter. We have some information about your brother Alex." Mark tried to mask his anxiety over the recent news and welcomed hearing about Alex. He missed his brother and hoped his betrayal would be easier to deal with than it really was. He enjoyed the money, the power and the rock-star attention, but deep down longed for the days back in Chicago. He missed working with Alex and his team, wearing jeans and T-shirts and eating pizza instead of wearing thousand-dollar suits and eating steak.

"Go on," Mark said with an air of attempted authority. As Brysen opened a file and scanned it, his brow furrowed.

"Alex Winter has returned to Chicago and is now staying with Peter North. Our sources spotted him entering a drug house outside of Colorado Springs last week. They spotted him leaving the drug house and returning to his Manitou Springs home. He left the next day for Chicago where he is residing with Mr. North." Brysen slapped shut the folder.

"Okay, so he is in Chicago. Thanks, Brysen. Good work." Mark was relieved that this was all there was.

"Oh...one more thing," Brysen said with his usual serious tone. "We intercepted a call to one Becca Valdez, widow to Xavier Valdez. It appears Alex will be making a trip to Mexico to visit Mr. Valdez's family. We would like to identify the significance of this visit."

Mark, puzzled, said, "So, he missed the funeral and wants to give his condolences to Xavier's family...maybe he feels guilty."

Brysen continued with his serious poker face. Mark never seemed to know what Brysen was thinking.

"That's what we thought, but we wondered if there would be any other reason, especially after what has happened in Tampa."

Brysen's last words echoed through Mark's mind. "So you know about Tampa?" Mark fought to remain composed but felt warmth in his face as it flushed red with blood.

"We know about everything, Dr. Winter. We just wanted to get your opinion regarding why your brother would go to Mexico. We must keep our bases covered."

"I understand," said Mark as he quelled the temptation to bolt out the door and continue running until his legs gave out. "What is your plan then?" Brysen appeared to enjoy watching him squirm.

"We have eyes on him and will follow him to Mexico. We will let you know if we discover anything significant. In the meantime, I will not take up any more of your precious time, Dr. Winter. I believe you have an important meeting?" Brysen got up from the chair and headed for the door.

"Oh, and by the way, contacting your brother is not a

good idea at this point, Dr. Winter." He walked through the door with Mark following close behind. Mark and Brysen bid goodbye and Mark again closed his office door and headed for his desk. He dreaded what he needed to do next with every fiber of his being.

Mark summoned Maggie into his office and requested that she set up an emergency meeting with Tando's CEO, Jim Barnes. Thirty minutes later Mark found himself in the elevator on the way to the forty-fourth floor. Mark tried to determine just how to explain this disaster to Jim. One death would be hard enough to explain, but twenty would be impossible. Jim would be livid, and after experiencing Brysen's cold and calculating hit man demeanor he feared for his life. He figured the best way would be to tell the truth about Jeff's report.

The elevator ride seemed to take longer than usual, but the cab finally came to a halt and the gold metal doors opened. Mark walked along a thick gold carpet down a long hallway lined with luxurious hardwood. There were fine oil portraits of the previous Tando CEOs, and Jim's was the last one before the large wooden doors to his office. He opened the perfectly balanced door with little effort and proceeded into the small waiting area. Sophia, Jim's assistant, smiled and motioned Mark to go right inside. The door cracked open to reveal Jim standing by the windows looking out at the L.A. skyline. "I never get tired of this view, Mark. It is especially beautiful right after sunset like this. Come in and have a seat. Can I offer you a drink? It's after five, maybe something strong?"

"Thanks Jim, I will take you up on that. Whiskey, please." Jim walked over to a bar on one wall of his expansive office and poured a drink. "Macallan Single Malt Highland Scotch it is, a fine whiskey at about $12,000 a bottle." Mark took the glass.

"Impressive, Jim. Thank you." Mark almost swallowed the entire drink in one gulp but left a little in the glass out of politeness.

"Must be something important," Jim poured more whiskey into Mark's glass.

"It is, Jim." The two men sat in large chairs facing each other.

"So, what is this all about?" Jim took a sip of his drink.

"Well, I'm very sorry, but it's bad news, Jim." Mark hoped the expensive whiskey would calm his anxiety. "It appears something went wrong with the first round of twenty patients. I mean something happened that we had no control over. It is...just that..." It took all Mark's inner strength to steel his nerves for what he said next. "All twenty patients have died." There was something about saying it out loud to Jim that shook Mark to his core. These were people, for God's sake, not numbers or things. These people had husbands and children and families. Tando had given them hope for a new life without cancer. Now there would be twenty funerals.

"I haven't' had a chance or enough information to conduct a detailed analysis, but it seems likely that our treatment killed them."

"I know all about that," Jim said. "My job is to know, and I make sure I know about everything going on in this company. I'm glad you came to me, Mark. It helps to show your loyalty." Mark was right. Brysen had informed Jim of what had happened in Tampa. Jim continued, "China knows too. This could be bad for us, especially if the other eighty or so subjects in the first group also die. We can keep a few deaths off the radar, but a hundred is impossible. What we need from you, Mark, is a plan...a plan for fixing this horrible problem." Mark thought hard for a few moments. The frequency machine with its quantum resonance and Xiu's resveratrol formula were way over his head. He had a rudimentary knowledge of how it worked, but the deep understanding had died with Xavier. Alex was the only other person in the world who knew as much about the machine as Xavier.

"I'll do my best," said Mark. "I need some time to

think."

Jim got up from his chair, walked over to Mark and looked straight at him. "Now, this is just an idea, Mark, but it could help us. Do you think there is any way to convince your brother Alex to join us?" This was not what Mark wanted to hear. This was supposed to be Mark's victory over Alex, but now they wanted to recruit him to save the day. A deep anger began to well up inside him replacing the fear and anxiety. He looked into Jim's eyes with resolve.

"Believe me; Alex will *never* work for this company."

"Never say never," said Jim as he turned and walked back toward his desk. "Everyone has a price. In the meantime, I will need your plan to remedy this situation as soon as possible. The press will have a field day with this, and China is already screaming. I'm counting on you, Mark."

33
CLARK RESIDENCE. TAMPA, FL... THE PREVIOUS DAY

*T*he Clark family finished dinner and Shelly retired to the family room to relax in her favorite recliner after a long day. Her husband Tom and their two children, Ben, age eight, and Kaitlin, age ten, began their nightly ritual of washing the dishes while Shelly relaxed. Tom always tried to make these mundane chores fun by joking and making up funny songs. He stood by the sink singing a rendition of Row, Row, Row your Boat but changed the words to "wash, wash, wash the grease, gently off the plate, merrily, merrily, merrily, merrily, this is just our fate." The children laughed at the silliness and made up their own verses until they finished the chore.

Tom put the last dish away while Kaitlin headed for the dining room table to begin her homework. Ben went to the family room where his mom was resting and watching TV. "Dad, there's something wrong with mom!" Ben called from the family room. Tom rushed in to find Shelly lying on the recliner as if she were sleeping. As Tom approach he noticed the normal healthy pink glow of her skin had been replaced by a bluish tint. She made small gasping sounds as if struggling to breath.

Tom shook her, shouting, "Shelly? Shelly? Wake up, Shelly!" No response. "Ben, get my cell phone...NOW!" Ben ran into the kitchen to retrieve his dad's phone.

Kaitlin came in and began to cry. "What's wrong with mommy?" she said, sobbing.

"We don't know. Dear; just be calm."

Ben ran in with the phone and Tom snatched it from him and called 911.

The paramedics arrived in what seemed like a long time to Tom but in reality was only seven minutes. They immediately took control of the situation by running an ECG, administering oxygen and starting an IV. Within minutes Shelly was in the back of the ambulance heading for Tampa General Hospital with Tom and the kids not far behind. Tom soon lost the ambulance in traffic but continued driving as fast as he could while doing his best to appear calm for the sake of the children.

By the time Tom reached the hospital Shelly was already in the emergency room. An ER attendant met Tom and directed him to the waiting area to fill out paperwork.

"Can't I do this later?" he said with anger. "My wife might be dying in there."

A nurse approached him and said, "The doctors are with her now and are doing everything they can for her." Both Ben and Kaitlin were crying.

"Try to be brave," Tom said, trying to deal with the situation by comforting the children. "Mommy's going to be all right. Let's read some magazines. Look, here's one with some cartoons." The children began to calm down as Tom read the cartoon out loud.

As Tom waited to get word from the doctors, he thought about the events of the past four months. Shelly's diagnosis of stage four breast cancer had occurred about a year ago. He remembered getting the news one day when he returned home from work to find Shelly in their bedroom sitting on their bed in tears. She had put up a strong face for the children but could only do so for so long and had slipped into the bedroom to grieve in private. Tom put his arm around her and reassured her that they would fight this together and that all was not lost.

Numerous doctor appointments filled the next months as Shelly underwent mastectomy surgery and subsequent chemotherapy and radiation therapy. Tom took a lot of time off from his job to be with her and support her as best he could. The cancer decreased a bit but the prognosis was grim due to the metastatic disease spreading throughout her body. Tom witnessed her grow sicker and weaker while she struggled to care for the children amidst his attempts to help. At one point they recruited Shelly's mother for help, and she had cared for the children several nights each week.

The routine visits to Shelly's oncologist brought grim news, making it difficult to maintain hope. The couple worked hard at hanging on to the smallest thread of hope. Perhaps more chemo would help, or more radiation, or some new vitamin therapy. They were running out of options, and what little hope they clung to had begun to morph into despair. Shelly showed signs of giving up and became depressed. Tom continued to search the Internet for cures or new trials.

Just as Shelly began to contemplate taking control of her own death through suicide, everything changed. During a visit in June, Dr. Hinton, Shelly's oncologist, told her and Tom about the revolutionary Tando Cancer Cure. Dr. Hinton said that Shelly would qualify for the first round of human trials. The couple lit up with the news as it revived their hope.

Shelly discovered she would be the first patient to receive the revolutionary new treatment. Tom accompanied Shelly to her appointment, and they soon found themselves sitting in a makeshift waiting are in the Tampa test clinic.

"Hello, I am Dr. Jeff Bradley, and I will be administering your treatment." Dr. Bradley seemed sharp and competent. Shelly signed the release forms and Dr. Bradley discussed the procedure with her.

A nurse who needed to administer an IV led Shelly to a small room. "I see you have a port; we can use that," the nurse said after examining Shelly. Shelly had had a chemotherapy port installed for her frequent treatments. The nurse connected her port to an IV bag containing the resveratrol solution. "This is a natural substance that gets into your cells in order for the second part of the treatment to be effective," the nurse explained to Shelly.

At the conclusion of the resveratrol infusion the nurse led Shelly to a larger room containing the frequency generator. "Wow, this thing looks like something out of Frankenstein's lab," remarked Tom.

"Yes, I can understand why you would think that, but parts of the machine are exposed so that we can access it," explained Dr. Bradley. "I'm sure you won't feel a thing."

The nurse instructed Shelly to stand with her back to an upright table that lowered into a horizontal position. Two large, half-cylindrical pieces closed around her, enclosing her in a clear Plexiglas tube. The technicians placed several metal rings around the outside of the tube. "This will all be automatic in the final version of the machine," Dr. Bradley explained to Tom. "Okay, now we need to go to the control area." Dr. Bradley led Tom to the computer station.

The technician entered some data into the computer and the machine clicked a few times. "We are getting the quantum resonance readings from Shelly's cancer cells," Dr. Bradley explained while Tom sat, concerned. "Initiating phase two," the technician said, and the machine clicked again. After several iterations of this the technicians removed the coils and cylinders and the table rose to a vertical position.

"How do you feel, Shelly?" Dr. Bradley asked.

"Extremely tired," she said.

"We expected that. You need to go home and get some rest. "

Shelly and Tom returned home, and Shelly went to bed. Tom checked on her every hour or so as she slept the remainder of the day and all throughout the night. When she awoke the next morning Tom asked how she was doing.

"I feel great," said Shelly. "I feel like I have so much energy. I'd forgotten how that felt."

Tom witnessed a dramatic change in Shelly over the next few days. In addition to the increased energy she exhibited, a newfound enthusiasm and hope was evident. Her appetite returned as well, and she gained a healthy amount of weight. A subsequent visit to her oncologist revealed that all the cancer had disappeared. "I would not believe it if I didn't see it for myself," Dr. Hinton said. "I know they are calling this a miracle cure, and right now I have to agree."

During the next four months the family regained their old lives. Shelly seemed to have an endless supply of energy and even began to train for triathlon events, which was something she'd done before her cancer diagnosis. Tom enjoyed the reduced stress of having a partner to help him raise their children. Life was good.

But this had apparently changed now that Shelly fought for her life in the ER. Tom sat patiently reading to the children and waiting for news. Shelly's mom arrived and took over reading to the children. Her presence comforted Tom.

"Tom Clark?" a nurse called as she entered the waiting room.

"Yes, here," Tom answered.

"Come with me, the doctor will see you now." Tom followed her into the ER and past a number of beds with curtains drawn. The doctor stopped him before reaching Shelly's bed. "Your wife is stable but in critical condition. We are taking her to intensive care in a few minutes, and once we set her up, you will be able to see her."

"What happened to her?" exclaimed Tom.

"We don't know yet. We haven't seen anything like this before." The doctor began asking a barrage of questions. "Any problems with you or the children? Had Shelly traveled to the tropics, or come in contact with anyone from Africa?"

Tom took a deep breath and asked, "Will she make it?"

"To be completely honest, we don't know." The doctor shook his head. "We need to make sure she's stable while we run some tests. It's going to be a long night." Tom thanked the doctor, and the nurse led him back to the waiting room.

Tom instructed Shelly's mom to take the children home; he would stay the night. About thirty minutes later the nurse returned to escort Tom to the intensive care unit. He hardly recognized Shelly; she was unconscious and on full life support which included a ventilator, ECG, several IVs and numerous other medical devices. Tom, in a state of bewilderment and shock, sat with his beloved wife.

At 12:30 am the ventilator began to beep as if it were going to explode and several nurses rushed in. They removed the covers to find a number of blue areas growing on Shelly's skin. They ushered Tom out of the room as doctors and nurses ran in and out. Tom overheard bits and pieces of their conversations as they worked on Shelly as fast as they could. Then, all of a sudden, all the activity stopped. He heard the words 'call it' and knew that the worst had happened.

The doctor in charge walked out to Tom and said, "I'm so sorry. We did everything we possibly could do to keep your wife alive but we were unsuccessful. Again, I'm sorry."

The doctor's words rang in Tom's ears. He had been dreading these words ever since Shelly's initial cancer diagnosis. He thanked the doctor and turned to make his way back to the waiting room. On the way he spotted a small chapel. He entered, sat in a pew in the back row, and began to sob.

34

CRISIS RESPONSE TEAM MEETING, TAMPA, FLORIDA: A FEW DAYS LATER

*T*he hot moist Florida air caused Mark to sweat as soon as he stepped off the plane and into the causeway. He decided the best way to handle this situation was to assemble the brightest and best minds that Tando had to offer into a crisis response team. The team included Dr. Jeff Bradley as well as a group of science experts consisting of Morgan Salzer, Beth Manning and biogeneticist Dr. Xee Ying. The team had a couple of days to analyze tissues from the Shelly Clark case, and Mark hoped there was something they could do to correct the problem.

Mark raced through the terminal and into a limousine waiting to transport him to the test clinic site. The test clinic, a rudimentary version of the final cancer cure clinic, contained a rough version of the frequency machine which was set up for the first human trials. It was not as sleek and shiny as the final version, but it did the job. The open design of the machine, complete with its maze of wires, allowed for easy access in case repairs were needed. The control room consisted of a table with a desktop computer. The machine resembled a high school science project on steroids.

Everyone was waiting at the site as Mark pulled up. "Must be nice to be a big shot," Morgan whispered to Xee after spotting the large black limo through the lobby window.

"I wouldn't want his job for anything right now," said Xee.

"Good afternoon everyone," announced Mark as he entered the lobby. The team followed Mark into the test area where a makeshift conference room had been set up complete with a large table and a projection screen.

"First of all, my thanks to you all for coming," Mark began after taking his place at the head of the table. "You are Tando's brightest and best, and not to put pressure on you, but you are the hope for Tando's future." Everyone sat around the table setting up their laptops in front of them.

"Let's begin with Jeff; he was in charge of the human trials," Mark said.

Jeff nodded his head and began speaking with a shaky voice. "Okay, as we already know, what we are dealing with is the likelihood of twenty deaths projected to increase to one hundred. This, of course, is the entire first round of human breast cancer trials. So far we know the first patient, Ms. Shelly Clark, a thirty-eight year old stage four breast cancer survivor passed away last week from multisystem organ disease. The pathology report stated gross cellular death occurring throughout her body. It was as if she was fine one minute and critically ill the next. I spoke with the pathologist and he said he had never seen anything like this in a healthy person. He said it reminded him of end stage sepsis, but there was no infection. Since the incident, Xee conducted a deep cell and genetic analysis with her biogenetics team. Xee, can you tell us what you've found?"

Mark sat twirling his pen with his fingers. Xee clicked some keys on her laptop and an image of a cluster of cells appeared on the screen. "These are, of course, healthy liver cells. I am using the liver as an example, but this anomaly will repeat in all major organ cells." Xee changed the slide to show a damaged group of cells. These cells showed extensive damage and many appeared broken into a series of pieces. The next slide showed similar damaged cells. "Here are the same kinds of cells after the anomaly. You can see that they appear damaged, almost like they exploded. We call this apoptosis, or cell death. This happens to cells when they die; they explode." The image changed to a picture of DNA. "We know cell death can be programmed by errors in the DNA such as chromatin condensation and chromosomal fragmentation, and it happens all the time in normal development. In other words, some cells are *supposed* to die, during differentiation for example. Nature programs these cells to die. This program is influenced by epigenetic factors, which is somewhat like the same mechanism used by our hydrocolloid resveratrol formula but with negative effects."

Mark interrupted: "So, do you think this was caused by the resveratrol?"

Xee continued, "No, we do not. Resveratrol is a natural substance with millions of people taking it every day. It is totally safe. We think the problem is with the exposure to the radio wave frequencies."

Morgan interjected, "What do you think the mechanism is, Xee?" Xee showed a slide of a butterfly. Everyone looked puzzled.

"It's a pretty butterfly, but what do butterflies have to do with cell death?" Beth asked. Mark sat back in his chair as if he were in deep thought.

"The butterfly is a symbol reminding us of the butterfly effect in chaos theory." Xee changed the slide to a picture of a hurricane. "You are probably familiar with the chaos analogy in which a butterfly flapping its wings in one part of the world causes a perturbation in the global weather system resulting in a hurricane in another part of the world."

Mark leaned forward. "You mean small changes in chaotic systems can result in large effects?"

"That is correct, Mark," said Xee. "Our team of geneticists came to the conclusion that the cell death was caused by the frequency treatment imparting a small chaotic effect on the cell's DNA and surrounding epigenetic systems. The natural error corrective mechanisms within the DNA held this effect in check, but could only do so for so long. We think the anomaly has a lifespan of about sixteen weeks."

Mark looked at the screen and then at Xee. "You mean to tell me that we programmed these cells to die in four months?"

Xee looked away from Mark as she felt his anxiety rise. "That is correct; we see no other way this could have happened."

Mark felt as though his entire world was coming to an end. His mind raced as it searched for answers but there was only confusion. He had sold out his own brother and sent hundreds of people to their imminent deaths. And for what? For money? For fame? He had never understood how people could commit suicide until this very moment. Everyone in the room sat still as the gravity of Xee's report sank in.

Finally, Mark decided to try to salvage what was left of the situation. "Jeff, why did we not see this in the rat trials?"

Jeff cleared his throat. "Mark, don't you remember? We didn't actually complete any rat trials? Instead we relied on the data that you provided from your own rat trials...you know, from your other project."

It now became clear to Mark. The Latro hit on Freetech's Chicago and Beijing labs had destroyed everything, including the rats. Since he worked with Tando during the rat trials, it was he who had provided the data to Tando. And they had never replicated the rat trials. He had made some terrible mistakes—fatal mistakes. He should have replicated the results, or at the very least kept the rats alive. He had given in to Jim Barnes' pressure to get the cure up and running in record time, and now he was paying the price for taking credit for something he didn't fully understand.

Still shaken, Mark attempted to compose himself. "Morgan, Beth, is there a way to fix this?" Morgan was the Tando engineer on the frequency machine and Beth was the quantum physicist. Since Beth was in a better position to answer she replied to Mark's question.

"We don't know yet. We don't know if we can produce a frequency mix that still cures cancer and keeps the healthy cells alive. We tune our frequency mix to the quantum resonance of the cells. To our knowledge, any variation in the frequency mix would be ineffective. So now we have a frequency mix that kills cancer cells but also instills a death sentence on healthy cells. So far, we have been unable to solve the chaos problem. There are probably only a handful of people in the world who have experience with quantum resonance, and of that small group there are only one or two with enough knowledge for any real chance at solving this. Plus we would need to start at the beginning with cells and work our way back up to rats and so on. It could take years."

Mark looked like a man sentenced to death. Jeff came over and put his arm on Mark's back. "We will all do our best. There was no way you could have known. It is not your fault." Mark dropped his head and nodded a few times.

"Thanks Jeff, thank you everyone. You are all fantastic at what you do. All I ask now is to keep me in the loop with regard to any new developments. Also, I'm planning to take the heat for this one. You all keep working on it, okay?" The others looked down and nodded.

Mark's original plans were to stay in Tampa and help the team find a solution, but after this hopeless and devastating news there was no point in staying. He returned to the limo and directed the driver to phone ahead to the Tando corporate jet to get it ready for departure to L.A. He had to inform Jim of what he'd heard as soon as possible. He feared what was to come.

35
BACK IN MEXICO

$\mathcal{A}$lex knocked on the door of the Valdez residence and a voice called out from inside, "Hola!" The door opened to reveal a young woman in her twenties with long dark hair. She wore jeans, a peach colored t-shirt and cowboy boots. Alex recognized Daniella from a picture he had seen on Xavier's desk.

"Hello, I am Alex Winter; I worked with your brother Xavier." Alex spoke slowly, not knowing if she spoke English.

"Oh, Alex, come...in!"

An older lady wearing a long blue jean skirt and a white blouse walked into the room as he entered. Alex recognized her as well; Xavier's mother Alma. Daniella explained to her in Spanish who he was.

"My mother says welcome to our house," said Daniella. "Please, come in and sit down." Daniella turned to her mother and told her to find papa. The woman directed Alex to take a seat on the sofa as she went to find her husband.

Daniella took a seat on a chair facing Alex. The small living room featured white stucco walls and a large fireplace. Flanking the fireplace were two small tables, each one displaying a picture of one of the fallen brothers.

Xavier's was on the right and Luis's on the left. Candles placed in front of each photo and rosaries draped across one corner of each frame illustrated the religious values of the family. Alex glanced at Luis's photo and remembered how Peter had explained the details of Luis's death in a Mexico City hotel.

"You come so far, Alex..."

"I could not face your family at Xavier's funeral, Daniella. Xavier was such a brilliant scientist and physicist, and he was a good friend, and I wanted you and your family to know how lucky we all were to be his friend, and work with him."

Daniella turned to face the picture of her brother and said something in Spanish to it. "Xavier is glad that you came."

Alma re-entered the room pulling a man along with her that Alex recognized as Carlos, Xavier's father. Daniella introduced Alex to Carlos and they shook hands. Carlos spoke to Daniella, who translated for Alex. "He says you are welcome to stay at our home."

"Thank you, but tell your father that that won't be necessary; I can stay at a hotel in town." Daniella translated and Carlos responded.

"He says it is not safe in town for gringos like you. This is not Mexico City. We don't get many tourists, and there are thieves. You are safer here. He insists."

Alex sighed and resigned himself to accepting Carlos's invitation.

"Tell him thank you very much, and I am grateful."

Daniella translated and Carlos smiled and nodded his head.

Alma appeared with a tray full of cups. She motioned with a nod of her head and a smile for Alex to take one. She presented the tray to Daniella and Carlos for each one to take a cup as well. She returned to the kitchen and appeared a few moments later with coffee, which she poured into each cup. Alex sipped his and signaled his enjoyment by smiling and nodding his head.

"Daniella, please tell your parents that I've come to say how sorry I am for their loss of both their sons." Daniella nodded and translated in Spanish to her parents.

They both responded. "They said thank you for coming so far to do so."

Alex continued: "Also, tell them it was an honor to work with Xavier; he was one of the most brilliant people I have ever known."

Alma and Carlos answered to Daniella: "They said that Xavier talked often about you and about his work." Alma began to cry and Carlos put his arm around her.

Alex asked Daniella about the kidnapping and she told him that the cartel had not harmed her. She explained the Sicarios carried out all the kidnappings and killings for the boss, El Jefe.

"They told me that their trouble was not with me but with Luis. Luis had worked for them for years as a Halcones, a Falcon, the cartel's eyes and ears on the streets. Many teens begin their cartel careers this way. Eventually, Luis worked his way up to Sicarios. He was nineteen at that time and separated from the family. When he visited on occasion, I could not stand to be in his presence; his soul was dark. He often smelled of death. My brother was lost to the devil.

"By his mid-twenties Luis had worked his way up in the organization to the level of lieutenant. He controlled a small territory under one of the drug lords. El Jefe took a special liking to Luis, and my brother looked up to him as a father figure. Luis preferred the power and riches that came with drugs to the hard work and struggle of a rancher.

"But Luis's ambition and love of power got the best of him when he decided to skim off the top of his Capos' cut. No one is trusted in the drug cartel, and Capos and El Jefe are always looking out for their own interests. They had their eyes on Luis, and in the end his own halcones betrayed him. The information went all the way to the top, and a hit was carried out by the cartel's sicarios. Luis thought he could hide in the crowds of Mexico City and jump to another cartel, but they soon spotted him and informed the boss.

"A group of sicarios took me to a farm house not far from Cheran and held me there at gunpoint in order to put pressure on our family and friends to turn Luis in, but our family had no clue as to his whereabouts. They searched nearby areas and asked questions but learned very little. Their luck turned when a teenage boy told them that he had seen the sicarios transporting a young woman to a farm house. That young woman was me, of course. The posse outnumbered the sicarios and surrounded the house. The sicarios had received word that Luis was dead, so they allowed me to go free."

Daniella seemed to have no sorrow over Luis's death. Because of his involvement in the cartel, the family had for some time existed under a constant threat. Their connection to Luis had ostracized them from the community as well. This was evident during the few dates with young men that Daniella had had during the past few years.

"The men I dated were good men, but they all knew about Luis; or if they didn't, then they soon found out and ran away in fear."

Luis's death had dissipated the dark cloud that hung over the family, and now Daniella's parents were hopeful that she would meet a good man and start a family, one that might someday take over their ranch now that both their sons were gone.

Despite Luis's deal with the devil, his family still prayed for him as evidenced by the candles and rosary on the table holding his picture. They were devout Catholics and prayed for God to have mercy on his soul. They also prayed that Xavier would somehow plead to Jesus in heaven to forgive Luis.

Dinner consisted of delicious homemade beef tamales and a chicken vegetable stew with tortillas and salad. Daniella struggled to interpret for both parents as they spoke at the same time. Alma seemed to dominate the discussion and asked a lot of questions about Xavier's life in Chicago. At one point Carlos decided to let Alma take over the conversation and turned his attention to enjoying his dinner.

"Did you show Alex your collection from Xavier?" Alma asked Daniella.

"Your collection?" said Alex.

"Yes, Xavier sent gifts from America. They were small things, but I cherish them because they made me feel close to him."

"My father will want to drink with you. I hope you like Tequila."

"I love it," said Alex although he had not had a drink since he returned from Colorado. Alex sensed that his visit was going well. These were good hearted, hardworking humble people, and he could see where these qualities had originated in Xavier. He missed his friend.

Carlos returned with a bottle of Tequila and poured a glass for Alex and one for himself. Daniella returned from the kitchen to act as interpreter.

"To our guest from America!" Carlos lifted his glass. Alex followed suit, said thank you and took a healthy drink.

"To Xavier, your son, my friend!" said Alex while lifting his glass. They both finished their Tequila and Carlos refilled the glasses. After another toast Carlos motioned to Daniella.

"Show him Xavier's gifts."

"Come with me, Alex." Daniella led Alex to her bedroom.

Alex entered the modest bedroom containing a single bed, a dresser and a night stand. One wall displayed a series of shelves containing a collection of objects. Most of these were kitschy souvenirs obtained from various cities in the U.S. There were snow globes from New York and Chicago, a frame made of seashells from St. Petersburg Florida, a miniature replica of the St. Louis Arch and other assorted knickknacks.

"These make me feel close to him." Daniella took each one off the shelf to show Alex.

"Which one is your favorite?" said Alex while shaking a snow globe.

Daniella walked over to her night stand and picked up a small ceramic statue. She turned to face Alex while carefully cradling the piece in her arms. "My favorite is this one," she said while presenting the statue to Alex. "I call it my bird of hope."

The statue, standing about seven inches tall, depicted a bird painted a bright orange and adorned with fine detail. With wings spread, head cocked toward the sky and mouth open, it stood on top of a flaming pedestal. A shiver ran up Alex's spine.

"Daniella, this is not just a bird. This is a mythical creature called a Phoenix. It represents life, death and resurrection. When did Xavier send this?" Alex's heart began pounding in his chest as he remembered his vision the night he almost took his own life. An eerie sensation came over him. Alex didn't believe in premonitions, spirits, or even religion for that matter, but he sensed that someone or something had been watching over him. Since his suicide attempt he had seemed to move toward something greater than himself with each passing day. He recognized Daniella's Phoenix must be yet another increment in his difficult journey toward some unknown destination. There was more to come and he needed to allow himself to follow his instincts.

Daniella handed the statue to Alex. "Actually, Becca sent this to me. She said he told her to send it the night that he died." The blood drained from Alex's face.

"He sent this the night he died? He turned it around

examining it closely for any kind of mark or writing. He found nothing. He turned the statue upside down to examine its mark of origin. It was a typical hollow ceramic piece with a hole in the bottom. Alex peered into the hole but saw nothing unusual. "Do you have a flashlight?" Daniella left the room to find one. Alex shook the angel but heard nothing.

Daniella returned with the flashlight and handed it to Alex. He turned it on and aimed it into the hole. There, taped to the inside of the statue, was a small black plastic object. "There is something inside here, Daniella. Maybe a message from Xavier!" Daniella looked shocked.

"Xavier sent a message inside?"

"I don't know, but there is something here. Do you have a screwdriver I can use to pry it out?" Daniella again left the room, this time bolting to find her father. Alex heard them speaking in Spanish, and both Daniella and Carlos returned as Daniella handed him a screwdriver.

Alex pried the small square object from the inside of the statue while being careful not to damage it in any way. It took some time to do this, and Carlos and Daniella crowded him on either side. He carefully peeled the object from the tape. He examined it up close and noticed some small flat gold metal pieces on it.

"This looks like a simcard! Xavier was trying to tell us something. There must be something important here." Alex reached into his pocket to retrieve his cell phone. He popped the back off, pulled out the simcard and inserted Xavier's instead. He turned on his phone and accessed the file manager to see what was on the simcard. Sure enough, there was one file. Alex opened the file and found that it contained a single string of numbers: 20236775, 967, 744, 390.

"This must be some sort of code. I'm sorry, Daniella, but I need to take this back to Chicago as soon as possible to figure this out. It could be very important. Would you mind if I borrowed the statue so we can analyze it? It may contain more clues." Alex popped the simcard out of his phone but made a copy in another file in his phone for safe keeping. He rushed to the door. He told Daniella to thank her parents for their hospitality and stopped to give Alma a goodbye hug and Carlos a farewell handshake before heading out. Daniella followed him to his car. He hugged and thanked her.

"Be careful on your journey, Alex. Do not stop until you get to your hotel in Mexico City. Do not be a stranger. You are always welcome here." Alex waved goodbye as he pulled the rental car around and headed down the dirt road into the night.

Alex dialed the long international number to connect with Peter as soon as he left Cheran and hit the open road. It was 9:30 pm in Chicago. "Hello, Alex? I thought you were in Mexico?"

"I have big news..." Alex barely contained himself. "Xavier gave us a message!" Alex went on to explain the story of Daniella's statue and the simcard. "I'm not sure, but there may be more information inside the statue once I can get it back to Chicago and into the lab."

Alex pulled the car to the side of the road. "Okay, Peter, get a piece of paper and write down these numbers." He relayed the numbers one by one and requested that Peter read them back to double check them.

"Got it!" said Peter. "I'll get the team on this right away. I can get Kira, Julie and Kevin to work on this. Xavier knew we would eventually find this, so someone in the original team should be able to figure this out. Wow! This is fantastic news, Alex."

"I'm on my way to Mexico City right now. I'll be at the Grand Hotel de Mexico and will contact you when I get there. It should be a five to six hour drive from Cheran. Can you work on getting me on a flight to Chicago tomorrow?" Alex pulled back onto the road.

"Will do, Alex; I should have something by the time you contact me. Drive safely, my friend." Peter hung up and Alex continued to drive through the black Mexican night.

Alex arrived at the hotel at about 1:00 am. The grand lobby was empty except for the cleaning crew. Alex was able to get a room on the third floor and headed there clutching the statue in one hand and his luggage in the other. He walked down the long hallway to his room and slid the key card into the lock which responded with a green light and a click. He opened the door to the dark room and reached for the light switch and flicked it on.

Alex's heart sank as the lights came on and illuminated a man sitting on a chair across the room pointing a pistol fitted with a silencer at him. Just as the image materialized, the cold steel of the silencer of another pistol touched the side of his throat. He dropped his luggage and raised his hands with one still clutching the statue.

"Dr. Winter, we are glad to meet you." The man on the chair spoke with a Hispanic accent. Who were these men? Had they followed him from Cheran? Were they part of the drug cartel?

"What do you want? Money? You can have it!" "We don't want your money. We just want what you are holding." The man holding the gun to Alex's throat grabbed the statue from Alex's hand.

"We also need the simcard that you found inside the statue." The man on the chair motioned to the other man to move Alex further into the room and sit him on the bed.

"Take his phone, empty his pockets." The man obeyed the instructions and found Alex's cell phone in one pocket and the simcard in the other. The man held up the phone and the simcard. Alex continued to hold his arms over his head.

"These are the items?"

"Yes, those are the items." said Alex, defeated. The man picked up a device resembling a walkie-talkie. "This is coyote seven. Tell the boss we have the items." He clicked it off and moved past Alex toward the door while still pointing the gun at Alex. "You will not call the police. They will not listen to you. And one thing more: your brother sends his regards..." With that, the door shut behind them.

Alex sat on the bed wondering how Mark had known about the statue so soon. But after a few moments, he pieced it together. I am so stupid! He realized that Tando had probably had him under surveillance all along. It would be a valid strategic move to keep an eye on him, and it had paid off. He felt terrible about how he had succumbed to his own excitement about discovering Xavier's statue, and by contacting Peter on an unsecured line. He knew his call to Peter had broadcast the information directly to Tando.

Alex also pondered why he was still alive. It would have been easier just to get rid of him. He surmised that either Mark had given the hit men explicit instructions not to harm him, or it would be better to keep him alive and under surveillance just in case he discovered any other important nuggets of information.

The ringing of the hotel phone in his room interrupted Alex's thoughts. He picked it up and heard Peter's voice on the other end. "Alex? Is that you? I was waiting for your call and I thought something might have happened to you. Are you okay?"

Alex sighed and responded, "I am okay, but barely. A couple of hit men just held me up. They took the numbers and the statue."

Peter was angry. "I was hoping we weren't bugged, but I guess I was wrong. I'm glad you are okay though."

"I'm sorry, Peter; I had to give it to them. They held a gun to my head. How could I have been so stupid as to call you and spill the beans on an unsecured line?"

Peter detected the shame in Alex's voice.

"Don't be too hard on yourself, Alex. It was only a matter of time until they found out. Plus they only have a series of numbers. Nobody knows the significance of the numbers, and knowing Xavier, he left us quite a puzzle to solve."

Alex felt a bit better. "Did you contact the others?"

"Yes. Good news on that front, Alex. Kira, Kevin and Julie all said they were in. They are heading here as we speak." Alex detected the excitement in Peter's voice and was happy to get the old team back together. "I also booked you on a flight to Chicago, direct; you leave at 9:45am and arrive at 2:30pm. I'll be there to pick you up." Alex thanked Peter.

"I don't think we should say any more. I will see you tomorrow." Alex hung up the phone.

36
EARLIER THE SAME EVENING: MARK'S CONDO IN L.A.

Mark, awake in bed and experiencing another restless night of sleeplessness, reached for his beeping cell phone. He had lived through the roughest days of his life and hoped to go to bed after an evening of television and vodka. After the Tampa meeting, he flew back to L.A. to report to Jim Barnes. Needless to say, Jim was not pleased and again put pressure on Mark to fix things as soon as possible. Mark directed the Tampa team to continue to work on the problem but understood the hopelessness of the situation. That was, of course, until he answered his phone.

"Mark, this is David Brysen from Tando. I have some important news. Please hang up and dial this number for a secure line." Mark cringed at the thought of talking to Brysen but hung up and dialed a long series of numbers. "Brysen here. As I said, there is important news about your brother Alex, and about the project." Mark became anxious; as the first thought that crossed his mind was that they had killed Alex.

"Alex? Is he okay?"

"Yes, your brother is fine."

Mark sighed with relief. "Okay, tell me the important news."

Brysen continued: "You are aware that Alex has been under surveillance. He was followed to Mexico City and to the Valdez residence in Cheran. Our operative witnessed him leaving the Valdez residence last evening. We intercepted a call from Alex to Peter North in Chicago. Evidently, Alex discovered some kind of message hidden in a ceramic statue by Xavier Valdez. He thought the message might contain a code leading to information about the project. We intercepted the code and alerted our Mexico City operatives to intercept him at his hotel. They carried out their mission and retrieved both the statue and a small simcard containing the code. We already had the code since we intercepted Alex's phone call to Peter North. I thought it prudent to give explicit instructions to keep Alex Winter alive. I had orders to do so by Mr. Barnes." Mark was excited and relieved.

"That's great news, Brysen. Excellent work! Can you give me the numbers?"

Brysen paused for a moment then continued: "Mr. Barnes has instructed me to inform you that a team has been assembled and is beginning work on the number string at L.A. headquarters. You are to join them immediately." Mark had figured that Barnes would bypass him and take over the project himself.

"I'm on my way. Thanks, Brysen."

Mark and Alex were once again competing, but this time the stakes were much higher. Mark concluded, since Xavier was one of the leading experts in quantum resonance and co-developer of the frequency machine, the hidden message must contain a critical piece of information. He figured Xavier had somehow discovered Mark's set-up and left town to save his life but had had just enough time to hide some valuable information in the statue. He must have instructed Becca to send it to Daniella with the hope that someone from the Chicago team would find it. Perhaps Xavier's plan was for Daniel to discover the simcard and alert Alex or Peter. Xavier was a genius, but this was an even more brilliant move than he might have expected. He had to crack the code before Alex did.

37
CHICAGO: LATER THAT DAY

The door to Peter's apartment burst open and Peter and Alex entered to applause and cheers from Kira, Julie and Kevin, all of whom had been working most of the night. The race was on to beat Mark in solving Xavier's puzzle. After greetings and hugs, the team gathered around Peter's dining room table.

"First of all," Peter began, "I can't stress enough about secrecy. No cell phone calls with any information whatsoever. I think we are okay if we work here, but I can't be one hundred percent sure. I did some searching and didn't find anything that looked like a bug, but you never know. I think we should keep the curtains drawn at all times and stay off the Internet. If you are working on a computer, make sure your wi-fi card is off or unplugged if you are wired in. So, with that said, any developments?"

Kira opened her laptop and read off some notes about what they had already covered. "First of all, it would help if we knew what we were looking for. What was he trying to tell us? Is this a warning about Mark? Or Tando? Of course, that would be a moot point now. Or is this something else?"

Peter's phone buzzed indicating a news alert. Peter's phone contained a news aggregate app that he had set to alert him with any news about Tando. These news services were much faster than TV.

"Hold on. Hold on... Something big is happening at Tando." Peter stared at his phone. "It says here that the breast cancer patients in the first human trials for the Tando cancer cure are all dead or dying. It says up to one hundred patients may be affected. This is going to hit the evening news like a ton of bricks. I certainly wouldn't want to be in Mark's shoes right now."

Alex sat back with his arms clasped behind his head. "So, this answers Kira's question, doesn't it? Xavier must have known about a problem with the machine."

Kira's face lit up. "Wait! I remember Xavier saying something about a chaos effect. I thought he was just mumbling quantum mumbo-jumbo to himself. You know Xavier; he spent a lot of time inside his own head."

Peter chimed in: "I remember him saying something about chaos too. In fact, Mark brought it up when he suspected Xavier of being a traitor."

Kira continued: "Now I remember. He said he was working on a solution to the problem and he was close to solving it."

Alex's face lit up as well. "Yes, yes, that would make sense. Xavier probably thought the machine created a chaos effect in the cells. Actually, it makes perfect sense now. An effect like this could create damage to the cells; in fact, if the effect grew strong enough, it could even kill the cells. That's probably what happened at Tando. They ran the trials and inserted a small amount of chaos into the patients' cells. The chaos grew enough to produce a programmed cell death."

"Apoptosis," Julie shouted. "Apoptosis is programmed cell death. Some cells are naturally programmed to die, but they could also be artificially programmed to die with something like this."

Kevin patted Julie on the back. "How did you know that, Julie?" Julie turned and smiled at Kevin.

"Hey, I took a few Bio courses."

"Mark knew about it too," Alex said. "I would say he either forgot about it or figured Xavier had already solved it with the solution included in the last data transfer."

"But it wasn't" interjected, Peter. "Which is why Xavier hid it... He must've thought it could be used as a bargaining chip for his life, or to keep our project alive." Alex grabbed his laptop from its carrying case and set it on the table in front of him. "Let's get going; we have work to do. We know what we are looking for now. The code should give us some kind of frequency information. We also can assume that Mark and Tando have a team working on this, and with their resources it probably consists of a slew of mathematicians and code-breakers."

The Chicago team dove back into the task of decoding Xavier's message. Peter brought in a large whiteboard and set it up on an easel next to the table. He wrote the numbers 20236775967744390, and anyone was welcomed to put their ideas under it. They began with looking to see if the numbers were in any way related to frequencies. They tried multipliers and a multitude of combinations without success but then concluded that this would be too obvious.

They thought the numbers related in some way to letters of the alphabet. For example, the number two might mean the letter "B" and so on. The team decided to break up into small subunits based on a specific hypothesis. Kevin decided to work on alphabet substitution while Kira and Alex worked on putting the numbers into a matrix. They soon found that the odd number of digits did not fit. Peter examined characteristics of the number and found it was not a prime number or Fibonacci sequence. Alex and Kira proposed that this might be a digital code, so they rewrote the number in a long binary sequence on the whiteboard: 1000111111001010011110110010010101110100111000011 0000110

The team tried again to match this number with various combinations of frequencies. Kevin also tried to relate the number to letters of the alphabet. By that evening the team began to grow weary of their newfound code-breaking task. Peter sent out for pizza. "We can't stop until we break it," Peter exclaimed. "Pizza is on its way. Help yourself to caffeine soft drinks as well."

38
TANDO BUILDING, L.A.: THE SAME DAY

Mark's team had already been working on the code as Mark was on route from his condo. He arrived to find no less than twenty scientists, engineers and mathematicians working on the number sequence. The lab consisted of a large room with two rows of lab benches and chairs. The room was bright with several banks of gleaming fluorescent lights. Every team member wore a white lab coat sporting the Tando badge. Mark felt a bit out of place with his jeans and t-shirt but grabbed a white lab coat off one of the many hooks next to the door to fit in. There were also two terminals for accessing a Cray XK6 supercomputer. The team worked on the solution as if their lives depended on it.

At the front of the room a large white board displayed Xavier's code. "Welcome to the boiler room, Dr. Winter." A middle-age man held out his hand. "My name is Alan Spearling, and I have been assigned to lead this code breaking project."

"My pleasure," said Mark while shaking the gentleman's hand.

"I've heard a lot about your work with the cancer cure. I'm sorry about the recent events though." Mark was glad the man showed some respect despite his diminishing status at Tando.

"I can help get you up to speed on what we are working on right now," said Alan. "We've divided the team into small units with each focusing on a different technique of code breaking. There is an alphabet team, a cipher team, and a team using powerful code breaking algorithms with the Cray XK6. This bad girl can scale up to five hundred thousand processors for a fantastic amount of computing power." Mark nodded his head in approval. "No big revelation so far, but it's only a matter of time. If there is a message in this number string, we will eventually find it."

Alan showed Mark to his makeshift office in one corner of the lab. He sat at the desk and noticed a flashing light on the phone indicating a message. He picked up the receiver and pushed the message button. It was from Jim Barnes.

"Mark, I hope you had a good trip from Tampa and are happy with the code breaking team. Despite the late hour, I want you to come up to my office when you get here. I need to discuss something important with you." Mark's heart dropped into his stomach. What now? Maybe Brysen will put a bullet in my head and end this misery.

A few minutes later he found himself in Jim's office with no Brysen in sight. During the elevator ride he conjectured that they would probably keep him alive because they needed to pin this massive failure on someone. The two men greeted each other. "I take it you find the team adequate?" Jim said with authority.

"Yes, very adequate," said Mark.

"Alan is a PhD from MIT and a world renowned mathematician. If anybody can solve this puzzle, he can." Jim seemed calm and confident. "We hope whatever message Valdez hid in these numbers will be a solution to this chaos problem. I'll be blunt, Mark. Both our heads are on the chopping block. Whether the ax will fall will depend on what happens with this code. Tando is positioned to lose billions, and may implode if we don't solve this, which is why I brought you up here."

"What do you need from me, Jim? I don't think I can be useful breaking codes, at least not as useful as the other esteemed scientists on the team." Mark was a defeated man. He didn't care what happened to him at that point.

"I'll get right to the point, Mark. What I need from you is your brother. We are sure he also has a team working on the solution, and who knows, perhaps they know about other clues from their time with Xavier. Maybe they can piece this whole thing together. Maybe they could even work with us here at Tando. You know we pay quite well."

Mark felt even more defeated. Once again, Alex had won before the contest had ended. Jim had cast Mark out of his own plan, and with one decision Alex could again be number one. He was sure that Tando would pay just about anything for Alex and his team to work for them. He also knew this was all in vain, because Alex would never sell out. Not only was he the smarter brother, but he was also the more ethical one. Alex had always hated what Tando stood for, which was why he'd shunned anyone that had anything to do with them. Alex had always favored the underdog, the little guy, the start-up taking on the giants and winning. He didn't care about money or fame. He only cared about making positive contributions to the world.

Mark surmised what was coming next, as Jim continued: "We want you to meet your brother and try to persuade him to work with us. We want you to call him to arrange a meeting. Now we can do this the easy way, or we can employ other more unpleasant ways. I wouldn't want to get Brysen involved, if you know what I mean. It's up to you. Once Alex agrees, we will talk further about what will be said." Mark felt dejected but sucked up his bad feelings and agreed to call Alex later that day. Jim said that Brysen had informed him that Alex was staying with Peter, and that he could reach him there.

Mark turned to walk away. He was already dead inside.

Jim stood by his office door and watched him walk to the elevator. "Keep your chin up, Mark." Jim said. "The game's not over yet."

39
CONFRONTATION

*T*he all-night cerebral session took its toll on the Chicago team. Pizza boxes and empty bottles of caffeinated soda formed an architectural structure, the boxes supported by the bottles. Kira crashed on Peter's sofa. Julie and Kevin left for a walk to clear their lungs and heads. Peter and Alex continued their relentless cognitive gyrations on the code as if trapped in an endless loop of metal masturbation. So far their efforts had resulted in nothing more than a disorganized mashup of papers riddled with numbers, letters and pizza sauce. At 9:00 am, Peter broke from Alex and snapped on the TV to see what was going on in the outside world.

Tando Pharmaceuticals headquarters in L.A materialized on the screen. "Hey, Alex, get this!" Peter sat down on a chair next to the sofa where Kira lay sleeping. Alex slid away from the table and joined Peter.

The TV announcer began, "The death toll mounts as nineteen more women died after receiving the revolutionary and now controversial Tando Pharmaceuticals cancer cure. No word yet from Tando CEO Jim Barnes or project leader Dr. Mark Winter. Tando did release a statement this morning that read: "We at Tando Pharmaceuticals wish to express our deepest sympathy over the loss of these heroes. We want to assure everyone that we are using all our resources to find a solution to this problem and are confident we will prevail so we can make the cancer cure safe for everyone."

"Tando stock has already plummeted forty-two percent with news of this tragedy and analysts are forecasting Tando, the world's largest manufacturer of pharmaceuticals, may be headed for bankruptcy if they don't resolve this issue soon. So far, Mr. Barnes and Dr. Winter have declined our requests for interviews, and there are no press conferences scheduled, but mounting pressure may force them to reconsider."

The camera cut to the living room of a grieving family.

The announcer continued, "Investigative reporter Helen Jung is with Thomas Clark, husband of Shelly Clark, the first patient to die from the Tando cancer cure."

The camera showed Helen Jung sitting across from a man sitting on a sofa flanked by two children. The man was upset and grief stricken. A box of tissues rested on the coffee table in front of them.

Helen began, "We are here at the Tampa, Florida residence of Shelly Clark, the first patient to die from the Tando cancer cure."

The camera zoomed in on Thomas Clark and the kids. The children sat quietly staring into space. Mr. Clark squinted with eyes red and swollen from tears. He displayed the demeanor of a beaten, confused and bitter man. It was as if this little vulnerable family had had all joy sucked out them.

"Mr. Clark, were you in any way aware of any problem with the cancer cure?" The camera zoomed in closer.

"They told us it was perfectly safe. They said it was a natural treatment. I should never have let her go into that death machine. Her doctors said she could have lived another year or so. Tando took that away from us. They need to be brought to justice for what they did." He switched from confusion to anger.

The interviewer continued, "Did you see any change in Shelly before her death?"

"Absolutely not; she seemed fine. She even competed in a triathlon the week before. There was no sign of any cancer or anything. We thought it was too good to be true. I guess it was." The camera cut back to the interviewer.

"You heard it; the miracle cancer cure may be too good to be true." Now, back to you, Al.

"Tando will self-destruct if they don't crack the code before we do," said Peter as he lowered the TV volume.

"I know Mark betrayed us, but I feel sorry for him. He's the only family I have left." Alex returned to the table. Kevin and Julie entered the room toting a tray of Starbuck's coffee.

"We thought this would jump-start our foggy brains this morning," said Kevin while he and Julie passed tall cups of extra-caffeinated coffee to Peter and Alex. Peter raised the cup to his lips and felt his pocket vibrate from his phone. He dug into his pocket to retrieve the vibrating device and glanced at the number.

"That's odd; it's not anyone I know, and the area code looks like California." He wavered for a couple of seconds deciding what to do as the phone vibrated, then dragged his finger across the screen. "Hello? Who? Excuse me, but is this a joke? Really? Okay, I will see if he will talk to you." Alex, it's for you. You won't believe it; it's Mark." Alex's jaw dropped as Peter handed him the phone. "You can take it in the bedroom, if you need privacy. Also, remember anything you say will be monitored by Tando."

Alex made his way into Peter's bedroom and closed the door. Everyone else sat frozen in silence hoping to glean bits of the private conversation.

"Hello, Mark..."

"Now don't hang up until you let me say my piece, Alex." Alex recognized Mark's voice.

"What's going on?" said Alex with suspicion.

"It's complicated," said Mark.

"Mark, Xavier is dead. I just spent time with his family and they're devastated. Your goons held a gun to my head," Alex informed.

"I'm sorry. I didn't intend for things to work out this way. I made a big mistake, and now I am paying the price." Mark spoke like a beaten man.

"So, why are you calling me? Aren't you busy enough with your code breaking team? I'm sure you are way ahead of us."

Alex hoped that Mark would give him a tidbit of information regarding the code. "I can't talk about that, Alex. I hope you understand. I didn't want to involve you in this, but there are no other options."

"Then this is not your decision to contact me? What's going on? What do you want from me, Mark?"

"I want to meet with you face to face. Will you agree to that? I can be in Chicago by tonight," said Mark.

"So I meet you and then get hauled off in some big black limo to who-knows-where and shot in the back of the head?"

"I give you my word that no harm will come to you. Think about it, Alex. Tando has everything riding on this, and you know more about this thing than anyone else in the world. There is no way in hell Tando would want you out of the picture."

"Mark, you can go fuck yourself!" Alex drew his right finger to the phone to end the call when Peter burst in holding up a piece of paper. He and the others had been listening at the door. The paper read: *You should meet him; we may be able to get information.*

Alex took in a deep breath and nodded his head to Peter. "Okay...okay...I will meet you," Alex said to Mark. "Alone. No Latro goons...no black limos or vans...in a public place. Clancy's bar. You remember, where we used to hang out in the old days."

"Thanks Alex. I'll be there at 8:00 pm." Alex swiped the phone.

Alex and the team returned to wracking their brains at the dining room table. Kira ran the numbers through custom, off-the-cuff software that she wrote containing sophisticated code-breaking algorithms. Some of the algorithms required such immense computing power that it took several hours to run one sequence. As Alex's meeting time drew near, the team was losing steam and exhausting their code-breaking options. They became tired and crabby and began to snap at each other. Kira broke the tension by suggesting that they play a game of Hadron, a frequent stress buster in their early days together. The group declined at first, but Kira insisted, "Let's play in honor of Xavier. It will be good to clear our minds by mindlessly blowing each other's brains out." They agreed, took positions on the sofa and chairs and logged in. The mood began to elevate as each player made last minute changes to their avatar donning an impressive array of virtual weapons. Kira equipped hers with her favorite automatic laser pulse rifle complete with exploding ammo. Kevin selected a machine gun with the highest maximum ammo capacity along with some electrical discharge grenades that paralyzed his enemy while he finished them off with the machine gun. Julie equipped her amazon avatar with an oversize pistol for close encounters, and a grenade launcher for distant attacks. Peter declined and dropped on his bed with instructions to wake him when they finished massacring each other.

Alex prepared to leave. "Wish me luck, and don't tear each other apart too much," he said while slipping on a light jacket. "I wish I could play with you, but maybe next time."

"Hurry back; we might still be at it when you get here," said Kira as she tapped at her keyboard.

The team was ready to engage in battle. The next step was choosing a location among the thousands available on the planet Hadron. Available were easy locations consisting of flat terrains with a few buildings for cover and advanced maps including entire cities, mountains or islands.

"I haven't been in here in a while," Kevin said as he got up to get a drink. "I wonder how my property is holding up?" he called from the kitchen.

"Probably infested with vagrants," said Julie. "They like to store their loot in abandoned properties."

Kevin returned and discovered that the others had chosen a mountainous terrain to begin the battle. They had already claimed starting places behind rocks or sniper positions on cliffs. Kevin manipulated his avatar out of the open, finding a cave for cover.

"I know exactly where you are, Kevin, and I'm coming to get you," said Julie.

"I really miss Xavier," said Kira. "He was so good at this game." The others nodded in acknowledgment. Kira activated her avatar's jet pack so she could jump off a cliff and hover over the others to get a good shot at them when she began to scream. "Wait! Wait! I got it! I got it! Everybody stop!"

"What's up, Kira?" said Peter emerging from the bedroom. "I can't sleep with all this shouting!"

"What's happening?" added Julie.

"I've solved the code! I've solved the code!" Kira jumped up from her chair and began dancing while continuing to shout.

""What do you mean?" said Peter. Kira stopped and pointed at her screen.

"Look at the top of your screens, everyone. Move your avatar and look at the top of your screens." The others followed. "Do you see the numbers on the top of the screen? Do you see them? They are coordinates, 3D coordinates. We've been so stupid!"

"I got it," said Peter. "We *are* so stupid. Instead of trying to break some exotic code by looking at the entire string of numbers, we should have left the commas in."

Peter rushed to the dining room to retrieve the

whiteboard as Kira began entering the coordinates. "I'm almost there. Still rezzing. It's a mountain on the other side of Hadron. I can't materialize inside of it but I can reach inside with my telekinetic powers." Kira continued to tap at her keyboard. "I got it. It's a box." Kira's avatar retrieved a small insignificant looking brown box. She clicked on the box. "It's a file with a whole bunch of stuff in it. Like journal entries. It looks like the final solution to Xavier's chaos problem. We love you, Xavier!" shouted Kira.

Ecstatic, Peter said, "Hurry! Save it to your laptop and delete the box so Tando can't get it. We beat them to it! We've won! We must tell Alex. Wait, he's on his way to see Mark. We have to keep this secret. Kira, put the file on your jump drive and delete it from your computer. We can make a copy, but we can't put this on any machine connected to the Internet. We'll tell Alex in person when he gets back from his meeting with Mark."

Two twenty-something female hostesses greeted Alex as he entered Clancy's Bar and Grille.

"How many?" one said while the other grabbed a menu.

Alex pointed to the bar and smiled. "Have a nice evening," they replied in a weird unison and motioned him inside. A large U-shaped bar dominated the room with twelve taps for various beers on one end and a large mirrored shelf full of bottles and glasses on the other. Small tables lined the outer perimeter of the darkened room. Alex reminisced about how he, Mark and the others would come here after work and blow off steam.

Mark sat alone at one of the perimeter tables, a half-empty glass of beer in front of him. Alex surmised that he had been waiting for a while. Mark wore jeans and a t-shirt, a sharp contrast to the expensive suits he modeled for TV appearances.

"Hi, Mark," said Alex with caution.

"Alex, please sit down. I understand if you don't want

to shake my hand. How are you?"

"How am I?" Alex was angry.

"I know I've been a real shit, and I am very sorry."

"What I want to know is why, Mark? Why did you do this? We had such a good thing going? How could you blow the whole thing?"

"Alex, my entire life has been spent in your shadow. You were always better than me at everything. Do you know how hard it was to grow up working your butt off for things only to see your little brother come along and show you up? Do you know what that's like, Alex, to work like crazy only to hear your own parents predict that your little brother will blow you away? Well, this was my chance to finally get some credit, to finally get some recognition, to finally be the star, to be rich, famous and powerful. This was my one chance, Alex. I'm sorry, but when Tando approached me and told me what they would do for me, and for the cure, I couldn't refuse. I made a huge mistake and betrayed my brother, and one of my best friends ended up dead. And here's the pinnacle of irony, Alex; now Tando wants you to come in and fix everything for them. A real shitty slap in the face that is! I betray my own brother and now they want him to save the day. Just like every other time in my life. I'm a cast-off to them now, and I'm going to hang for this. You know they need a scapegoat." Mark struggled to hold back tears.

Before his journey to Colorado and his suicide attempt Alex would have told his brother to go to hell, but now he understood Mark's motives. He sensed the deep regret in Mark and felt sorry for him. "Mark, you did some stupid things, but I am still your brother. I didn't realize how hard it was for you during those years growing up. You know I would never work for Tando. I don't believe in what they stand for, and I could never live with myself if I did." Alex could see the pain in Mark's eyes. "Anyway, there's nothing I can do to help. I am assuming you are here because you haven't cracked Xavier's little puzzle, and I know I shouldn't be telling you this, but we haven't cracked it either. Maybe we never will. Maybe what Xavier tried to tell us will die with him."

Alex hated what Mark had done, but he still loved him. But Mark made his bed and now had to sleep in it. "If I could turn back the clock, I would turn it back to the time when we all worked on the project together, but I can't, and now I am forced to play out this sick twisted affair," said Mark. He finished his beer in one gulp.

"Why don't you just resign?" said Alex.

"Do you think they would let me off that easily? We're talking about people who don't flinch at killing, especially traitors. You know what they are capable of. My career ends with Tando, and I will be grateful to get out of this with my life." Alex knew Mark was right. He knew firsthand how ruthless Tando and the Latro could be.

"Well, if it's any consolation, I forgive you," said Alex as he reached forward to put his arm on Mark's shoulder. "Maybe this isn't as bad as you think. Maybe you can ride it out and get your life back together. The future is yet to be written."

"Thank you, Alex. I don't deserve a brother like you. I would understand if you disowned me. I'm sorry, and for what it's worth, I love you." They sat in silence for a few moments. Alex figured that they had said what they needed to say. He said goodbye and headed into the night.

Sounds of rock music and happy voices echoed through the halls of Peter's apartment complex. *Somebody's having a good time.* Alex approached Peter's apartment and realized the sounds were coming from there. He opened the door to see Julie and Kevin dancing and holding up glasses of what appeared to be champagne. Kira and Peter also held champagne glasses and led a cheer when Alex entered. "Have you all lost your minds? When I left, you were burned out and exhausted." Peter poured another glass of champagne and handed it to Alex.

"Join the celebration. Kira cracked the code!" Alex

turned to see Kira who took an impromptu bow being careful not to spill her glass.

"Did I hear you correctly?" said Alex with a puzzled expression. "I thought I heard you say Kira solved Xavier's puzzle." Peter grabbed Kira by both cheeks and kissed her on the forehead.

"Our genius here figured it out. It was a set of 3D coordinates. They were playing Hadron and she made the connection. We were so stupid, Alex. The code was an address in Xavier's favorite game. It was so obvious; but we made sure that Tando will never their hands on it. We deleted it and have the only copy."

Alex could not believe Peter's words. "What did you find in Hadron?" Alex sipped the champagne.

"It was an extensive file containing Xavier's last notes. It solves the chaos problem. Evidently, he was working the final settings when he discovered that the Latro was after him." Alex thought that what Peter said made perfect sense. "By the way, how was your meeting with Mark? Did you learn anything?" Alex's demeanor changed from disbelief to sadness.

"Well, they don't have anything. They also asked if I, or I should say we, would come to work for them. They offered a million to start. That jump drive could be worth billions."

"I hope you told him to shove that offer where the sun don't shine?"

"Well, of course I did not take the offer, but he also said he was sorry for what he did." The music stopped and everyone gathered around Alex and Peter. "He's a broken man, Peter. I've never seen him this way."

"He should be sorry, especially about Xavier," said Julie.

"I know, I know...and he is ...and he is paying the price for what he's done. What's important now is what to do next. We have the cure for cancer, but no way to implement it. No money, no clinics, nothing but what you see right here." Alex hadn't thought about the consequences of cracking the code before Tando did.

"I got it covered." Peter could not contain his happiness. "I placed a call to our old investor, Sam Foulton. I was careful not to divulge anything but was able to finagle a meeting with him tomorrow morning at 9:00 am sharp. I figured he would know what do to."

Hope took root in Alex. "Excellent job, Peter; I think we should all go together. In fact, I want to propose a toast." Alex raised his glass. "To Kira, our genius, for cracking the code!"

Everyone raised their glasses and cheered. Kira blushed.

40
SAM FOULTON'S OFFICE: 9:00 AM

Sheri, stunning as usual in a black business suit and electric blue blouse, contrasted the unshaved, un-showered, disheveled, jeans and t-shirts clad Chicago team. Her ever-present smile and perky greeting welcomed them as they filed into the reception area. "You can go right in; he's expecting you," she said while nodding in the direction of Sam's office.

Alex and Peter led the way into Sam's expansive office. Sam sat at his desk tapping away at his keyboard flanked by stacks of paper. A disorganized aura always seemed to accompany Sam, like a Pig Pen in a fine business suit. Only it wasn't a cloud of dirt swirling around him but financial news, reports, and volumes of papers requiring his valuable signature. Sam used a stacks-of-paper filing system with various stacks representing each project. Important stacks occupied a position closest to him, while less pressing matters were pushed to the far reaches of the desk. Sam's system drove Sheri crazy whenever she attempted to find something. Peter had witnessed this firsthand when Sheri had entered Sam's office during a meeting and asked for the Canyon Project file. Sam pointed at the far end of his desk and Sheri began ruffling through the large stack. After more than a few moments she became frustrated. Sam intervened, took one look at the pile, and pulled out the right file like a magician executing a precision card trick without one pause in his discussion with Peter.

"Alex, Peter, come in. This must be Kira, Julie and Kevin as well. Come in. Come in. Let's go over to my private conference room." Sam clicked a button on his phone. "Sheri, we will be in conference, no calls." He looked at the others while still holding the intercom button. "Can Sheri get you anything? Coffee, tea, water, soft drinks?" Everyone declined except Kira, who ordered a Mountain Dew.

Everyone took seats around a large oval table. The spectacular view of the Chicago skyline was displayed through large tinted windows and served as a dramatic backdrop.

"So, Peter, I was surprised to get your call last night, and I understand you not wanting to disclose anything because of the threat of surveillance, but what can I do for you?" Alex was surprised at how cordial Sam was since he had not seen him since the night of Mark's betrayal. Evidently, Peter had smoothed things over with the app project.

"We have some big news, Sam. You're familiar with what's been happening at Tando?"

"Yes, the shit really hit the fan over there, and I'm loving every minute of it. Serves them right after what they did to us," said Sam.

"Of course you are familiar with how the Tando cure is killing people... Well, let's see, how can I explain this in simple terms?" Alex saw how Peter struggled to find the words.

"Peter, let me try to explain this," said Alex. "The reason the Tando cure is killing people is because of a flaw in the settings. Xavier discovered the flaw and fixed it the night he died. He hid the solution and left a clue to its location. It's a long story as to how we got the clue, but the bottom line is we found Xavier's solution to the flaw." Sam sat looking up at the ceiling for a minute, as if to process the information.

"Now let me get this straight," said Sam as if trying to solve a riddle. "You are telling me that you can fix Tando's problems with the cancer cure?"

"That's right," said Peter while the others nodded their heads. "All we would need to do to get the correct settings would be to enter them into the system," said Peter. A huge smile erupted on Sam's face.

"Well, my friends, this changes everything, doesn't it? You are sure this cure will work?"

"Sam, we would bet our lives on this," said Alex.

"Very interesting, very interesting," muttered Sam in a low voice while rubbing his chin with his thumb and forefinger. "Have you all been following Tando's stock prices?"

"Well, we've seen the media blitz on the deaths and all, and we did hear something about stock prices, but we are clueless," said Peter.

"Gentlemen...and ladies, this is what is known as a sell off. Tando is a sinking ship, and everyone on board is jumping off. Their stock is plummeting, and if it continues this way, and I see no reason why it shouldn't, Tando will be forced into bankruptcy, and at this rate it's coming down pretty quick. When a company kills people, it doesn't matter how much money or power it has, it's going down and that will create an opportunity for us. I have a plan." Sam was licking his chops.

Sam outlined a scenario whereby bankruptcy forced Tando to sell off its assets. He explained how a subsidiary of Foulton Enterprises could purchase the cancer care division of Tando, including all the clinics under the guise of converting them to MRI imaging centers. If they could pull this off, they would control a complete set of clinics already in place. All they would need to do is to reprogram the computers with the new settings. They would of course need to go through human trials again, but they could be up and running with the cure centers within a year. Peter and Alex knew that Sam had a head for business and were impressed with how Sam came up with such a brilliant plan off the top of his head.

They agreed to go forward. Sam said he would get his legal team on it right away. For now they were to sit, and wait, and protect the information at all costs. He said it would take some time to get the front company in place, but he was sure that Tando would jump at selling off the clinics and washing their hands of the cure if given the chance. As long as Tando had no clue as to how to solve the problem, the Chicago team and Sam were safe. They were to sit back and enjoy the show as Tando fell apart. After a brief discussion, they all agreed that the safest place for the data was the safe in the heart of Sam's building.

Sam led them to the security operation located in the basement of his building. They passed what appeared to be a large records room while making their way down a long narrow corridor. Alex identified numerous security cameras along the way. At the end of the corridor stood a large metal door flanked by an armed guard sitting at a desk reading a newspaper. "This must be the safe room," muttered Kevin.

"Right you are," said Sam while placing his finger inside a hole in a device on the wall. They waited a few seconds while the device read his fingerprint. A loud clunking sound signaled the movement of large steel bolts and the door cracked open.

"This room is bullet proof, explosion proof, and even earthquake proof, plus I'm the only one who can enter." Sam led the others inside. The entire room appeared to be made of some kind of heavy steel. One wall contained smaller drawer-like components with small video display screens on each. A metal table stood in front of the drawers and held a curious device resembling something out of an optometrist's office. It contained a camera and keypad at one end and two semicircular pieces of plastic on the other.

"I keep all my important documents in these safes," said Sam while entering numbers into the keypad. He placed his head against the circular plastic pieces as if lining it up for an eye exam. His forehead fit into one while his chin rested on the other. His face glowed red as a laser passed across it several times while flashing after each pass. "Retinal scanner plus facial recognition," he said. "I love tech!"

One of the drawers opened. "You can put it in here. Also, to show our trust, I will set this up to allow one of you to have access. Now, who will it be?" The group conferred for a minute and announced that Kira should be the one to have access since she discovered the solution. "Kira it is! Come over here, dear." Sam led Kira to a computer terminal. He entered some numbers and led Kira back to the drawer. "Okay, now put your face in this thingamajig and look straight ahead; try not to blink. The scanner will pass over it three times. Try not to move." Kira followed his instructions and the scanner passed over her face illuminating it in a red flashing glow. "Now you can come into this room and open this drawer. Only you and I can get into this room and open this drawer. Kind of like being married." chided Sam. Kira let out a small nervous laugh. The team felt more at ease after seeing the extensive security. Sam was right; Tando could get to any one of them. Plus Alex and Peter were the prime targets. It would be better if neither one were able to access the information.

Sam walked the team out to the lobby to bid them farewell. "Now, all you have to do is sit pretty and wait. Oh, and by the way, I'm sure your funds are running low. Does anyone need cash?"

Everyone perked up at this news since funds were indeed running low. Alex was camped out at Peter's apartment, and with the exception of Peter, the others survived on meager fellowship stipends. "I'll deposit one hundred and fifty thousand dollars into an account for your expenses for the next few months. Does that sound like enough, Peter?"

"That is more than enough, and thank you, Sam," said Peter as the others smiled, shook hands and hugged him.

"I will set up a business account and let Peter know when it's ready; should be a couple of days. Also, think of a name you'd like to use. Peter, I will be in touch. I'm excited."

"Thanks again, Sam," said Alex while shaking Sam's hand. The team left the building full of hope.

Back at Peter's apartment they discussed their next steps. "I know what I have to do next," said Alex. "I need to get my butt over to Beijing and beg Xiu for forgiveness. Excuse me, but I have to work on finding a flight as soon as possible." Alex excused himself to the dining room table and began tapping on his laptop.

"Now that the information is secure, we must lay low, maybe take vacations and split up, or we could continue working at our jobs," said Peter as he sat on the chair next to his sofa.

"We might be better off sticking together. This way each one of us is less of a target for Tando," said Julie as she sat next to Kira on the sofa. They all concurred that it would be best to continue their lives as if nothing had happened. Tando would think they were unsuccessful at breaking Xavier's code, and they would be safe.

They all discussed how much they could now enjoy their lives since the pressure was off. Alex interrupted the happy talk with, "So, what should we do about Mark?" The question echoed through the room, killing the conversation.

"What about him?" said Kira. "He can rot in hell for all I care."

Julie chimed in, "I don't care about him either. Think of poor Xavier."

Kevin added, "Mark is getting what he deserves."

Peter added, "We know he is family, Alex, but there is nothing we can do. He created his own reality on this one. I understand it's especially hard for you, but this will all blow over and he will have to rebuild his life."

Alex walked back into the room and stood facing the others, his brow wrinkled with tension. "I hope you're right, Peter. I'm worried he won't come out of this alive."

41
TWO WEEKS LATER: TANDO HEADQUARTERS, L.A.

Mark had never witnessed an adult man engage in a temper tantrum, but that was exactly how Jim Barnes reacted when told of Alex's refusal to cross lines and work for Tando. He threw objects, balled his fists, and cursed and stomped his feet. Imagining Jim as nothing more than an overgrown baby had helped Mark to regain a more balanced perspective.

Tando Pharmaceuticals was like a jet plane attempting to remain in flight after three of its four engines had fallen off. In public, Jim tried to act like the proverbial pilot of the troubled jet, telling everyone to remain calm while the plane struggled to remain in flight. Tando's stock experienced a similar phenomenon, and dropped over seventy percent as the media continued their nonstop barrage of negative stories. Some stations even began broadcasting stories about the negative stories.

Channel 37 News:

"We have breaking news about the Tando cancer cure. It appears that World Economic News has reported that Tando's stock is ready to lose another five points. Stay tuned for more after these messages..."

To make matters worse, each of the original trial

subjects had succumbed as predicted to multisystem organ failure. In an attempt to contain some of the negative news, Jim forced Mark to hold a press conference with him. Within minutes it became a feeding frenzy, despite Jim's strategy to continue stating how sorry they were and how they were working hard to correct the problem. An excerpt of the conference went like this:

Reporter: "Mr. Barnes, are you aware other scientists are questioning your destroying the rat subjects before beginning human trials?"

Barnes: "No I am not aware of this and I assure you we are using all our resources to find answers."

Reporter: "What have you said to the families of the deceased women?

Barnes: "We have expressed our deep condolences and are working out a settlement as we continue to do the best we can to find a solution to this problem."

Reporter: "Will you be submitting your resignation from Tando anytime soon?"

Barnes: "I have no intention of submitting my resignation. We are doing our best here."

Reporter: "What are you telling Tando shareholders who are seeing their stock plummet?"

Barnes: "We are telling them that we are doing our best."

The remainder of the press conference continued in a similar fashion. Mark fielded a few questions but the press seemed to target Jim. At one point Jim turned so red with anger at the reporters that Mark thought he might have a stroke.

Mark spent his days in his fishbowl office adjacent to the code-breaking lab and passed the time playing solitaire and video games. The Tando team of mathematicians continued to beat their brains to break Xavier's code, but two weeks passed with no solution in sight, and everyone grew tired and frustrated. Mark wondered when Jim would pull the plug and cut his losses.

Jim's plan to make Mark the scapegoat had backfired, making Jim even more manic. The media and the public were far too savvy to be taken in by such a tactic. Nobody was inclined to sympathize with rich CEOs or greedy corporations. They wanted heads to roll, and Jim's was first on the chopping block.

Mark's more subservient personality gleaned a modicum of public empathy. Jim's tactic of attempting to drag Mark through the scandalous muck with him came across as an obvious diversion tactic. Mark came across as a victim, and most people knew how Tando manipulated scientists.

Mark was taking his medicine for his actions. He came to work on time, killed whatever time he could, and returned to his downtown condo at night. He saved his money for whatever lay in store for him.

The Tampa team reported to Mark every week. Jeff tried to remain upbeat as the team attempted to fix the chaos problem. Jeff was confident that they would find the correct frequency mix in time, but progress was slow given the almost infinite number of corrections that needed to be tested. Jeff figured they could get up to Xavier's level in about a year.

42
BEIJING

The ramp leading to the greeting area at Beijing International Airport seemed longer than before. Alex thought about the last time he'd walked along this ramp toward his first meeting with Xiu. Then his excitement originated from the unknown of a new relationship; now he was equally excited about the hope of regaining what he had lost. He was a different person than had walked up the ramp a few months ago. He appreciated life more deeply. He appreciated Xiu more deeply as well.

Alex and Xiu had connected only a few times since Alex left the team back in June. Alex had needed to be careful not to disclose anything about Xavier's message, or about Sam's plan to take over Tando's cancer care clinics. Alex hoped she would find it in her heart to forgive him.

As soon as Alex cleared the ramp, their eyes met. Xiu waved her arms and ran to greet him. They embraced so tightly that Alex couldn't breathe. "Alex, my dear, dear Alex, you have come back for me. I am so happy."

"I am happy too, my love," said Alex with tears streaming down his face. The embrace led to a long deep kiss that stirred all the loving feelings between them. "I wanted to tell you in person how sorry I am for what I did." Alex wiped the tears from his face.

"I understand," said Xiu as she did likewise. "I know you thought you needed to be a success to be with me, but I want you to know you were wrong to think that. You are a success in my eyes, no matter what happens. I chose to be with you because of who you are inside."

They returned to Xiu's apartment where Alex told her all about Xavier's puzzle and how Kira solved it and how they were just waiting for Tando to enter bankruptcy so one of Sam's companies could purchase the cancer cure division. Xiu was happy to hear this, but even more happy that Alex was with her. They celebrated that night by strolling down Wang Fu Jing Street and eating at one of their favorite restaurants. Alex and Xiu had never been happier.

43
A FINAL CONFRONTATION

*T*he past few months had gone as Sam and the Chicago team expected. In due course, Tando did file for bankruptcy and began selling off its assets. Sam formed a new company called X-Image (the X was in honor of Xavier) and was ready to purchase the Cancer Cure division including all the clinics under the guise of converting them to imaging centers. Later they planned to form a subsidiary of X-Image called X-Cure. Tando seemed to have no suspicions about the Chicago team's knowledge concerning the cure.

A neutral legal office in Chicago hosted the closing for Sam's deal on February first at 2:00 pm. Sam's company, X-image, would pay fifty million dollars for the entire string of clinics. Sam appointed a new CEO and business team to run the venture, while the various members of the Chicago team remained incognito. Peter and the others would assume management roles once the deal was signed. Everything was ready to go as planned.

That morning Mark began his work at 8:00 am, as usual. He had not done much actual work in the past couple of months but had spent his time in his office playing video games. The code-breaking team had now dwindled to just a few people, as the deal to sell off the division was imminent and Tando needed to cut expensive personnel. Mark spent most of his time playing one game in particular, the same game he remembered playing with the Chicago team when they all had worked together. He liked it so much that he recruited one of the remaining mathematicians to play with him during breaks. They played Hadron a few times until Jerry, a mathematician, made the discovery.

"Hey, Mark, have you ever noticed the 3D coordinates at the top of the screen?" said Jerry.

"Why would I care?" said Mark with sarcasm.

"Well, you might care if you knew that these numbers are much like the code we have been trying to break."

Mark's heart began to pound as he remembered that this was Xavier's favorite game too. Jerry and Mark both rushed to enter the numbers into the game and immediately found their avatars in front of a virtual mountain. "It looks like the coordinates are pointing to something inside the mountain. We can't enter, but we can retrieve it externally. I'm reaching in but there is nothing here," said Jerry with disappointment. "Do you think the other team got there first?"

Mark already knew the answer. He decided to play it cool and not pursue the subject. He resigned himself to the fact that he'd lost this contest a long time ago. He decided to help Alex by keeping his mouth shut. Jerry had a different idea. "I think we should contact Mr. Barnes right away," said Jerry with enthusiasm.

"And tell him what? That we found nothing in this video game?" Mark tried to dissuade Jerry from taking further action.

"No, Mr. Barnes should know about the solution to the code." Jerry got up to return to his desk.

"Wait a minute. Jerry; that's not such a good idea. I mean, hasn't Barnes been through enough? This is just another dead end." Jerry bolted to his desk and picked up the phone.

"I don't care; I'm calling him now." Mark raced toward Jerry.

"Don't make that call, I'm warning you, Jerry." Jerry saw the anger in Mark's eyes and pressed the security button on the phone just before Mark grabbed his arm and wrestled the phone from it, smashing it to the ground.

The two men wrestled as Mark unleashed his pent-up anger on Jerry. He pinned Jerry to his desk while punching him in his face, chest and whatever other body part he could hit when two security guards pulled him off and wrestled him to the ground. The few remaining scientists cowered around them.

"He attacked me! He attacked me! I tried to call Mr. Barnes. This is of the utmost importance," said Jerry wiping blood off his mouth.

"I think we should all pay Mr. Barnes a visit," said one of the security guards and reached for a small radio on his hip. "We have a code red for Mr. Barnes. Brysen should be there too," he barked into the microphone.

The guards led the two men to Jim's office. Jim sat facing the window with Brysen standing by like an automaton. The clock on the wall read 11:30 am. "So, what's this all about? Not like you Mark to lose control like this. And who is this?" Barnes swiveled his chair to face them.

"This is Jerry Hickson, one of the mathematicians on the code-breaking team," said Brysen.

"Do you mind?" said Mark while lifting his hands. Brysen nodded and the guards unlocked the cuffs.

"This man was assaulting Jerry in the lab," one of the security guards said pointing to Mark.

Jerry struggled to talk while his lungs heaved and he held tissue to his bleeding mouth. "Mark tried to stop me from contacting you, Mr. Barnes. We solved the code, and he tried to stop me."

Barnes perked up. "You solved the code?"

"That's right," said Mark. "We solved it only to find it led to nothing."

"That's not entirely true," said Jerry still wiping blood from his mouth. "It was a location in a video game leading to an area that probably did contain something."

Brysen chimed in, "Mark, why would you try to stop Jerry from reporting this to Mr. Barnes?"

Mark composed himself and took a deep breath for his next lie. "Well, since the solution led to nothing, I didn't want to bother Jim. We've all been through so much these past few weeks. I guess everything that's happened made me lose my temper. I'm sorry for attacking you, Jerry." Mark tried to smooth things over but Brysen was too smart.

"I think Mark is hiding something," said Brysen while picking up the phone.

"I agree with you, Brysen," said Jim. "Jerry, please go to medical; we will take it from here."

A security guard escorted Jerry out of the room leaving Mark with Jim, Brysen and the other guard. Brysen excused himself and exited the room to make a call. The events of the past few months were building up inside Jim. "Is there anything you want to tell me about this code, Mark? We can do this the easy way, or we can do it the hard way."

"Nothing to tell," said Mark staring at his feet.

"Do you think your brother has the solution to the code?" asked Jim.

"No, I don't think so," said Mark.

"Okay, you leave me no choice but to do this the hard way."

Brysen rushed into the room with two other guards as if he were carrying out a special ops mission. These were not the typical Tando building security guards. These were armed Latro operatives. "Take him," Brysen ordered, and each guard grabbed one of Mark's arms. They led him out of the room and into the elevator where they rode to the basement. The elevator doors opened and the guards escorted Mark past the security offices and down a long dark hallway. They took him to what looked like an interrogation room.

Mark was placed in a metal chair and his arms were restrained by short chains and steel handcuffs. Brysen stood in the shadows in one corner of the room while the other two guards flanked Mark. There was a video camera and large LCD TV in front of him. Brysen's phone buzzed and he answered it. "The target is on its way, ETA fifteen minutes," a voice said coming from Brysen's phone. Mark was confused over what he heard. What target?

Brysen turned to Mark. "Okay, we have fifteen minutes. Is there any other information you would like to tell us about the code?" Mark remained silent. "Okay, have it your way," Brysen said.

Mark sat with his head down while he replayed his life in his mind. He thought about his childhood with Alex and all the games they had played, projects they'd built and fun they'd had as children. He thought how much he loved his brother and how much he missed his parents after their fatal accident. He thought about how shitty he had been to everyone he loved. He thought, this was what I deserve; to be locked up in some fucking interrogation room with people who don't care if I live or die. He realized that the chain of events set in motion when he first made the decision to sell out to Tando had led him to this point. Ever since that moment he'd known that he was on a path to something awful. The money and fame had worked to cover up this feeling to an extent, but in the end it surfaced to make his life a living hell. He thought that whatever horrible thing might happen, he would do his best to protect his brother.

Brysen's phone buzzed again. "The target is acquired. Ready to broadcast." Brysen nodded to one of the guards who flipped a switch that turned on the TV. Mark's darkest fears came true when he identified what it displayed. There, sitting at a similar table, was his brother Alex.

"What's going on? Mark, is that you? Where are you?" Two Chinese Latro guards armed with assault rifles accompanied Alex.

"I'm not sure what this is all about, Alex. They brought me here a few minutes ago. I'm in L.A.," said Mark as his voice cracked.

Brysen spoke up. "Alex Winter, we just want you to answer a couple of questions about this secret code. We can do this the easy way or the hard way. It is up to you."

"I don't know what you are talking about," said Alex.

"Let him go!" Mark yelled. "He has nothing to tell you."

"Did Alex tell you they solved the puzzle and possessed the solution during your Chicago meeting?" said Brysen in a slow methodical but hideous voice.

"No, no, he said they had not solved the puzzle," said Mark. "Now let him go!"

Brysen became more authoritative. "Alex, do you have the solution to the puzzle?" Alex figured that if he told them he didn't, he would be telling the truth since it was locked up in Sam's safe.

"No, I do not," said Alex. "I will ask you only three times," replied Brysen with an even stronger tone. This time Brysen signaled to one of the guards who again lifted his pistol fitted with a silencer and held it to Mark's head.

"I will ask you a second time. Do you have the answer to the puzzle?"

Mark began to cry and yelled, "Don't tell them anything, Alex! Don't tell them anything! They can shoot me, but don't tell them anything. I won't let you do it, Alex."

Alex also began to cry as he sat helpless, watching his brother begging him not to speak. He could not bear to see his brother executed this way, and he knew they would kill him. He wondered if they would execute him as well out of revenge. He glanced at his watch. It was now 1:45 pm Chicago time. If he could just stall them a bit longer, then Sam's deal to purchase the Tando clinics would be completed and there would be nothing they could do to stop it. He searched his mind for an answer but concluded any indication of knowledge of the solution would be cause to stop the deal, and all would be lost.

Alex lifted his head and looked at the camera but just as the words began to come out of his mouth he witnessed a most unusual and horrible sight, one that would forever haunt him.

There, on the screen, a series of events enfolded lasting about five seconds. Mark had worked himself into such a frenzy screaming, "Don't do it! Don't do it!" In a fit of extreme rage and adrenaline filled, superhuman strength he managed to stand and lift the heavy metal table while still chained to it. The table, not attached to the floor as it should have been, allowed Mark to lift it high enough, and in a split second he turned and knocked the gun out of the guard's hand. The stunned guard stepped back but then tried to reach for the gun which had fallen on the table. He was a split second too late. Mark wasted no time grabbing the gun, firing at the guard and at Brysen and hitting both. As fast as his actions were, they weren't fast enough for the third guard. The third guard, standing on Mark's left, instinctively drew his pistol and fired a fatal shot into Mark's head. Mark immediately slumped forward, his bloody head hitting the table.

"No!" Alex screamed as he witnessed his brother's execution. He sat in shock as the screen went blank.

Brysen had suffered a stomach wound and lay on the floor oozing blood. The guard who had held the gun on Mark had taken a fatal wound to his chest, and the other guard rushed to help Brysen. Brysen's phone buzzed again. It was the Chinese Latro awaiting further instructions. Brysen gasped a few times and said, "Let him go." He then clicked off the phone. The other guard had already called

911.

Alex again felt a hood placed over his head as the guards dragged him out of the room and shoved him into the van that had brought him there. Twenty minutes later the doors flew open and two men pulled him out. He could see a tiny sliver of his surroundings at the bottom of the hood and recognized a brick street, steps, and then a building. He heard voices and objects clanging around him as the men led him through a room and placed him on a chair. In an instant the hood flew off his head, blinding him for a few seconds. After his eyes focused, he found himself in the back room of what appeared to be a small restaurant. The abductors clicked off the handcuffs and disappeared out the back door. An older Chinese man approached him and motioned for him to exit the restaurant. "*Likai, Likai!*" he said pointing to the front door.

Alex exited the front of the restaurant and discovered that he was on an unfamiliar street. This was not unusual because Beijing was so immense and Alex only knew the streets around Xiu's apartment. He began wandering down the street in a state of shock while continuing to replay the image of Mark's death in his head. He could not accept that his brother was actually dead. It had all happened too fast for his mind to process. One moment he pleaded with Alex not to talk, and the next he was dead.

Dawn approached as the sun diffused through the dense pollution casting a red-orange hue on the almost vacant streets. It was quiet as the city began to wake and engage into another day of human complexity. Alex thought how odd it was that this immense city would go on with its millions, or perhaps billions, of human interactions as if nothing had happened. His life, however, had changed forever.

After walking in no particular direction for a while, the cobwebs began to clear in Alex's head. *I must get back to Xiu.* The sound of her front door bursting open had awakened them in the early hours of the morning. Three men had entered their bedroom and carried Alex away. He knew nothing of what had happened to Xiu. Perhaps they were holding her as well. He remembered her screams as they forced him out of the apartment.

Alex found a busy street and managed to signal a lone taxi. After a few clumsy attempts he was able to communicate Xiu's address to the driver. The driver nodded and he arrived at the apartment building after twenty minutes.

He bolted out of the taxi as soon as it pulled up to Xiu's building and ran up the five flights of stairs to her apartment. He found the door propped half open as it hung from its damaged frame. He called for Xiu as he swung open the door. She sat on her sofa, sobbing.

But her face burst into happiness when she saw Alex. He ran to her and they embraced as if all the love they had for each other poured out of them in one primal moment.

"I thought I would never see you again," said Xiu with her head cradled on Alex's chest. "I love you so much," she said as she again began to sob.

"It's over," he said. His own tears began to flow as he placed his head upon her soft shoulder. "It's finally over."

44
CHICAGO: EIGHTEEN MONTHS LATER

$\mathcal{A}$lex and Xiu exited their limo and made their way to the entrance of the International Hotel in downtown Chicago. "Doctors Alex Winter and Xiu Ling have arrived," a uniformed attendant announced into his headset as he held open the large glass doors leading to the luxuriously decorated lobby.

"Alex! Xiu!" Peter called to them from across the room. "You look fantastic! Xiu, you are absolutely beautiful in that dress...and Alex, I've never seen you in a tux before. Very dashing!"

"Sam went all out on this one," said Alex as he surveyed the scene. The lobby, packed with people dressed in formalwear, reminded him of watching the Academy Awards on TV. Ornate bouquets of flowers framed several fountains. A large banner beckoned everyone to the grand ballroom. The banner read: *X-Cure Grand Opening Celebration.*

People filed into the elegantly decorated ballroom along a red carpet. They passed by a small staging area where reporter's cameras flashed and television cameras swung into motion covering the entrance of VIPs. A small orchestra played jazz as attendants dressed in 1940s costumes escorted guests to their tables. "Looks like a royal wedding celebration in here," said Alex as attendants escorted him and Xiu to the front table.

"Hey everyone, it's Alex and Xiu!" exclaimed Kira as the couple approached the table.

"Kira? Is that you?" Alex was shocked to see Kira in a formal dress. "Wow, you are the second most beautiful girl in the room!" Alex looked over at Xiu as she blushed. Kira stood and came over to Xiu and rubbed Xiu's belly in a small circular motion.

"How's the bump?" Kira said as she chuckled. "You guys are not wasting any time. Get married and a few months later there's a bun in the oven." Everyone laughed and was happy to be together again as they celebrated the grand opening of the new X-Cure clinics.

Sam had successfully formed X-Image, Inc. and because of Mark's sacrifice, signed the last minute deal with Tando as they sold off the Cancer Cure division. He then created the X-Cure division of X-Image, which took over the clinics. Once the team programmed the new settings into the frequency machines, the cure was ready to go. After Tando self-destructed it was no problem publishing research and obtaining FDA approval based on the new human trial research. The trials were successful and the FDA awarded full approval of the new cure for breast cancer. The public embraced the new company and the clinics were booked solid for the next year.

After Mark's death, Alex remained in China for a few months except returning for Mark's funeral. Brysen had the interrogation room and basement strategically bombed, eliminating any evidence of the truth. Brysen's statement to the police was that he had witnessed Mark's breakdown over the Tando implosion. He said that Mark had probably set the bomb in the basement of Tando headquarters to damage Tando's information infrastructure. Brysen told police that he and the other guards had attempted to stop him, but Mark was armed and shot at them. Jim Barnes naturally backed up Brysen's statement, leaving Alex with no way to substantiate his version of the story. Brysen survived his wound but his life was never the same since he now wore a colostomy bag. He retired on disability from Tando.

Alex and Xiu married a couple of months after Mark's death. They had ceremonies in China and again in Chicago when Xiu returned with Alex. They purchased a luxury high-rise condo in downtown Chicago and were inseparable. They expected their first child in about four months.

The other members of the Chicago team also fared well with the new venture. All were already millionaires and slated to make millions more. Every team member remained in Chicago and either purchased lavish homes in the fashionable northern suburbs or luxury downtown lakefront condos. Kira loved showing off her Lamborghini, and Kevin and Julie started dating and purchased a condo together. Hans retreated to the suburbs and loved his old tudor home.

The team also made sure that Xavier's share of the fortune went to his family. In an instant they went from poor ranchers to millionaires. They continued to live in Cheran and donated large sums to their church and to the local school system.

"Daniella, so good to see you," said Alex as he waved to her table. She came running up to hug him.

"I am happy to meet your beautiful wife," said Daniella. "We are also so grateful for the money."

"We are forever in debt to Xavier, Daniella; it was the very least we could do," said Alex while Daniella hugged him. Alma and Carlos soon appeared and surrounded them with smiles and greetings. Alma grinned and pointed at Xiu's belly and winked at Alex in approval.

Tando survived the bankruptcy but its weakened state reduced its immense power to a fraction of what it had been. Word on the street was that the Latro had disintegrated with its members moving on to look for work in more troubled parts of the world. Tando still produced chemotherapy drugs, but the X-Cure was making such treatments obsolete. The company's demise marked the beginning of a new era of freedom in the pharmaceutical world, allowing for an acceleration of new research and development by other companies. Companies like Frank McElroy's Biopharmco, as well as other nutraceutical companies, operated without fear of retaliation by Tando.

Jim Barnes took the hit for Tando. The media dragged him through the muck of Tando's failure, and the board of directors fired him. Word was that he was close to a nervous breakdown and had become a hermit in his mansion in the California Mountains. But as these things usually go, he drew a large multimillion-dollar severance package before Tando hit bottom. The team surmised that he would surface at some point in the future.

"Now that you are super rich, you can't say hi to the little people?" a familiar voice from the adjoining table shouted.

"Tommy, so good to see you, my friend." Alex dodged the crowd to Tommy's table. "Wow, you guys all look great! I'm so glad you could come," said Alex.

"I had a premonition you would be successful," said Angie while Adam and Bill remarked about how beautiful everything was and asked for the name of the decorator.

"How's Biopharmco these days, Frank?" said Alex while shaking his hand.

"Business couldn't be better since we signed with X-Cure to produce all the resveratrol. I thank you again."

"No Frank, I'm the one who should be thanking you for introducing me to my dream girl." Alex put his arm around Xiu and lightly kissed her on the cheek. Alex and Xiu took turns hugging everyone.

"Hey, where's Sam?" said Alex as he spied Sam's empty

seat at the table.

"You know Sam. Always the showman. He's waiting to make his big entrance," said Peter as the emcee began to announce:

Ladies and gentlemen, I would like to present to you the person who brought you the X-Cure. Please welcome Sam Fulton and his date, Sheri Pearson.

The crowd erupted in applause, and cameras blinded the couple with flashes.

Kira remarked, "Sheri looks stunning in that gown, but I've never seen anyone in a tux and cowboy hat before."

Alex and the others laughed, and a good time was had by all.